FINDING
MY WAY

FINDING
MY WAY

USA Today bestselling author
HEIDI MCLAUGHLIN

Wake Up by Eric Heatherly
© 2013 Eric Heatherly/Psychobilly Music/ASCAP
D.O.C. 10/5/13
Cover Designed by:
Sarah Hansen at © OkayCreations.net
Edited by:
Michael Burhans
Formatted by:
Tianne Samson with E.M. Tippetts Book Designs
Photography by:
Toski Cover Photography
Models:Tanner

Belcher & Emily Hackman

ACKNOWLEDGEMENTS

First and foremost: I have to thank the fans because without you The Beaumont Series isn't possible. Your continued support and encouragement means the world to me.

And to Yvette: who once again has slaved tirelessly over my rambling to make it sound nice and pretty. You brought Jimmy to life and for that I can never thank you enough.

Jessica & KP: Thank you for all the work that you do on a daily basis to not only support me, but authors everywhere.

Sarah: I love how you can take an image and make magic. I've enjoyed working with you immensely.

Emily: I thank you once again bringing The Beaumont Series to life.

Toski, Tanner & Emily: Words cannot express the gratitude I feel. Thank you for helping bring Liam and Josie to life.

HB, Holly & Yara: Thank you for taking a chance and reading something different from me.

Eric Heatherly: How you can supply the perfect song is beyond me, but I love it. Thank you for being on this journey with me and providing my guys with the music that they needed to complete their stories.

To my Bitches: I love you hardcore. We're family through and through.

Indie Inked: You're friendship and support is unwavering for that I thank you.

To my family: Thank you for your continued support. Thank you for encouraging my crazy ideas and for helping create new ones.

To my girls: You're both so creative and your imaginations are wild. I can't wait to see what you do. You both have your own amazing stories ready to be written and I can't wait to help guide you through the process.

CHAPTER 1

Liam

Senior year. Today's the day that starts it all. The one day I've been looking forward to since my freshman year. Three weeks ago I started my last year of high school football, once again taking the helm behind center as the starting quarterback at Beaumont High. This is my second year as captain, earning the title at the end of my sophomore year. That alone is an achievement. Most of the time, the outgoing seniors give the honor to juniors, but not that year. My father said I should've had it my freshman year especially since I was leading the team. He's always like that though. Westburys are the best at everything they do. According to my dad, no one is on the same level as us. It's not something I agree with.

I rest my hands behind my head and stare at my ceiling. Mine and Josie's names are written in glow in the dark paint just above my bed so it's the last thing I see before I close my eyes at night. She did this over the summer. She stood above me in her tiny cut-off shorts with her long, tan legs straddling me as she stretched her arms above her head writing on my ceiling. I did what any normal red-blooded male would do – I sat up and bit her ass and tried to get her to stop what she was doing so she could focus on me.

I love this girl. Josie Preston. We've been together since our sophomore year. I remember asking her to homecoming on a whim. I then made a mistake and told her I'd call her that night but couldn't because my dad was on my ass about football and homework. The next day she wouldn't even look at me. It killed me inside. I didn't know what to think, but knew that Josie was going to be someone special. I just never realized how special. I can't imagine my life without her now.

I'm not afraid to admit that I'm whipped. When you have someone as sexy as Josie Preston on your arm, you're bound to do anything she asks. Everything about her makes me crazy. If I'm not staring at her long legs, I'm playing in her brunette locks. I love that she enjoys running and wants to stay toned. Her eyes, they're the gateway to her soul and I can stare into her blues orbs until she pushes me away. Most guys balk, but not me. I love her and I know she loves me. We're going to spend the rest of our lives together whether my parents want me to or not. I'm not like my father. I refuse to turn my nose up at people who have less than my parents. Material possessions don't mean anything if you don't have someone to love and share life's experiences with.

I listen carefully for my dad to leave the house. I've been setting my alarm so I can get up and practice my guitar without him being home. I know my mom knows.

I've seen the hallway light come on and the shadow of her feet stop at my door. She won't knock or even ask me when I am coming down for breakfast. She's operating under the *if I don't ask my son a question I won't have to lie to my husband* policy. It doesn't bother me, not anymore. After years of her being despondent I'd probably be shell-shocked if she actually opened her mouth to ask me a question.

This house is strictly football. Day in. Day out. Even when I'm playing baseball, football is the focus. I don't mind, but there are other things I want to try. One of those things is taking a music class, but my dad approves my schedule. All the classes I take are NCAA regulated according to the clearinghouse. A strings class isn't on the approved list, I know because I asked my guidance counselor. It was a long shot, I knew that, but I still tried. Now I'm self-taught.

I get up and move slowly in my room. In my closet, deep in the back behind a few boxes, hides my acoustic guitar. I bought her at a yard sale and had her tuned up at the local music shop. She's a Yamaha with a spruce top with a rosewood fingerboard and bridge. My favorite part is the tortoiseshell pickguard. It makes her look old and used. Since then, I've been practicing each morning after my dad leaves for work before my day needs to begin. That was six months ago.

I haven't told Josie. I plan to. I'm just waiting to finish a song so I can show her how the music I create makes me feel. She's the only one that will understand. She's the only one that will appreciate what I can do. I want her to see that there's more to me than being QB1 and captain of the football team.

Carrying my guitar to my desk, I pull out my chair and sit down. I slide the drawer open and pick up the yellow notepad that I've been taking notes on. I don't really know what I'm doing. Aside from playing the piano when I was younger, it's foreign to me. But I'm willing to learn and teach myself until I can get to college and find a tutor. My dad won't be able to stop me then. I'll be on my own. I'll be able to roam freely around campus and do what I want, when I want. My only concern will be Mason. He won't understand. He doesn't have much, but what he does have, his father works hard for.

Mason Powell and I have been best friends since I can remember. We've always played football together and he's always been on my left. He's my running back and a damn fine one at that. He's also the reason I noticed Josie. He's been dating her best friend for a bit longer than Josie and I have been together. The summer he started dating Katelyn, I left for football camp. He was so pissed, but got over it quickly. When I came back he pointed out Josie and I was smitten. I just had to get up the nerve to ask her out.

Mr. Powell is someone I respect. He's there every game, rooting on his son. Mason can run for ten yards or a hundred and his father will be outside the locker room with the biggest smile on his face, waiting with open arms to give his son a hug. I want that. I've wanted that for so long. I don't know when I realized I'd never have that relationship with my dad. Seventh or eighth grade, maybe? My memories run together now when I try to think about it. I can't remember a time when my dad hugged me, instead of only handing me piece of paper telling me everything I did wrong.

After my games, he'd sit down and go over and over the list until I was a walking mantra of his advice. He's Sterling Westbury, he knows everything, even if he couldn't finish out his college career. Westburys excel at everything they do. And if that's the case then I'll succeed at learning how to play this guitar and I'll create music that everyone will love, even if it's only Josie that I'm playing for. If I can make her smile with music I'll be on the right path.

I strum the strings, closing my eyes as I take in the melody. In my head, when I imagine what it should sound like, it's soft, romantic. I know I'll achieve that sound, it just takes time. I love that when I play my guitar she sounds like she's talking to me. She's telling me a story and each note is a letter or a word that I need to decipher. I need to decode her to figure out what makes her tick and she's just waiting for me. Together her and I are going to create a masterpiece, we'll create magic, happiness.

I play a few more chords before picking up my pen and writing down some words. I can't call them lyrics, not yet. I'm not there. These are just words. Feelings that take control of my body every time I think of Josie. Each song I've tried to write is about her. One day I'm going to get it right and she's going to sit on my bed and I'm going to surprise her.

My parent's bedroom door opens and closes. I count her steps and watch the shadow of her feet as she stops in front of my room. I like to think that one day she'll knock, but it won't be today and not likely tomorrow either. I could engage her in a conversation and maybe she'd ask me how I'm doing or how things are with Josie, but she'd just stare and smile softly. She's a robot. A shell of who she used to be. My dad did this to her. He comes home late. He's demanding and ignores her. He's the poster child for a shitty husband and father, but she doesn't leave him. She won't. Bianca Westbury likes the prestige he brings to her: The country club, dinner parties and gala events. Those are the things that she looks forward to and when she doesn't have one to prepare for, she drinks until she's numb and walking through a fog.

She continues down the hallway and I wait until I hear the water running for her coffee which she'll be adding Baileys to. Everything has booze in it and I'm sure she's oblivious to the fact that I know this. I'll go down in a minute for breakfast and pretend like today is just like any other day, except it isn't. It's one hundred and eighty days until I graduate and can start packing for college, that's when the real countdown will be begin. Josie has one of those eighteen-month calendars and the last days in July are marked in red. I'll leave then, for some college, away from her.

CHAPTER 2

THE traffic to Josie's house is heavy, which makes no sense since she lives three blocks from me. But those three blocks can stretch on. It always does on the first day of school and even though I'm heading in the wrong direction there's no way I'm letting my girl ride the yellow submarine. I rest my head on the back window and tap on my steering wheel. I'm currently stuck behind said yellow submarine while we wait for the train to finish crossing. You'd think the rail company would make a conscience effort to make sure the train doesn't interrupt school traffic, but no. It's like this every morning. Tomorrow, I'll just have to leave earlier.

My dad detests that I pick Josie up every day, but I don't care. I stopped caring after he called her trash our sophomore year. He doesn't get it. Not everyone has to be like him. Hell, *everyone* I know doesn't want to be like him. I know I don't want to. I just want to get through this year, go off to college, do my four years and get drafted into the NFL. The day I'm drafted, I'm asking Josie to marry me. It might be a few days later after I get paid, but I'm buying her the biggest diamond ever. I'm going to let the world know that she is mine.

When I finally had enough nerve to talk to Josie that day before football practice I was so nervous that she'd turn me down. I was just a pimply teen going through bodily changes that I don't want to mention and I had no clue how to talk to her. I had to ask Mason for advice because he had spent the summer messing around with his girl and Josie's best friend, Katelyn Cohen. I felt stupid and if I'm honest, a little bit embarrassed. I mean, I should know this shit, shouldn't I? Still, Mason's words of wisdom worked.

Shit hit the fan when Sterling found out I was taking Josie to homecoming our sophomore year and since then it's just gotten worse. Josie rarely comes over and when she does, he's not around. I look forward to him going on business trips. The peace and quiet is a welcome relief. Even my mom is visibly relaxed when he's not around.

The school bus finally moves across the tracks allowing me to get to my girl. She's waiting on her front step with her arms bent and resting on her knees and her fingers playing with her lips. Tomorrow she'll be in her sassy little cheerleading uniform, which drives me insane. I can't keep my hands off of her and I can't keep guys from staring at her.

As soon as I pull up, she's standing and shouldering her bag. I wish she'd wait for me to come get her, but she says we'll be late if I do that each and every time. She doesn't understand that she's worth being late for. I lean over and open the door for her and watch as she jumps in, dropping her bag by her feet. I grab her hand and pull her to me, cupping her face so I can taste her delicious lips. I can't get enough of her. I'm sure it's not healthy, but I don't care. I need her like I need water.

"I missed you, Josie."

I feel her smile against my lips and know today is going to be torturous. "I saw you yesterday."

"It's not enough. Let's runaway together."

Josie laughs and pulls my hand away from her face. She threads her fingers in with mine and snuggles into my side. This is where she belongs, next to me. She rests her head on my shoulder as I put my truck in drive and take off down her road.

"You didn't answer me."

"About what?"

"Running away together. We should do it. We should leave Beaumont and go someplace where no one will know us."

"What about Katelyn and Mason? We'll miss them."

I set my hand down on her knee and give her a gentle squeeze. "They can come too."

"And college and the NFL?"

I smirk as I look out the window. "You're right, baby. We're living the American dream right now, aren't we?"

Nothing is said the rest of the way to school. We have a plan and sometimes I think she's afraid to deviate from said plan. My path has been chosen for me and while I'm grateful for the opportunities I've been given, I can't help but wonder what else is out there for me. For us. Are we destined to be what I made her into? She's captain of the cheerleading team this year. We'll be homecoming and prom king and queen this year. There are expectations and we'll follow them because we're both afraid of letting people down. But Josie could've been something different. I never stopped to consider her dreams. I just expected she'd be a part of mine and we'd be happy. But what if she's not?

I pull into the school parking lot and take the spot next to Mason. He has Katelyn pressed tight up against the car with his hands all over her body. I'm surprised they're not pregnant by now. I really wouldn't put it past him to try to knock her up before college. He's so stupid in love it's ridiculous. Katelyn's smarter than that though. She has plans and this lug of a best friend of mine isn't going to ruin that for her.

"Hey guys," Josie greets them when we come around the truck. Katelyn pushes Mason off her, well she tries to at least. He doesn't let her go, but hangs onto her waist with his hands.

"Are you ready for the game tomorrow, Liam?" Katelyn knows everything there is to know about football courtesy of Mason. They spent one summer going over everything so that he could talk to her when I wasn't around. I was only gone for that one summer and he's never let me live it down.

"I'm ready," I say, adding, "this year we're breaking all kinds of records." I high-five Mason over the top of Katelyn's head.

"My dad's fired-up," Mason adds as we walk into the school, nodding to the right of me as we walk. "Someone's snaking your girl, Westbury." I look and sure enough Nick Ashford is watching Josie.

"I thought he graduated last year?" I ask.

"No, he's the same age as us," Josie informs us. How she knows this is beyond me.

"He's a douche. I don't like him staring at you. I might have to teach him a lesson."

"Oh my God, you're horrible, Liam."

Josie moves out of my reach and pulls Katelyn along with her. Nick Ashford has a thing for my girl, I know he does, but he needs to keep his eyes on his own property. The way he watches her, I did the same thing until I had the nerve to ask her out. I see him look at her, watch her when she walks down the hall. The subtle way he brushes up against her arm when they pass in the hall. He's messing with fire because Josie's not up for the taking.

"What's with her?"

I shrug. I don't pretend to understand her when she's like this. She knows I'm protective and jealous and I hate it when guys gawk at her. Only I should be able to gawk at her openly. "She doesn't like it when I get jealous."

"Your girlfriend is hot. I'd tap that if I didn't have Katelyn."

I punch Mason in the shoulder and keep moving into the school. When I turn the corner, Josie is bent over at the waist with her ass in the air for the whole school to see. I step up behind her and grab her hips, pulling them to me. I do this a few times until she yells at me.

"You're going to get us into trouble, Liam," Josie scolds me playfully as she stands and turns in my arms.

"It's the first day of school and the whole town knows we have sex, Josie. We got caught at the movie theater, remember?"

Josie glares at me. "Only because you hit the parking brake and we started rolling."

I laugh, remembering the situation all too well. It's funny now, but wasn't so funny when we were scrambling to get our clothes back on. The thing about car sex is that it's easy for the guy, just whip it out, but unless your girl is wearing a skirt, which mine wasn't, it's a bit harder for the girl to get her clothes back on.

"Josie, we're teenagers, teenagers have sex."

"Well we don't need to broadcast it."

I step until her back is pressed against her locker. "I think we need a trip out to the dugouts. We haven't been out there in a long time."

"Lunch?" she asks, knowing exactly what happens out there.

I lean in and kiss her quickly. "I'll be the one with no pants on." I leave her there and make my way down the hall to class. First day is starting off quite nicely, I'd say.

CHAPTER 3

ROLL over and look at the illuminated numbers of my clock staring back at me. I've tried to sleep, but to no avail. My mind is racing and is full of 'what ifs'. I've never been this nervous on game day, but the pressure is on. The naysayers doubt me. The papers, the ones who support our rivals, think I'm done for. They say there's nothing left and I'm already past my teenage prime. We've won three straight games, all on the road and we're the league target. Everyone is gunning to take us down and it starts tonight at seven p.m. under the lights.

Josie, Katelyn and the rest of the girls will be there to meet us as we come out of the tunnel. Their pom-poms will be shaking. Their mouths will be cheering as we rush by. I'll come out last. I always have. I need that one moment of peace before I step out onto the field and see the bright lights shining down on me. I need that solitude that I feel when I look at the thousands of fans who are gathered on a Friday night to watch us battle it out with our opponent.

What I don't look for are the scouts. I don't want to see them. I don't want to know that they're sitting in the stands with their notepads writing furiously about everything that I do wrong because according to my dad, I can't do anything right. My passes aren't hard enough. I run too slowly. I don't zig and zag like I should when heading to the end zone. I don't score enough. What he doesn't understand is that each time he says something it makes me want to quit and I hate having that feeling. I love football. It's my life. I know I'll do great, but each time he opens his mouth I want to yell at him. I want to tell him to go to hell and that I quit. But I won't. I have dreams. Josie and I have dreams. I can't let her down.

It's three in the morning on game day. I should be sleeping, but it avoids me even though I need it. I sit up and swing my legs over the side of my bed, my bare feet touching the cold hardwood floor. I don't know how to shut off the voices inside my head, but staying here isn't the answer. I put on the t-shirt I threw on my chair last night and my sweatpants and slip on my Nikes.

The window in my bedroom moves up easily and the early morning air causes my skin to pebble. This isn't the first time I've snuck out and won't be the last, but after the first time I was afraid the noise would alert my father, so I oiled it. I don't know what he'll do if he catches me and honestly, I'm not willing to find out. But I need to see her. I need to feel her and hold her against me. She'll help calm my nerves and ease the anxiousness that's building.

I shimmy down the rose trellis and take off in a dead sprint toward her house. The run is what I need. I'll be nice and tired when I crawl in through her window. Sleep won't elude me once I have Josie pressed tightly against my chest.

I don't knock or even worry about waking her parents when I open her window. She leaves it unlocked for me each night. The first time we were caught I thought her dad was going to shoot me. He should've. I can't imagine what was going through his mind, but he knows how my father is. I know Josie tells him about the way he talks down to her. I'd like to think Mr. Preston feels sorry for me. Instead of calling my parents he sat us down and talked about responsibility and college, and how he has hopes for Josie and doesn't want to see her give up on her dreams because we were being stupid. I sat on the couch holding her hand and listening to her father tell me that I'm a good kid, instead of beating the shit out of me for sneaking into his daughter's bedroom.

My shirt and shoes come off before I slide into her bed. She's facing the window, almost as if she's waiting for me. On her nightstand is my senior picture. I paid for extras so she could have one. It pissed me off that my mother would be so selfish and wouldn't order enough so I could hand them out. Of course, she knew they were going to go to Josie, but what should that matter? I know I should be used to it, but shit, Josie's my girl and she's not going anywhere.

"Hey, Josie," I murmur as I pull her comforter over me. I touch her hip lightly before moving my arm over her waist, pulling her to my chest. I bury my nose into her hair and close my eyes, inhaling her scent. I would stay like this forever if it could make my head stop spinning.

"What's wrong, Liam?"

"How do you know something's wrong?"

Her body sighs against mine. "You're shaking."

"I'm sorry," I say, as I try to release my grip on her waist, but she holds my arm there.

"You don't have to be sorry, Liam. If something's wrong, you can tell me. I'm always here for you. Are you nervous about the game?"

I nod and try not to smile, but can feel my lips turning up. I kiss her below her ear and sigh. "How do you know me so well, Josie? Not even my parents know me like you do."

Her fingers trail up and down my arm. I should be sorry that I woke her, but I'm not. Now that I'm lying next to her, I need her.

"We're soul mates, Liam. You'll always be a part of me."

How she knows this is beyond me, but I feel something when I'm with her. She's my sun and moon, the air that sustains my life. She can bring me down and make me weak in the knees with one look. If this is what it means to have a soul mate then I guess she's right.

"Can I hold you, Josie?" I whisper against her skin. "I just want to hold you."

Josie rolls over so she's facing me. My eyes close as she softly runs her finger down the side of my face. She rubs the stubble on my chin before leaning in and kissing me. The feeling of her lips against mine never fails to take me by surprise. It's like I'm kissing her for the first time, the way my heart rate increases, the tingling that I feel from her mouth brushing against mine. I get lost in the moment every single time. It's the sweetest kind of heaven and for that moment, her kiss helps me forget about the shitfest that Sterling brings with him.

"I don't know what's going on in that head of yours, but I'm here for you. You know that, right?"

"I know," I reply, pulling her closer to me. Our foreheads rest against each other's, our noses touching. All I have to do is turn slightly and I can press my lips against hers again. I know that if I do, it's all over for me. My desire for her is already peaking and if I start kissing her, I'll have her undressed and beneath me before I realize what I'm doing. As much as I need her, it's a game day and I have a routine. I'm too superstitious to veer off course. No sex on game day, not until after.

We'll win and after we do, we'll meet at the tower and hang out. We'll get in my truck and find a deserted road or go to the overlook where she'll show me how much she loves me. And she does love me. There's no doubt in my mind that Josephine Preston loves me. I just hope I'm enough for her.

CHAPTER 4

THE school day drags on. I'm anxious to get out on the field and start warming up. I'm ready to put on my pads and helmet and hit the field. I need to feel the vibrations from the stands. Its opening night and I know the fans will be out in droves. We're playing our cross-town rivals, a game that is usually played on Homecoming, but someone higher up thought this would be a good way to kick off the season. Honestly, I don't care who we play, as long as at the end of four quarters, we have the winning number on the board.

The only highlight is watching Josie walk around in her short as sin skirt and tight shirt. No, I take that back. The highlight would be when I get to saddle up behind her and press into the flimsy excuse for briefs that she has on. I've told her over and over again those aren't briefs but a true testament to a guy's ability to wait, because each time I see her do a split I imagine myself sliding them down her legs, which is exactly what I'm thinking about now as I watch her walk down the hall.

I don't know why I'm not up there next to her holding her hand. Sometimes I want to watch her. I love seeing her interact with our classmates. Does this make me a stalker? Maybe, but there are times that I feel like I need to hide in the shadows, like today. Don't get me wrong, I love the praise I receive on game day, but we're in school, we should be learning. Watching a game film in history class or discussing what scheme we're going to run tonight in English is over the top. I love football. I study the game. I run each play over and over in my head every single day so when it comes to game day, I want to relax. I want my mind to focus on the War of 1812 and not the Wing T offense our opponents are going to run.

I know the teachers can't help it. They're excited. I get that. We've won the last three state championships and are going for an unprecedented number four. Mason's expected to break the state's rushing record too. That's what I worry about, his record. I know he needs to break it to get some decent college looks and I can help him. I'm not worried about college. The scouts will be in the stands with their notepads writing down everything that I do right and even things that I do wrong. The phone calls will start soon. The coaches will make their intentions clear. I'll sign in February and seal my fate. Division I football is all but guaranteed for me. My dad' made sure. The high intensity camps since I was eight. The elite summer programs that took me away from friends each year. I'll give him credit; he saw potential and capitalized on it. I just wish he cared more about me as a person rather than a player. Why can't I be more to him then

QB1 of Beaumont High? Why can't he see me as his son?

Why? Because he doesn't care the way Mr. Powell does about Mason. Sterling only wants front page news. He wants to parade around in his business suit talking about stats and what college I'll pick. As much as it would kill me, I'd laugh if no one came forward. That would show him… and me because I need college to make it to the NFL, but the look on his face would be priceless.

I step behind Josie and slide my hands up her legs and over her hips until they're resting on those ridiculous briefs. I lean in and press my lips to the back of her neck. Her long dark hair is up in a ponytail. The ends are curled, making it look a lot shorter than it is. As much as I love my cheerleader, I look forward to the days when she's not wearing her uniform. I love running my fingers through her hair and burying my face in her locks. Games days are all about looks. She has to look her best. Only her best are days when she's wearing sweatpants and my jersey or one of my t-shirts. That's when she looks beyond beautiful.

My fingers run along the edge of her briefs, teasing her. She shivers lightly. I'm driving myself crazy and she knows it. Josie won't hesitate to use this to her advantage. I haven't learned my lesson yet because right now I can't do shit about the bulge in my pants. Not sure why I torment myself like this. All this is going to do is make me want to get tonight's game over with so I can have her. So I can feel her skin against mine. I need her to keep me level headed and focused. After spending the night with her in my arms, I think I might need to break tradition and skip the tower. I need my girl, desperately.

"What are you doing, Liam?" she asks, her voice heavy with anticipation. I relish the way she responds to me. She may be my first girlfriend, but I've heard enough locker room talk to know that she wants me. When we're together she's not a cold fish like some of the guys have described their hook-ups to be. Her body knows my touch and craves me just as much as I crave her. I often ask myself why it took me so long to notice her. Why it took until sophomore year, and for Mason to get me to notice her, before I had the courage to speak to her. The only answer I can come up with is that I was so focused on making varsity and securing my starting spot that I had blinders on. I don't know what it was about that day I asked her to homecoming, but I knew then that I wanted to be in her life forever.

"You know what I'm doing. I'm giving you a preview of what's to come."

Josie's head hits the front of her locker as she sighs. She turns slowly in my arms, her fingers move along my shoulders and to the base of my neck. I love that my girl is all natural. She doesn't dye her hair or spend hours tanning her skin under fluorescent lights. Her nails are real and kept short, but just long enough to dig into my skin at the right moment.

"Are you trying to break your self-imposed rules, Liam?"

"No, I'm just showing you what's to come later tonight. I thought maybe you'd want a little preview before we have to focus on other shit."

Josie teases my freshly shaved sides with her nails, causing my spine to tingle.

"What I want is for my super sexy boyfriend to go out there tonight and kick some ass so we can celebrate later." She finishes me off with the lightest, but almost deadly kiss. I hate my life right now.

When she pulls back I look into her blue eyes and know she's the voice of reason. I need my stamina for the game. I can't let anything get in the way of the prize. Beaumont needs to win this game to prove we're still number one and show them that it's going to take an army to bring us down.

"I love you, Josie."

"I love you too, QB1."

MY hands are resting on the collar of my jersey, pulling it away from my neck. I've been standing here watching Josie work a routine for the past twenty minutes. She's left me with a walking hard-on since early this morning and I'm still hours away from being able to do anything about it.

I turn as Mason slaps me on the shoulder. He stands next to me, eying Katelyn, I'm sure. "Man, our girls are hot."

I nod in total agreement. We do have the two finest chicks in school on our arms.

"Are you going to show her the eye black that you made?"

"Yeah, just about to put it on and go see her. It will piss coach off, but whatever."

"All right, I'll see you in the locker room." I nod as Mason walks away, unable to take my eyes off my girl. She throws her head back with laughter, her smile bright and happy. I take one last look at her before the rest of the team comes out. I slip my helmet on and run out last. I purposely stop before I get to her and take off my helmet, sneaking up behind her.

"Hey beautiful," I say, picking her up and spinning her around. She squeals, but laughs so I know she likes it. I set her down on the ground and face her. I watch her eyes as she takes in what's on my face.

"You know you're wearing the name 'Jo' on your face?"

"Of course I know. It says Jojo."

"Yes it does." She laughs, covering her face.

I pull her closer, kissing her deeply in front of everyone. The coach has a strict 'no fraternization with the cheerleaders on the field' policy, but I don't care.

"I love Jojo more than anything," I profess against her lips.

"You do, huh? Should I be worried?"

I shake my head, holding her face in my hands. "You're my Jojo. Just mine," I kiss her again before I turn and run toward the field leaving her on the sidelines ready to cheer for me.

I stop and turn, catching her ogling my ass. I smile and yell, "Hey, Jojo."

"Yeah?" she yells back.

"I'm going to marry you someday." Her mouth drops open and her eyes go wide. I wink before pulling the helmet onto my head and run out to meet the rest of the team. I know I'm young and just committed myself for life, but it feels like the first right thing I've done all year.

CHAPTER 5

'M twenty-one; at least that's what my driver's license is telling the clerk at the store outside of Beaumont. Her attention flicks between me and my license as she inspects it, before she hands it back to me, seemingly satisfied that I'm legal. This is all a game to her. We do this every Friday night and sometimes Saturday. Each week it's the same silent stare down as she pretends to calculate my birthday in her head.

She doesn't tell me the total, she just holds out her hand for the cash. I hand her the wad that was waiting for me after the game and smile. She shakes her head as she bags up the cases of beer.

"Are you ever going to tell me your name so I can thank you properly?"

"Nah. I don't know you and you don't know me. This way when you get busted I can deny everything."

I nod and gather the four bags that she's given

me to hide the beer. No one needs to fill me in on the consequences I'd suffer if I got caught; it's the reason I volunteer. I want to see just how far this town is willing to go to protect their *golden boy*. How far will Sterling go to make sure the local police turn a blind eye? I have a feeling I could rob a bank and would walk out of the police station with nothing but a slap on the wrist. Sterling Westbury owns this town and it disgusts me.

I set the bags in the back and hop into my truck. It's the only thing I own, besides my guitar, that's mine. No, that's not even correct. Sterling owns this truck, because I'm too young to have any assets of value. He just wants me under this thumb, wants me to be dependent on him. I am. I don't have a choice. I'm a two-sport varsity athlete. I could quit playing baseball and get a job, but my father won't let me. No one is going to hire me to work during the winter and summer. That doesn't make me very dependable. He likes to monitor my cash flow and I know he hates that I spend the majority of it on Josie. Knowing that pisses him off just means I'm going to spend more.

I pull into the field where our water tower is located. Only a few cars and trucks are lined up, most with their lights on to give us enough light to party. Music is low so people can talk without yelling and a bonfire has been started. I see a few couples walking off into the dark. No need to try to figure out what they're going to do. From the looks it, we'll be here a while. Normally I wouldn't care, but I *need* some time with Josie. I have this ache that I can't describe, but know that she's the reason for it.

The second I throw my truck into park, Mason is there to get the beer. He pulls a bottle out, pops the top and downs the beer before I'm even out of the truck. Like

I said, it's going to be a long night. He had a good game, but it wasn't enough to make much headway on his goal. Their defense was constantly blitzing and my offensive line kept missing tackle assignments. I'm lucky my ass didn't get sacked a few times. The constant blitzing was enough to keep me on my toes.

My passes were weak and not as hard as they should be and Mason's running game was only as good as the blockers allowed. It took him a while to find his groove. I can't make too many excuses, everyone had a bad game and we won so I should be happy, but it's not enough. It's not enough for Mason or Sterling. Both have goals that I need to meet.

I grab a beer out of the bag before Mason takes off with them and look for Josie. It doesn't take me long to find her. I can find her in any crowd. That's how well I know her. Her presence makes the hair on my neck stand up. My body tingles when she's looking at me. I don't pretend to understand how love works, but I feel it. She's in my bones. I need her to survive. I have no doubt when I'm on the field and she's in the stands I'll know exactly where she is. I know I'll be able to look into the crowd and see her, feel her watching me.

In my Home Economics class we were asked to write a paper about what we'd be if our goals were different. As I looked around my class I saw people who didn't have a clue about what they wanted to do once they graduated. I mean, seriously, we're seventeen/eighteen years old and we're told from the time we enter high school to start thinking about our future. What if you don't know? What if you make it to your senior year and haven't figured it out yet? Where do you go? What do you do?

These are the questions that I have and don't know the answer to. I don't need to, technically. My path is chosen. I've worked hard to get where I am and now it's just a matter of waiting for the right offer to come in. Nothing but the best for Liam Westbury, that's the motto I've lived by. I'll have my pick of all the top schools that want to provide me with a stellar education. And all they want from me is to run their offense and win. I'll do my four years and enter the NFL draft. Once I'm drafted, I'm asking Josie to marry me. I want her to finish college and make sure that my path is her path as well. I'm all she's known. My fear is that she gets to college and meets someone else and realizes I'm not the man she wants. She could find someone whose parents accept her for who she is and not by the amount of zeros that are in her bank account. What if I don't want to play football in college and become a number cruncher?

As much as I want to go to her and take her away from her friends, I don't. I climb the ladder leading to the top. This tower has been here for years, but no one knows if it's still working. As soon as I could drive we started coming here. At first it was just me so I could get away from Sterling. Then I brought Mason and a few of the other guys. The next time I brought Josie here.

I sit down next to Mason and heave my beer bottle over the edge, watching it fly down to my truck and shattering in the back.

"I love that sound."

"How can you hear it over the music?" Nick Ashford butts in. I close my eyes and wish he'd go away. He's dense and thinks he's better than me. I see him staring at my girl all the time and it pisses me off.

"I just can."

"Look at Katelyn," Mason changes the subject to avoid any confrontation from starting and brings his current bottle to his lips.

"What about her?"

"I love her."

"And she loves you," I reply against my better judgment. I love Mason, but sometimes when he's been drinking he gets so girly that I have to watch what I say. If I'm not careful, he'll cry on my shoulder and tell me how much he loves me for being his QB1 and I don't want to hear it right now.

I twist the top off my beer and take a long pull as I survey the crowd. The cops should be here busting this up, but they won't come. If they bust us, our winning streak goes out the door and they'd be the most hated people in town. They'd likely get fired. Beaumont takes their football a bit too seriously if you ask me, but whatever, it's allowing me to drink out in the open and fuck my girl in my truck without getting busted.

"Mase, come down here. I'm lonely," Katelyn yells up at him.

The laughter between the girls and us is just enough to keep a constant flow of noise in the air.

"I love you, baby," Mason yells through cupped hands. "I'm going to marry that girl and make beautiful babies with her." We start laughing, but I know it's true. Katelyn walks on water where Mason is concerned. I know the feeling. I look down and see the silhouette of my girl standing by my truck, my letterman jacket making me jealous because it's wrapped around her. But this is tradition, being here after a game.

"I know man," I say, patting him on the back.

"Double wedding," he shouts as I spew my beer out of into the open air.

"Dude, you're a dude. You aren't supposed to be talking about weddings and shit." Jerad says before chugging his beer.

Mason shrugs. "When you love someone, you just know."

His words keep me silent because he's right. I know I love Josie and want to be with her. I told her this much tonight. I see her as my wife of fifteen/twenty years and I'm confident that she sees me as her husband, but is it enough?

"Do you ever think about knocking her up so she has to stay with you?" I turn slowly at Mason and he meets my eyes.

"What?" I ask as utter confusion runs through me.

"I don't know. The thought of college away from Katelyn scares me and sometimes I think if I got her pregnant she'd follow me wherever I go."

I turn away and look at Josie.

My girl.

My Jojo.

I can't even begin to think like Mason.

"Nah," I say, taking a swig of my beer before tossing it to the bed of my truck.

CHAPTER 6

MONDAYS. I hate them. They're literally the worst day of the week. Not only are most of us tired, but teachers come to work in a bad mood. None of them are chipper or happy go lucky. They're pissed off and sucking down cups of coffee to keep themselves awake. You'd think that after our win on Friday night they'd be happy, but no, they'll save that for Friday when they can "pretend" to teach by way of talking football.

I set my books down on my desk and wait for class to start. Ms. Barnes walks in with bags under her eyes. Rough weekend for her, I'm gathering. A few of the guys snicker in class probably making assumptions about what she did, but I can't be bothered. My eyes are focused on the courtyard next to my class. My girl is out there with her P.E. class doing yoga and slowly killing me. I don't know what *dog facing forward* is but if that's what she's doing, we need to find some time to practice it together.

"Mr. Westbury, do you plan on joining us today?"

I turn at the sound of my name and find Ms. Barnes standing just to the side of me. She's leaning toward me, her cleavage prevalent in my face. I guess I don't have to assume why she has bags under her eyes. I smirk and shake my head before turning my gaze back out the window to watch Josie.

"Mr. Westbury, eyes forward please," she commands as she walks away from me. I roll my eyes and keep my focus on the outside. It's more entertaining and far more educational than whatever Ms. Barnes is going to teach us about globalization.

When Josie and her class start rolling their mats up a huge sigh washes over me. After staring at her in spandex for the last forty-five minutes, I'm ready to see her, to touch her. I look at the clock and count off the seconds until the bell rings. It will take me approximately a minute and a half to get across campus to her locker, piece of cake.

I'm up and out of my seat before the sound of the bell echoes through the school, realizing then that I never took my textbook out of my backpack. It's Monday, right? School is very overrated in my opinion anyway.

When I come around the corner I see Katelyn and Mason with Josie. This instantly brings a smile to my face. They're my family and the only ones who truly understand me. Josie is leaning against her locker, her face pensive.

"Wait until Liam sees this," I overhear Mason say as I approach them.

"Sees, what?" I ask as I bend down to kiss my girl before turning to Mason. "What's this?" Mason hands me a piece of paper. It's folded into fours like the notes girls would pass to us in class back in middle school. I open it and read it, wishing my eyes were deceiving me, but they're not. I take a deep breath and look at Josie. "What's this, Josie?"

"I don't know. Katelyn brought it to me. I don't even know what it says."

I look at Katelyn who shrugs as if this is no big deal when in reality it's huge. I'm going to kick someone's ass, someone who deserves to have a freaking beat down for even looking at my girl.

"He gave it to me in history class," Katelyn says as Mason wraps his arms around her. I know he knows what I'm thinking but if he thinks I'm going to take it out on Katelyn, he's nuts. She's like a sister to me.

As pissed off as I am I can't help but find the humor. Does this asshole really think a love letter to my girl is going to win him any brownie points? I look at the paper and try to contain my laughter.

"It says," I start.

"*Dear Josephine, Do you realize how beautiful you are? I see you in the halls and wish I had the courage to talk to you, but I don't. I wouldn't know what to say. I would like to get to know you better. Call me.*
Yours, Nicholas Ashford."

Mason and I bust out laughing as soon as I'm done reading it. Josie rolls her eyes and walks away from us. I look at the letter one more time before folding it back up and slipping it into my pocket. I'm keeping this shit for later and after my fist is done reminding Ashford that

Josie is mine, he can have his letter back.

I run to catch up with Josie before she enters her class. I don't say anything to her as I guide her out the double doors and toward the football field. No one will come out here, especially if they saw us heading this way.

I spin her around and push her up against the concrete wall of the concession stand. I know she's angry with me for being a Neanderthal, but I can't help it when it comes to her. She's mine and I don't share well. My hands cup her ass, her legs wrapping around my hips instantly. I move my hand to her face, cupping her cheek as my mouth captures hers. "Do you want to call Ashford?" I ask as my other hand moves under her skirt.

Josie shakes her head and that's enough for me. I know my girl is faithful. She's never given me a reason to be jealous, but I know I am of Ashford.

"He's jealous of me, baby. He wants everything I have. Please don't give it to him."

"I won't, I promise."

In my heart I know she won't, but right now that's not good enough. I need more. I work the buttons on my jeans and release myself, plugging right into her. It's stupid having sex without a condom, but right now I need this from her.

The moment her mouth drops open, I take advantage with my tongue. Her nails are digging into my neck, encouraging me. I'm trying to be gentle and not slam her against the wall but she feels too good and I'm having a hard time controlling myself. I pull back a little and slam into her again. She whimpers into my mouth before biting my lower lip. Our eyes are open and focused on each other. I love this girl with everything that I am.

I thrust a few times before saying the words that are going to piss her off. "I need to pull out."

"What, why?" she asks, moving her body in rhythm with mine making it hard for her to keep control.

"No condom," I say as I pull out. I have to set her down quickly and move away from her so I can finish myself off. It only takes a few seconds, which is not a good sign. I wipe my hands on my jeans and right myself before going back to her and pulling her into my arms. "I love you, Jojo."

She leans her head on my shoulder with her arms around my waist. "We can't be stupid like that, Liam. A baby would totally mess up your future."

"And yours," I say.

"I could handle it. You don't need the stress. You're so close to achieving all your dreams," she says in between the kisses she's placing on my neck. This isn't the answer I'm looking for. She's supposed to be angry with me and she's not. She's too freaking worried about my goals and dreams and not her own. She should have her own damn dreams for the future and not brushing off that we just had sex without a condom.

I step away from her and make sure her hair isn't messy and her clothes are straight before we walk hand in hand back to school. We ditched class and she'll probably get a call home even though I know that I won't. That's how this school works. The *golden boy* can do no wrong. Maybe I need to use that fact to my advantage more often.

CHAPTER 7

THE calls from scouts are starting to come in and it pisses me off that my dad is fielding them. He bought me a cell phone for this exact reason, yet coach still gives out my home number. Sterling will not choose my college for me. I refuse to allow that to happen. This isn't an opportunity for him to relive his life through me. I will not live in a state that I don't like or that is too far from Josie. She's far too important for me to be away from her.

Another evaluation period is coming up and knowing this has me on edge. These coaches and scouts are snooping around my life and there isn't shit I can do about it. They talk to teachers, coaches and whoever else they want so they can find out what type of kid I am. "*A rich, snobby one who gets away with everything because of what he's done for his school*" needs to be the answer they give, but they won't. I'm sure their responses are all scripted to suit each recruiter that comes through town.

If this were a recruiting week, they'd all be waiting by my truck when I get out of practice. That will be a nice week.

We're sitting pretty at number one in the standings. Four wins with one of them being too close for my liking. Winning by three is not how I like to end my games. We played well, but they played better. I'm just thankful that there were no scouts out that night. Not only am I worried about myself, but I'm also worried about my teammates. Everyone wants to play at the next level and that falls onto me. If I perform well, they do too. We're a team, a family.

I take my helmet off when coach blows the last whistle of the day and head toward the locker room. The mood of the team is somber. It always is after a close game. As their captain it's my job to reassure them, and I do. We won't have another close game like that. Not on my watch.

When I get to the parking lot, my girl is lying on the top of my truck. She's wearing those sassy little cut-offs with her hair in braids, a plaid shirt and cowboy boots. And she's the farthest thing from a cowgirl. But she is sexy as hell. I have to stop and stare at her for a minute, just to get the full effect. That girl right there is mine and she's waiting for me. I smile and cock my head.

"Whatcha doing, Jojo?" I feign innocence as I step up to her. She winks at me as she slides off my truck and into my arms.

"You know the only thing you're missing is a hat."

Her eyes raise and a cute little grin appears. She's up to something. Josie leans forward and nuzzles my neck making me thankful that I took a shower after practice.

"I have dinner for you."

Yes, my girl knows what I like to eat. "Are your

parents' home?"

Josie leans back and slaps me across the chest causing me to laugh. "What?"

"Really, Liam, is that all you think about?"

"Since I popped your cherry, yes. I'm a guy and I have a hot fucking girlfriend who I happen to love and thoroughly enjoy being with, and she also happens to be standing here in a pair of shorts that are tempting me. They're so short and I can easily slide my fingers up your legs to where I know you want me. Forgive me if my mind is in the gutter."

Josie kisses me hard, running her hands through my still damp hair. "I made you dinner," she tells me again, pulling away too soon. She rests her forehead against mine briefly. "There's a picnic basket in the back, I thought we could go to the Cliffs and watch the sunset."

"I'd like that." She doesn't know how much her doing this means to me. I kiss her once before throwing my football gear into the back of my truck. I open the door and let her slide in first before following her.

I rest my hand on her leg as we drive out of the school parking lot. For October, it's still warm, an Indian summer they call it. I don't care what the name is I love it. The weather allows me to roll the windows down and feel the wind in my hair, well what I have for hair. I love the fact that Josie doesn't say anything about the wind messing up her hair. I feel her move closer, her hand resting on my leg and her head resting on my shoulder. I don't know what she's thinking, but for me, I'm thinking I don't want this to ever end. I want to stay where we are and not have to grow up and move away from each other, but staying here doesn't provide a future for us. I have to take one for the Westbury/Preston team, her and I, and do what I need to do to support her.

We pull into the Cliffs. They're not really a part of anything but a roadside destination created years ago. They were dubbed "the Cliffs" because of their high elevation. That scares some people, but I think they're worth it. If you walk down the well-worn path you'll find some open spaces that look out of the river where you can watch the sunrise or sunset on any given day.

Aside from two other cars, the place is deserted. Just the way I like it. It means Josie and I can be alone with no one bothering me about the upcoming football game or what college I'm going to choose. It means we can sit here and have some peace and quiet. Although quiet is the last thing I want.

I take her hand in mine and pick up the picnic basket from the back of my truck. Josie made sure we'd be prepared and has a blanket in her other hand. I pull her close and kiss her before guiding her down the path. She takes the lead and finds a spot for us, spreading out the blanket and taking the basket from my hand.

I walk to the edge of the cliff and look out over the rocky slope that feeds into a vast river. The water is flowing after the rainfall we had. We swim here every now and again, but most of the time we prefer Katelyn's pool. The girls really don't like the river anyway. They're afraid they're going to catch something.

Josie's arms come around my waist. I lean into her and tighten my hands on her arms, holding her in place. She's my peace. My calm. I just need her in my life to make everything okay.

"We should eat," she says, whispering into my back.

I nod and let go of her hands, but grab one to hold while we walk back to the blanket. It dawns on me that in four years I can be hearing those words from her all the time and yesterday that seemed like a long time, but tonight, it seems like tomorrow. I know I'm going to spend the rest of my life with her.

We sit down and eat chicken and pasta. I know her mom made it for us and she's a damn good cook. Mr. Preston always jokes that's why he keeps her around and that Josie better learn how to cook if she plans to keep me happy.

Once we're done she crawls in between my legs and rests her head on my shoulder. I hold her in my arms as we watch the sunset, casting the perfect glow over the river. I could sit like this every day and not have a care in the world. Unfortunately, it will be back to reality for me as soon as I get home. The pile of college letters will be sitting there and Sterling will be looking at his calendar to schedule visits. None of which I want to go on. I want to sit here and hold my girl and watch this sunset over and over again because right now it's my favorite time of the day.

CHAPTER 8

MY father's office light is on when I pull into our driveway. I was hoping that he wouldn't be here when I came home. The last thing I want to do is talk to him. We have nothing civil to say to each other and we definitely don't agree on my college career path. He wants me to play in the SEC and I want to do anything but. The schools in the SEC are fantastic, but it's the fact that it's what Sterling wants that makes me want to avoid every single recruiter that comes knocking, just to spite him.

I carry my football gear into the house through the garage and leave it by the basement door for my mom to wash. Drunk or not, she's a master at getting out the grass stains. The kitchen is dark and empty with everything from dinner – if they even had dinner – put away. My mom wasn't waiting for me to come home at all and if she was, I have no doubt that Sterling told her that I would not be eating since I didn't go home after practice.

I have rules that I break often. My father doesn't think I need a social life unless he approves of who it's with. I can date any of the socialites from the country club or any of his business partners' daughters, but he won't acknowledge that I'm in love with Josie Preston. She's not good enough for me and she doesn't deserve to be on the arm of a Westbury.

Imagine being fifteen and asking a girl out for the first time only to have your father tell you she's trash. I don't know if it was that moment that I knew I hated my father or not. What I did know was that it didn't matter what he said about Josie, I was going to be with her.

The television is on in the family room and I can hear ice dropping into a glass. I could stop in there and say hi to my mom, but by now she's had so much vodka that she's in a haze. And what's the point? It's not like she's going to ask how my day was. But I want to talk to her. I want her to ask. I want her to care. I don't think it's too much to want at least one parent to give a shit about you, is it?

Standing in the foyer, I need to make a decision before it's too late. I can climb the stairs to my room or I can go in and try to communicate with my mom. I step toward the family room only to be halted by the clearing of his throat. I stalled too long. I should've dropped my gear off and high-tailed my ass upstairs as soon as I got home. He usually doesn't bother me if I'm in my room, but out here I'm fair game.

"Where have you been?"

"Out," I say, knowing this answer will not suffice and only piss him off more. I turn around to face my father.

He's still dressed in his three-piece business suit with his tie barely loosened. Sterling Westbury stands at six feet two, one inch taller than me. He was also the starting quarterback in high school. He was awarded a full-ride to Auburn, but was red-shirted by the coach his freshman year and tore up his ACL the next day. My dad never started a college game and the one he played in ruined his career. I've heard the story many times growing and when you are six and seven, you want to be like your father. But then you start having dreams of your own and most parents let you run with those, except *I'm* his dream. Everything he didn't accomplish is now on my shoulders.

"With Mason?"

I shake my head. "Josie."

"How many times do I need to tell you to get rid of her? She's not the right one for you."

"I love her," I retort, trying to keep my temper in check. It wouldn't bode well for me to get angry with him. He doesn't care and can take away my truck, and I need my truck.

"You don't know what love is, Liam. You love football. That is your focus. Get rid of the girl before it's too late."

"What do you mean too late?"

Sterling moves toward his office and I know I'm to follow even if I don't want to. He sits down at his desk and hands me a pile of letters. They're all addressed to me, but are opened and have notes on them. Each one is from a different college and placed in order of preference according to Sterling. Auburn sits on top, followed by Ole Miss and Arkansas. They're all interested in me.

He folds his hands on his desk and clears his throat.

"I didn't raise you to get trapped by the town harlot."

I bite the inside of my cheek and shake my head. "You don't know shit about Josie. I'm her first boyfriend. It's not like she's out sleeping around or messing with other guys. We're in love. I don't know why my happiness isn't important to you."

"Your happiness is on the field and you don't need to be some teenage statistic."

"Meaning what?"

"She's trying to trap you, get herself pregnant. You better not be having sex with her. You're too good for her." I want to reach across and slam his face into his ornate desk. I can see myself smashing his head repeatedly until there's nothing left. Who the fuck does he think he is talking about her like that?

"You don't know shit," I mutter weakly. It's no use with him. "You're such an arrogant prick thinking everyone is beneath you."

"Everyone is, especially that Preston girl."

I hold up the letters he just handed me. "Thanks for these, I'm not interested," I say, tossing them back on his desk and walking toward the door.

"Liam, stop," he demands. When I don't, he yells it again. I turn and look at him and for the first time in my life I wish he were dead. He's standing with his hands pushed down on his desk. I could rush him and throw him through his floor to ceiling window if I wanted. My mom would probably clean up the mess before calling the paramedics and that thought makes me laugh. We're the perfect fucking family on the outside.

"I don't want to do this, but you're leaving me no choice. I'm forbidding you from being with that girl. She's trouble and you need to focus on college. You're thinking with your dick and not your head. Don't be an idiot, Liam, she's not worth it."

"That's where you're wrong. She *is* worth it. I'm eighteen, Sterling. You can't ground me and you definitely can't hit me," I inform him as I walk toward him. "You've already made my life hell so what are you going to do, kick me out? I do everything you ask, but I won't let go of Josie."

"You'll see it my way, soon enough."

"I doubt it." I turn and leave, slamming his door in my wake. I almost run into my robot mother standing in the hall, listening.

"Why are you married to him?" I ask. Her eyes look sad and it makes me wonder why she stays. She knows how he is and how he treats me. Am I not enough for her? Isn't a mother's love supposed to supersede everything?

"He's my husband."

"Am I not important? Do you think it's okay for him to say that shit about Josie?"

She looks over my shoulder briefly before bringing her glass to her lips. "You know how he is. Just break it off with the girl, pick his school and keep him happy." She doesn't wait for me to respond before she moves to the bar that she keeps fully stocked.

My parents make me sick to my stomach and there isn't shit I can do about it until I leave for college, but then what? Come home to *this* for breaks and holidays? No thanks.

CHAPTER 9

TAKE the stairs to my room two at a time. I throw open my door, head for my closet and take out my guitar. This is a risk, but I'm willing to take it. I need to get out of this house and if Sterling and Bianca see me with my guitar, so be it. If I have to hide it at Mason's from here on out, I'll do it. Right now I need an escape and this is going to be it.

I'm back down the stairs and into the garage undetected. I feel as if I'm doing something illegal and sadly, in the Westbury house, this qualifies. Opening the door to my truck, I hop in and place my prized possession on the seat. I'd give anything to have Josie by my side right now, but I'm not ready to show her yet. I want to be good enough by Christmas so that I can play her a melody that will mean something to her. I want to write words that will mean something to us. I'm not foolish. I'm not looking to make a career out of strumming my guitar, but it's a good release and I hear chicks dig rockers. Even if I am a wannabe.

My favorite clerk is working when I enter the country store. She looks up from her gossip magazine and directly at the calendar. I try not to laugh, but I know she's looking to see if it's Friday. I'm a few days early.

It only takes me a minute to spot what I want. I open the glass door, reach into the cooler and grab a six-pack. I don't know if she's going to sell it to me with it not being my usual day, but we're about to find out.

"It's not Friday," she says, as she stands up.

"Yeah, just think you get to see me twice this week."

"You alone?" she asks, her eyes pointing to the beer.

I look out the storefront window and into the empty cab of my truck. "Yep."

The clerk sighs heavily. "Look kid, I know what you do on Friday nights and know you're not the only one drinking all that beer, but tonight..." she shakes her head and I know what's coming out of her mouth next. "Are you going to be driving?"

"No ma'am," I lie. "I have to pick up my buddy. He'll be with me and my girl." I'm shocked at how easily the lie comes.

"All right," she says, reluctantly as she takes the cash out of my hand. She bags the six-pack and I'm out the door and heading toward the Cliffs. No one will be there at this time of night and that's the way I want it.

I pull into the same spot that I was in earlier. Being here with Josie a few hours ago makes me wish I had gone to get her, but I really want to perfect this melody for her. I want to be able to play something that makes sense even if I'm the only one who understands the way music makes me feel.

Climbing out of the truck, I have my guitar in one hand and my six-pack in the other. I turn on my pen-flashlight to light the path to the opening and get as close as I can to the edge. I can hear the river, but can't see it. The pitch-black abyss is rumbling down below waiting to swallow whatever comes its way.

For a brief moment I consider stepping off the side to see if I can tame the river. I'd lose, of course, but the thrill of trying might be worth it. What would Sterling think when I turn up missing only for them to find me miles down the river? His dream would be shattered and there isn't a damn thing he could do about it. The only consequence would be that I'd hurt Josie and I can't do that to her.

I step away and sit down on the cold hard ground, popping the tab on one of the beers. This is going to be a night of firsts for me. I've never been here by myself. I've never drunk alone before. I've never drunk beer out of a can before either. I've never played in the dark. I've never played my guitar out in the open. What if the wildlife doesn't like me? I guess there's only one way to find out.

I down my beer and pop the next one before picking up my guitar. With it resting on my leg I let my fingers glide over the strings. I can't look at it to watch my fingers. This will be blind playing for me and from memory. I don't have the confidence I have on the field with my guitar. For all I know my positioning will be wrong and even though I'll think I sound good, the reality is I probably sound like complete shit. I go over what I've learned from books. G, C, D, E and A, as I move my fingers into the shapes that I remember, repeating them over and over again. They sound right, but I can't be too sure.

Over and over until I'm confident that I can play the melody I've been working on. I haven't felt this relaxed since school started. There's something so peaceful about making music with your hands, maybe all athletes should do this. Whatever it is, it's working.

I close my eyes and let my fingers recall the notes I have written down at home. They may not make sense, but they will… someday. But that moment will have to wait. I'm eager to show her what I can do, what I've taught myself. I know she'll be proud of me.

The song I'm playing echoes off the rocks and through the valley creating a lullaby for the lurking animals. That's what I'm telling myself at least; to keep the fear away that any second I'm going to get mauled by a deer for disturbing his slumber. When I stop playing my tune carries on, almost like the surrounding scenery is my own personal orchestra. I smile, despite being alone. It's a good feeling to have, being able to hear something you've created. That's not something that can be done on the football field.

On the field, I'm a puppet being controlled by the giant. Do this, run this, throw there. None of those are my decisions. I'm trained to do what I'm told and when. I know every offensive scheme in our playbook. I can run any route thrown at me and pass with the best of them. Double team coverage is a joke because I'm hitting my target in their numbers each and every time. But I'm not free.

Right now I am and I love this feeling.

CHAPTER 10

I WATCH as the seconds tick off the clock before running into the locker room. We have a twenty point lead at half-time and I can't think of a better way to start our homecoming celebration. My coach hates this part, but it's tradition. I know he wants to go over what we need to execute, but Mason and I are due on the field for the coronation.

I jog out of the locker room with Mason by my side and find our girls. I hop into the back of the rented convertible and lay one on her. She doesn't push me away or tell me that I stink. She cups my face, holding me to her lips.

The car lurches forward, making me pull away from my girl. We're about to enter our stadium and drive around the track. The marching band is in front of the first car, leading the parade. The rest of the guys from the football team, lining the sidelines, in a show of solidarity.

Josie and I are dressed not to impress, that will come later tonight. I'm still in my uniform and she's definitely in hers.

"I love you, Jojo," I say, kissing her one more time before we're visible to the crowd. My parents are here and have voiced their displeasure of me accepting my homecoming court invitation. This type of thing may not be what Sterling wants, but it's important to my girl so this is where I'm going to be. I just have to keep him away from her and we'll be good.

We do one loop around the track before the cars stop and we're told to stand by the make-shift podium. I hold Josie's hand while she exits and even though my parents want me to keep my distance, I don't. I refuse to let her go of her hand. She's done nothing wrong. I'm not some fifteen-year-old kid anymore. The first time they told me to stay away from her just drove me to be with her even more. Then I fell in love and it was all over from there. I didn't care what they said then and I definitely don't care now.

Most of the girls hoping to be crowned queen tonight are dressed in their formal dresses. Personally, I think it takes away the element of surprise of when your guy shows up on your doorstep, rings the bell and stands in your entryway waiting for you to make an appearance. Last year when Josie and I were nominated for Princess and Prince of the junior class, I asked her not to change into her dress at half-time because I wanted to see her in all her beauty when I knocked on her door later that night with her corsage in my hand. If I have to be in my uniform, I want her to be in hers as well.

"I'm sorry I smell," I whisper into her ear, nuzzling

her as I do. She giggles and pushes me away slightly.

"I'll forgive you."

"After I make it up to you later?" I waggle my eyebrows at her only for her to turn beet red. Our school administrators are standing behind us and one of them is snickering. I shrug and place my arm around her waist, pulling her as close as she'll let me.

The microphone is tapped and the crowd goes silent. "Each year we're honored to bring forth the finest in our student body for coronation and this year is no exception. The student body nominated two boys and two girls from each class to represent Beaumont High in the annual homecoming parade tomorrow. We use an anonymous ballot voting system here at Beaumont and this year we've had a record number of votes."

"It's a popularity contest," I mumble. Josie tries to jab in my stomach but my shoulder pads prevent her from reaching me before I grab her arm. "What it is, Josie? Do you think any other senior couple stands a chance with me and you and Mason and Katelyn in the running?"

She rolls her eyes but she knows it. I'm captain of the football team and she's captain of the cheerleading squad – again it's the popular vote.

"Please hold your applause as I announce this year's coronation court. This year's freshman prince and princess are: Garrett Plice and Simone Santoro."

This is the part of the process that takes forever. Securing the nomination and voting was the fun part. Right now we have to watch each couple or 'non-couple but only a couple for this moment and a single dance tonight' take their spot on the podium.

"Our sophomore prince and princess are: Aiden

Hansen and Riley Wade," the Principal announces. She beams with each name as if she had a hand in making sure they were chosen.

"Our junior class prince and princess are: Ryder Whitley and Maddy O'Sullivan." Ryder is on the football team. He's our tight end and is quicker than shit. No one gets by him. He started dating Maddy over the summer after talking to her all of last year. He finally got up enough nerve to ask her out. I'm sure Mason and I ragging on him didn't help much, but it's all locker room talk.

"Our senior class prince and princess are…" I wish this moment wasn't happening. It's between us and our best friends. It's not going to matter who wins; either Mason or I will be consoling our girls. I'll be sad if it's not Josie and me because I know how much she wants this. I faintly hear their names being called. It's when I see Mason and Katelyn walking toward the podium I know.

"And this year's king and queen are Liam Westbury and Josephine Preston."

Josie and I make our way to the center where crowns are placed on our heads and she's given a dozen red roses. Looking out into the crowd, her parents, the Powell's and Mrs. Bishop, Katelyn's mom, are all standing and cheering. They're trying to take pictures from the stands. Mine are sitting front and center, with their heads down no less.

All the girls are waving to the crowd as we're being ushered back to our cars. Our driver opens the door and I help Josie in, keeping my hands on her waist. I can't wait to see her in her dress tonight. She's kept it a secret just so she can surprise me tonight.

We loop one more time around the track before we're

through the gate and back into the parking lot. I hop out, holding her hand so she can step out of the car.

"I love you, babe," she says, kissing me quickly so I can get back to the field. I wink and smack her on the ass as I leave to catch up with Mason.

Once inside the locker room, Coach goes over our strategy for the second half of the game. He wants to run a lot of pass plays and stay away from the ground attack. I feel Mason sigh next to me. I know he doesn't like to think about the record, but I do. It's always on my mind. It's going to happen. The only way it won't is if coach benches me.

"Coach, the receivers are going to have to show me their numbers if they want the pass. I can't get a mark that isn't there."

He nods and repeats what I just said before excusing us back to the field. I lightly bump Mason with my shoulder hoping he waits for me. Because of tonight's activities our half time has been about an hour long so we have to warm-up again. I stay back and wait until everyone leaves the locker room.

"What's up?"

"Nothing, man."

"I call BS. Is this about the record?"

He shrugs.

I put my hand on his shoulder. "It's gonna happen. I promise you."

Mason attempts a smile but it ends up being half-assed. "Are you getting looks?"

He shrugs again. "Mostly II's. A couple lower I's, but nothing big."

I don't want to tell him what's waiting for me at

home. I'm sure he knows and I'm not one to pour salt in open wounds. "They'll come around, especially after you clinch that state leading rushing yard. You're close. It's going to happen." That earns me a smile as we walk out of the locker room. I slip my helmet on just before our tunnel ends. I don't want him to see the expression on my face because it's my problem to bear, not his. I'll get this done for him. It's the least I can do.

CHAPTER 11

"WHERE are you going?"

Why I stopped in the hallway to adjust my tie is beyond me. I survey my dad through the mirror. He has a cigar hanging out of his mouth, which means my mother is either passed out on the couch or she's out with her friends. It's the night before the Beaumont Homecoming Parade and while she may be a drunk, she's every bit the socialite and wouldn't miss being with the women gathering to watch the floats come alive. Maybe she doesn't drink when she's not at home, although I can't blame her for her stupor sometimes.

"Homecoming," I inform him as I step away from the mirror. I don't want to look at him, let alone stand near him.

"And you think you're going?"

"Yes, I'm going," I answer without hesitation. I walk into the kitchen and pull Josie's corsage out of the

59

refrigerator, smiling as I examine the tiny pink roses. This is our last homecoming in high school and it's all too bittersweet. I shut the door to find Sterling scrutinizing me. He breathes deeply and when he exhales and I can smell Scotch on his breath, lovely.

"Are you thick headed or just stupid? Help me figure it out here, son, because I'm certain I told you to get rid of that trash."

My blood boils as I step forward, my finger pointing in his face. "You —" I step back again and shake my head. "You don't know shit about Josie. I'm in love with her. That in itself should be enough for you, but it's not. You should care about my feelings. I don't want a life like yours, can't you get that through your head?" I brush by him, my shoulder bumping into his. He may be my father but I have no doubt I can take him down if I have to.

I get into my truck and slam the door angrily, resting my head on the steering wheel to cool down. I don't know how much more I can take of Sterling and his hatred for Josie. It might not be so bad if my mother stood up for me every now and again but she just tells me to do what he says. I know I can't sit here any longer. We're already late for the dance because of my game and it's not fair to keep Josie waiting because of my douchebag dad.

When I get to Josie's I hop out and leave the truck running. I'm eager to see her in her dress. One knock and the front door opens with Mrs. Preston standing there, beaming. I walk in and she immediately straightens my tie. This is how tonight should be. My mom should've been there to do all of this for me.

"Oh you look so handsome Liam."

"Thank you, Mrs. Preston." I lean down and give her

a kiss on the cheek. It's pretty sad that I can't wait for her and Mr. Preston to become my in-laws so I can have a normal family.

The clank of heels catches my attention. I turn and see Josie walking down the hallway. Her dress is black and, oh man, does it do things to me. There's a slit strategically placed just for my hand, which reaches so far up her thigh that if she moves just right, I'll be able to see my promised land. I continue to admire her as she spins in front of me. The back of her dress is black sheer lace. I know this from the many trips to the mall that we've made. She's turned me into a girl. When she turns forward again I realize her neck is bare and I immediately realize that I need to rectify that. I should be buying my girl necklaces and bracelets, showing her that I love her.

I step forward, our eyes lock. "If this is what you look like for a semi-formal I can't wait to see what you wear for prom."

"Do you like it?"

"I love it, Jojo," I whisper as slide her corsage onto her wrist. "Are you ready to go?" she nods as I take her hand in mine. "Mr. and Mrs. P, I won't keep her out too long."

"We know, Liam," Mr. Preston says as he walks us to the door. It warms me that they're so welcoming. Why can't I have that at home? As we're walking down her stone path, I stop suddenly.

"What's wrong?"

"Pictures, we forgot to take some." I turn her back to the house and walk in, spotting her mom right away. "Can you take a picture of us, please?"

"Of course, dear," she says as she picks her camera up off of the table.

Josie and I stand, arms wrapped around each other, posing. I know a few of the images are going to show me looking at her and those are the ones I want to keep.

"I'll take these to be developed tomorrow after the parade."

"Thank you."

We rush out of the house and to my idling truck. I open the door for her and she slides in all the way to the middle. I run around and get in, kissing her quickly before driving down the street.

The school parking lot is jam packed, forcing me to park in the back. Not that I mind. It's more secluded back here and that means more privacy for later. I don't know how I'm going to keep my hands off her and away from that slit. She had to know something like that would drive me absolutely crazy with lust. That's probably why she bought it, to test my resolve. Well I hate to tell her this, but my resolve has been gone for a very long time when it comes to her.

"We better put these on." I place her tiara on her head, careful not to mess up her hair. I lean forward and capture her lips with mine. "My queen," I murmur against her lips.

"My king," she replies as she sets my far from masculine crown on my head. I never wanted to be homecoming king, but I'd be anything she asked me to be if it made her smile, and this does so it's worth it.

We walk hand in hand into the gym. I have to give the student council credit; the decorations aren't cheesy, but definitely dance-worthy. The theme is 'Bring Back the 80's'. I guess they need a revival or something. For me, though, I keep them around. The music is sexy and it's the perfect mood enhancer.

I lead Josie to the dance floor and take my girl in my arms. We start swaying to *Open Arms* by Journey. I glance around quickly and notice that most of the student body are either dancing or walking back to their tables. It's the music. There's something about a decade's worth of artists that can take it slow with a love song or change the beat and make it a hard-core melody but still give you the same affect.

My hands begin to wander over her body, from her back to her ass, to her back again. I don't know how I'm going to go to college for four years and not see her every day. It's going to kill me, both inside and out.

The song switches to *Purple Rain*. This is the first song we ever danced to. I'll remember our first dance for as long as I can. I held a girl in my arms, afraid to look at her. But when this song came on, I kissed her and made her mine.

I slide my hand up the outside of her thigh, adjusting myself in the process. She glances at me with her beautiful blue eyes. They drop to my lips and back again as my hand moves into the slit of her dress. Like I said, this is what she wanted when she bought this bad boy.

Her forehead rests on mine as our bodies move to the lyrics that Prince sings so passionately. I want her and she knows it, she wants me too. I can feel it in the way her body is pressed against mine. My fingers brush against her, moving what little scrap of fabric that she calls panties out of the way. I shield her as much as possible from prying eyes as my fingers dip into her folds. I stifle a groan when I feel how wet she is. Her head moves down to my neck, she bites me lightly as I increase my movements. She moans softly in my ear as she grinds against my hand.

We need to get out of here before we get suspended for having sex on the gym floor or caught in the bathroom. I reluctantly remove my hand and take her hand in my other one. I pull her behind me, her feet shuffling to keep up. I take a chance and look over my shoulder, to make sure she's okay with leaving and her eyes tell me she is. She's biting her lower lip as she looks up at me with desire. I'm not stopping to talk to classmates as they call out our names. The tension is building and I need the release that only she can provide. I'm on a mission and her name is Josie Preston.

"Get in" I demand as I open the passenger door. She does, moving in far enough to let me follow her. I throw my keys into the truck, only for her to put them in the ignition and turn on the radio. I don't know what's playing and I don't care. Her and I are about to make our own music. I take off my suit jacket and pull my shirt out from my pants all while meeting her lustful gaze. My movements are rushed as I climb into my truck, my lips crashing against her with my crown falling onto my face. I forgot it was there. Josie removes it before she starts working on the buttons to my shirt. I pull my wallet out from my back pocket, taking a condom out before throwing it on my dashboard.

"I want you, Jojo," I unbutton my pants and sit back, slouching against the seat and watch as she hikes her dress up over her hips. I tear open the condom and roll it onto my shaft, eager for her.

"Come here, Jojo," I whisper against her lips as I pull her to me. This isn't the first time we've had sex in my truck and likely won't be the last. I enjoy the thrill of it too much. The tight quarters makes it feel more torrid.

She moves her leg around me as I hold her hips in my hands. My fingers are digging into her, anxious for her and I to connect. "Leave it on," I say to her as she starts to remove her crown. "You're so fucking beautiful, Josie. God, how I want to see all of you right now."

"You can, Liam." Josie slides the shoulder strap down, showing me her breasts. I lean forward, taking her nipple in my mouth. Her fingers dig into my scalp, urging me on.

"I need you. Please I need you so bad, Josie." I beg her to sit on me, to ride me. I need to feel our connection and know she's not going anywhere.

She moves ever so slowly. I growl when I feel myself enter her. Her hands grab onto my shoulders for leverage as she moves up and down. As much as I want to sit back and watch her work me over, I can't let go. I put my head in the valley of her breasts and listen to her heart tell me that she loves me and that she's never going to leave.

CHAPTER 12

NO one has ever asked me what I want to do with my life. It's been planned. I never questioned anyone's intentions and I never thought to add my own two cents, for whatever they're worth. Now I'm sitting in this office, with these ridiculously ugly drapes, the smell of stale smoke and a legend quarterback sitting in a king-sized chair because he's let himself go after he retired from the NFL. That is not going to be me.

But I can't say that because my father won't shut up. He keeps talking like the NFL is the only option that I don't need a college education because nothing is going to happen to me. How does he know that?

The man behind the desk wants me to commit today and if Sterling has his way, I'll be signing before I leave here. Except I can't and I seem to be the only one who knows this. There are rules and regulations and I'll be damned if I'm going to let some overzealous legend ruin my eligibility status. I've read the rules. I've watched the films. I know what I'm allowed to do and what will get me in trouble.

I look down at my pants and remember what I was doing in them when I last wore them; they were around my ankles, just a few nights ago. I can still see her sitting on top of me, working us into a heated frenzy. She looked beyond sexy riding me with her tiara on top of her head. My very own queen.

"What do you think, Liam?"

My head jerks up at the sound of my name. "I'm sorry, what?" I don't dare to look over at Sterling. I can feel his scowl already glaring at me.

"What do you think? Are you ready to become a Tiger?" Tigers, oh yes. It's all coming back to me now. My legit attempt to avoid coming to Auburn failed miserably. Because here I sit while my dad discusses my future with his alma mater, not giving a shit about what I think.

I told my dad no, that Auburn was not on my list. He didn't listen and booked me for a visit anyway. It wasn't until we landed did I realize what he had done. And what am I going to do, call my mother? No, I can't do that and he knows it. So here I sit, zoning out of a conversation about my future because right now I just don't care.

"Liam?"

I roll my eyes and sit up in the chair. I run my hands down my pants. "I'm not sure what I think," I answer as I clear my throat. "I'm eighteen years old and all I've known is football and I feel pretty damn lucky to have my choice of colleges, but with that choice comes a lot of responsibility. I think before I put my name down or verbally commit to someplace I need to know the teammates. I need to know that they're one hundred percent committed to winning just as I am. I've never lost and I know that's unrealistic when I get to college, but I want to win. I want the Heisman and a BCS Championship and if Auburn and Tennessee can't offer me that, but Ole Miss can, I'm taking my game to Ole Miss." Sterling stiffens next to me and I know that a lashing is coming. Maybe he'll grow a set and hit me so I can beat the shit out of him. Honestly, I'm surprised he hasn't tried yet.

The coach sits back in his chair and rubs his chin contemplating the fact that I just told him if he can't guarantee me everything that I want, I'm not coming here. I'm not going to sign my life away for four years without meeting the team. Without having some type of workout with them. I know it can't happen on campus, but I can definitely make time to meet them at the park for a little flag football.

"You have a very vocal son, Sterling. I have to say, I'm shocked."

I bite the inside of my cheek and wait for whatever my dad has to say. He grunts and clears his throat.

"The boy is foolish and doesn't know what he wants."

I roll my eyes and keep my gaze on the orange carpet.

"He's dreamed all his life about being a Tiger. He's just listening too much to these other colleges feeding his mind with empty promises. Don't you worry, Hal, Liam will pick Auburn on signing day."

No, Hal, you *should* worry because I most definitely will not be picking Auburn on signing day. My dad thanks Hal and they promise to get together soon for a round of golf. It must suck having to kiss everyone's ass all the time and while it should be my dad kissing Hal's, it's not. Hal wants me to suit up for him and that's just not going to happen.

The car ride is silent. I watch the scenery as we drive to the next university. The radio is on NPR or some other political talk radio that I care nothing about. I just want to go home, back to Beaumont and Josie. I wish she could've come with me on these trips, but since one of my parents has to be present I knew it would never happen. But having her here would make the decision so much easier. I'm going to ask her if she'll apply to wherever I decide to go. I know it's a long shot, but I don't think I can be away from her. Not like this.

I close my eyes and block out the noise from the road. My head rests against the window as he speeds down the highway. My life was supposed to be simple and I thought it was until recently. Now nothing makes sense. Last year if you've asked me about college, I could rattle off a million things I want to do with the NFL being my top priority. Ask me now and the answer is going to shock you.

"We're here." His voice is gruff and full of anger. The University of Alabama is not on his radar, but they're on mine. We get out and he straightens his jacket immediately, sucking in his gut as a group of girls walk by. I shake my head and walk ahead of him.

"Now any one of those girls is worth bringing home."

I stop and look at their retreating backsides. "Really? They're colors are crimson and white and I thought for sure you only saw blue and orange."

"You're looking at this the wrong, Liam. If you go to Auburn, you'll have special liberties that others won't."

I shake my head. "I don't want special liberties. I want

to earn my achievements on my own merit. And I don't want one of those." I point to the girls. "What makes them any better, huh?"

"They're here getting an education."

"So? Josie's going to college."

He scoffs. "She's waiting until the right moment to get pregnant so you have to support her for the next eighteen years." He walks away before I can give a rebuttal, which is probably for the best because the next thing out of my mouth would've been, "*so what if she is*" and something tells me that Sterling wouldn't appreciate that too much.

CHAPTER 13

BEING called out of class and told to report to the principal's office is never a good feeling. I rack my brain as I walk to the office. I know I'm passing all my classes and all my absences from this week have been excused. I can't imagine that I've done something so wrong that I'd have to meet with the principal.

I open the door to the office and stand at the counter while the secretary files her nails. She looks up, snapping her lips as if she's moving her false teeth back and forth. Why they keep her around is beyond me. You can't understand her when she talks and her hearing is too far gone to hear the phone ring. She motions for me to go into the office, not even calling the principal and tell her I'm coming.

I knock once and open the door. Mrs. Craft is sitting behind her desk, her head down and fingers flipping through a magazine. "Mrs. Craft I got a message to see you."

She looks up and smiles. "Oh yes, Liam, come in and sit down." I do as she asks. I bite my lip and wait for her to deliver the bad news. Only she doesn't. She continues to look through her magazine while I sit across from her not knowing what's going on.

The door opens. I turn and see my coach walk in. He's not smiling and that puts me on edge. His normal smile when he sees me is gone. I don't even know what to think or what I've done to be called down here. He nods in my direction and steps aside so a man in a dark blue business suit can enter.

"What's going on?" I ask, my nerves on edge.

"Liam," Mrs. Craft says. "Coach Randall has some news."

I turn in my chair and look at my coach for some help here. He smiles and while that would normally put me at ease, it doesn't help with my anxiety. "Liam, I've never had a player like you and I probably never will. Last year you came so close to making the cover of *Sport Illustrated* that when they called this year I did everything I could to make it happen. Son, let me introduce you to Chris Bailey, he's a sports writer and he's here to interview you."

I stand and shake his hand, probably a bit too eagerly. This has been a dream of mine since they started profiling high school students.

"It's very nice to meet you, Mr. Bailey."

"You too, Liam, but please call me Chris. Do you need your parents here while we do the interview?"

Hell no, I want to yell, but don't. "No, Sir, Coach can stay."

"All right well let's get started, shall we?"

The three of us move Mrs. Craft's chairs into a circle and start talking. I like that coach stayed here with me and made sure I didn't answer anything I wasn't supposed to. To be honest, I was nervous the whole time, but when Mr. Bailey said he had everything and would be sending a photographer to take my pictures I think I smiled so big that I stretched the muscles in my face to permanently look like this.

As soon as I leave the office, the class bell rings. I rush to meet Josie. I'm excited to share the news with her.

"Guess what?" I say as I wrap my arms around her. I nuzzle her neck, disrupting her attempt at putting her books away.

"What?"

"Someone is going to be on the cover of *Sports Illustrated*."

Josie pauses and turns slowly. Her face lights up as her arms come around my neck. "I'm so proud of you."

"I couldn't have done it without my girl," I say, kissing her full on the lips. She tenses, afraid to get caught, but I'll take the blame if we do. They can suspend me for all I care. I need to kiss my girl.

"We should go celebrate," she says, pulling away.

"What are you thinking?" I ask, raising my eyebrows. She smacks me in the chest. I can't help it. She's sexy and she turns me on. But she wants it too. She shrugs and pushes her fingers into my hair, adding more pressure where my hair was recently shaved. I close my eyes and relish in the massage she's giving me.

"Are your parents' home?" I look into her blue eyes and see the answer before she shakes her head. I don't say anything as I slam her locker shut and pull her down the hall.

"W ANT to go meet Mason and Katelyn?" Josie plays with the hair on my arm, her fingers rubbing up and down along my skin.

"I guess we should do something before your parents get home."

"You mean like get dressed?" she laughs and rolls over in my arms. "I'm very proud of you, Liam. You set your goals and you're achieving each one of them."

"I couldn't do it without you, Jojo." I angle my head so I can kiss her deeply. When our tongues meet I have to control myself from picking up where we left off. Her parents may know we have sex, but getting caught by them isn't something I'm comfortable with. "We should get dressed," I say, in between the soft kisses I place on and around her lips. My hand slides down her body and slaps her ass. She smiles against my mouth before moving away.

"You're trouble, Liam Westbury." She stands next to her bed, naked as the day she was born. She watches me watch her and all I can think is what it's going to be like to wake up to her every day. I need to find the courage to ask her to follow me to college because I don't want to be away from her. I won't be able to handle it. Right now, she's the only person keeping me grounded.

Once she's dressed, I finally move. Allowing my eyes to take in every one of her moves is bad news for me. I have to turn away from her, not so she can't see what she does to me, but so she won't ask to take care of me. We can pick this up later. Right now I want to take her out. Treat her right. Aside from homecoming, we haven't been out on a date in a while. Football takes up so much of my time that it limits what I'm allowed to do, but not tonight. Tonight I'm going to hang out with my friends. Maybe catch a movie, have some dinner and just relax. There will be no need to talk about the future, football or what's looming in front of us… the high school championship game.

As soon as my clothes are on, Josie and I are out the door and on our way to meet Mason and Katelyn at Deb's. It's an old diner that my parents hate and will probably ream me out for even stepping foot in, but the food is good and she doesn't skimp on quantity. It's the perfect place for growing men like Mason and myself.

When Josie and I walk in, Deb waves and motions to the booth where Katelyn and Mason are huddled in the corner. Sometimes, when I look at them, I think something's up. Like they're hiding something. If they are, I'm sure they'd tell us though, so I really need to stop letting my imagination run wild. I have no doubt they think the same thing about Josie and me.

Deb takes our order as soon as we sit down. We've been here so many times we have the menu memorized. My girl is tucked into my side with my arm resting on her shoulder. This feels good. It feels right. If I can stay like this forever, I'd have no worries.

"What are you both giggling about?" I ask, breaking up Katelyn and Mason's interactions.

"Nothing," he replies, as he kisses her on her forehead. "We've just been planning the future." I roll my eyes and pick up the glass of water in front of me. The future is the last thing I want to talk about.

"Oh, I love the future talk. Tell me, what are we

doing?" Josie asks.

Always 'we' never just 'them'. We're the foursome that's destined to be together for the rest of our lives. It shouldn't matter to me, but a little separation in life isn't necessarily a bad thing. It allows us to grow, even though I know it's not what I want. They're my family. This is where I want to be.

"Well we were just thinking that it'd be nice if the guys got accepted to the same school and we could all go together," Katelyn says. I agree with her, I'd love it. I'd give anything to continue to play with Mason for another four years. With me at the helm and the right blocking, we'd be unstoppable.

"Oh we could have a double wedding," Josie adds. I almost choke on my water and have to try to hold in my coughing attack. I know I said I was going to marry her... someday, but I never said anything about planning a wedding.

"A football wedding is a must," Mason adds. I shake my head and wonder what goes through his mind. He's so whipped it's not even funny. I know I am too, but I'm not about to start talking weddings and shit and I definitely don't want a football themed wedding. I want to see my girl have the fairytale wedding she deserves.

"Speaking of football," Mason starts. "We have one game left Westbury, and I need one hundred yards. I'm going to get it, right? I mean I'm getting some decent looks and all, but I think that record just sets the bar a little higher..." I zone him out. Because the pressure of everyone's expectations resting on my shoulders that I've been feeling every day, where my head is about to explode, is now back. I want one night with my friends where the word football isn't discussed. I want one night where I can just be Liam, boyfriend to Josie and best friend to Mason, instead of Liam, QB1 of Beaumont High about to play for an unprecedented fourth state title.

I know it's probably too much to ask, but it's what I want. I smile at Mason and nod. "You'll get it man. It's just a hundred yards, no biggie."

Josie beams at me and leans in for a kiss. "You're the best, you know that, right?" I nod, but don't feel that way. I want her to tell me I'm the best because she loves me for me, not for what I'm about to do for Mason.

CHAPTER 14

ORNS are honking. Kids are yelling. I know the minute I appear at my window, I'll have to go down there and join them. My teammates are outside, pumped for today's game. This has become tradition, showing up at each other's houses at the crack of dawn. The whole town is ready for tonight. So am I. This is what I dreamed of when I was in middle school and now this is my chance to play for my fourth title. It doesn't mean anything less, that this is my fourth, if anything it means more. This will be my last night taking the helm behind center in a Beaumont uniform. My last night taking a snap under the Friday night lights and I'm ready.

I open my blinds and the yelling gets louder. Some of the guys are in my yard, putting up a sign and the others are standing in the back of Mason's truck, all wearing their jerseys. The cheerleaders are in front of and behind them in trucks, singing our school fight song. I wave, letting them know that I'll be down. I grab my jersey from my bed and slip it on before heading down the stairs. I jump down the last three, much like I used to do when I was younger.

"Where are you going so early?"

I freeze at the sound of Sterling's voice coming from behind me.

"It's game day," I answer curtly, without turning around so he can't see the look of annoyance on my face. I really wish he'd just stay in his office and not talk to me. If he did that, my life would be a little bit less stressful. "We've been doing it this way since my freshman year."

Sterling huffs. "Tomorrow things change around here. Hal sent me the team's workout; you'll be starting that first thing."

I close my eyes and count to ten. It's the only way I'll stay calm. "I'm not going to Auburn," I say, weakly.

"What'd you say, boy? I don't think I heard you."

Trying to keep my breathing normal and not lose my temper, I turn slowly to face my father. He's standing there with his hands on his hips like an authoritarian. He won't be paying for my college, yet no doubt he's forgotten this fact. I've secured my future at any school I want because of my ability. Yes, he may have helped me achieve said ability, but I am where I am because of *me*. He's not out night after night taking a pounding. He's not busting his balls on the field to make sure his team is taken care of. That's all me.

I clear my throat and look him in the eyes. "I'm not going to Auburn, *sir*." Sir was added for emphasis because he demands respect, which I never give him.

"And you came up with this decision on your own,

smart ass?"

"Yes, I did. They don't have a program I want to study."

"You're going to the NFL, Liam. That's the plan. Don't you dare deviate now because you're getting a little pussy and she wants you to stay around. Once you get to college the chicks will be spreading their legs every day for you if that's what you want."

I close my eyes and shake my head. When I open them again, he's glaring at me. "This has nothing to do with Josie. I want to go to a school that is right for me, not you. Why can't you understand that? Why can't you support me? Everything I've done, I've done because you made me. I'm not going to Auburn."

Sterling storms toward me, but I hold my ground. "In February, you will pick Auburn if you know what's good for you." He stalks away before I have a chance to say anything in rebuttal. I bang my fist against my head in frustration. Why can't shit just be easy? It's a fucking school for God sakes, nothing more, nothing less. Going to Auburn isn't going to make or break my career in the NFL. Why can't he see that?

I take a deep breath and walk out the house, pasting a ridiculous smile on my face. As soon as I step out, Josie is on the ground, running to me. I catch her mid-stride and bring her into my arms, burying my head in her neck. I hold her to me, with her legs wrapped around my waist and her arms over my shoulders.

"I heard him yelling," she says, her voice muffled.

"Don't worry about him," I tell her as I put her down. As soon as I look into her eyes, I can see that it's bothering her and it should. For all I know she'll reconsider marrying me because of him. Fuck, I would. Who wants to marry someone whose family doesn't accept you?

I hold her face in my hands, pressing my forehead against hers. "You can't listen to him, Jojo. Promise me that you'll never listen to a single thing that man says."

"I promise, Liam."

"DO you hear that crowd?" Mason yells at me before we leave the tunnel. This is it, our last game ever in high school. Mason is so close to breaking the state record for rushing yards. It's going to happen in this game. It has to. I already broke the record for passing earlier, days after my *Sports Illustrated* cover came out.

"Yeah man, I hear it. Crazy, right?"

"There have to be more people than last year."

We aren't supposed to be out of the locker room yet but I needed to see things one last time before I slip my helmet on. I want to take it all in because this is it. After tonight, win or lose, it's done and my life changes. I wish I could go back and make time stop. Makes everything slow down, but I can't.

The smell of popcorn and hot dogs wafts through the air, making me hungry even though we had dinner already. We ate as a team, our last meal together. For some, we'll never play together again, but for others they'll move onto basketball and even baseball.

The band becomes louder as the clock ticks down. In just a few minutes I'll be running out of this tunnel and will either make history tonight or go home with a second place trophy. Sadly, for the other team, second place isn't going to cut it.

I slap my girl's ass as she passes by with her white, gold and red cheerleading skirt flipping up as she runs.

She turns around and saunters up to me with that look in her eye. I know what she's expecting and I plan to deliver, both on and off the field. Josie is everything I could ever want in partner, I just hate that I'm going to have to leave her. Not once have I considered schools close to home, mostly because of their coaching staff and records. I want to win when I'm at college. I want to be someone. If I stay close to home though, I can be with Josie. See her on the weekends once the season is over. Have her on campus with me. But my choice won't keep me close to her. My only hope is that she'll come with me wherever I go.

"You know how sexy I think you are when you bite your lip? You have this look in your eyes, Liam. Do you have plans for us later?" she whispers into my ear, pulling on my earlobe. My focus is now solely on her instead of the game as her hand sneaks under my t-shirt. There is nothing better than her skin against mine.

"Knock it off you two," Mason teases us as he slaps me in the back of the head. "If you give him a stiffy during the game, some linebacker is going to break his pecker."

We all start laughing. She kisses me goodbye, telling me to kick ass. She's never, in the years we've been together, wished me good luck, just to kick ass.

I slip on my helmet just as we're signaled to take the field. We run through the cheerleaders and the student body with pom poms in our face and hands slapping our backs. They're pumped and ready for victory. Parents and fans are on their feet in the stands, yelling loudly.

Mason and I go off to the side and warm-up. We've done it this way for as long as I can remember, always together. We have a routine and we aren't about to break it now. As we throw the ball back and forth, my chest tightens. It's almost over and it hasn't even begun yet.

Captains are called to center field for the coin toss. The other team wins, electing to defend first. Whatever they want, I'll give it to them.

When the whistle blows, I take center with Mason on my left. The play is for him. He needs only one hundred yards to break the state record for rushing and I'm going to make sure that happens tonight. I have to make sure it happens for him. Our first play is a hand-off to him; he breaks the first tackle for a thirty-yard gain. I look at his dad and nod. I called him last night and asked that he help me keep track of Mason and he said he will after he thanked me for making sure his son gets the record. Mason's my best friend. He deserves it.

Every play in the first half goes to Mason. We do this over and over until his dad holds up a sign showing 100 and I know. I call a time-out and hand Mason the ball and watch him jog it over to his dad. They hug and the fans go nuts because Mason Powell just set the state's all-time leading rushing record with nine thousand five hundred and two. I dare anyone to try to break it.

As the clock ticks down, I stand behind center and look out over the field. I look to my right then left. My teammates all wait for the call. We've won this game. The other team can't catch up. I squat and call out my cadence. When the ball touches my hand I drop back, one step, two step, three and take a knee. The second my knee touches the ground I'm tackled by everyone. I hold the ball to my chest. It's my prized possession.

I'm hoisted onto shoulders and paraded around the field. The band is playing so loudly that they drown out the fans. I hold the ball high, pumping my fist into the night air. When I'm let down, I catch a five-foot nine brunette cheerleader in my arms. I drop my helmet, but not this pigskin, as I wrap her tightly in my arms.

"I'm so proud of you, Liam."

I nod because in this moment I *am* proud even with all my misgivings. Maybe I just need some time away from football to get my head straight. Maybe it was just the pressure of the season that got to me and maybe Auburn isn't such a bad choice after all.

"Next stop the NFL, Westbury," someone says behind me, breaking my moment. The pressure never goes away, does it? It just stops for a brief moment.

I look at Josie and smile, knowing it's not legit. If I can't have a night without pressure about my future at least I can have my girl in my arms.

CHAPTER 15

WISH I could say the past month has been stress free, but the truth of the matter is, it hasn't. Sterling is on my case every day about school. If it's not Auburn, it's another SEC school that's willing to bend the rules while they discuss business on the golf course. I thought that after winning the state title and Mason getting his record, things would cool down for a bit. But they haven't. If anything, they've gotten worse. The expectations are there, even if people aren't intending them to be. Just one day, I want to go to school and not be asked where I'm going to play football. If they're not careful I'm going to tell them nowhere and become a hobo.

As soon as the day is over, it's Christmas break and I plan to spend most of it with my girl. My parents left this morning for a cruise, one I conveniently forgot about and acted all distraught about being home by myself for three weeks. Of course, Sterling took those pretend moments to remind me of my looming decision and how wise it would be to have it done by the time he returned. His words went through one ear and out the other while I was counting off how many hours of freedom I'd have.

This morning, after they left, I played my guitar and I played it loudly. I sang at the top of my lungs because no one was home and no one was going to barge in on me and tell me that I'm wrong for wanting to play. Freedom. That's what I had this morning and I loved it.

As soon as the bell rings, I'm up and out the door making my way down the hall. There are parties being planned, get togethers arranged, all places Josie and I will end up, but not tonight. Tonight we're going to celebrate our own Christmas, in my house. This will be the first time Josie's been over in years. I've kept her away for obvious reasons, but tonight and any night thereafter that she's allowed to come over while my parents are away, she'll be with me.

With her hand in mine we walk to my truck. She doesn't have a clue about my plans. She just knows that I'm bringing her to my house. I can tell she's apprehensive, nervous. I don't blame her. It's usually how I feel when I'm at home.

"Are you sure we won't get into trouble?" She whispers, clearly afraid that someone might hear her. I hate that she feels like this. I just shake my head as I pull her through the garage and into the house. I grab two bottles of water from the refrigerator before taking her by the hand and leading her upstairs to my room.

"Hold these," I say, stopping in front of my door. I pull the silk scarf she's wearing and come up behind her. Her neck is exposed, vulnerable and taking my attention away from the task at hand. I have to touch her, my lips burn when they touch her skin. I'm going to take a risk, live on the edge so when I feel her breathing pause as I tie her scarf over her eyes, I get excited knowing that she's welcoming my attempts.

"What are you doing?" she asks, still keeping her voice low.

"Trust me," I say against the back of her neck. I hold her hips in my hands, my fingers under her shirt, with her pressed against me. Her body sags against mine, ready for whatever I'm going to do to her. I open my door and guide her into my room. She jumps when my door slams shut. Even though my parents aren't home, I'm not taking any chances on someone walking in. I plan to have her naked and saying my name over and over again until the sun comes up. That thought alone increases my breathing. I want to take her now, but I have a plan. One that I've worked incredibly hard on since I found out the 'rents were leaving the country.

I reluctantly leave her standing in the middle of my room and take the bottles of water from her, dropping them to the floor. I pull her forward, she stumbles, but I catch her. I'll always catch her when she falls.

"I'll never let you fall, Jojo."

The back of my hand caresses her cheek causing her to blush. I love that her other senses are heightened right now. "I love it when you blush." I don't give her time to respond before I put my lips to hers. My plan is going out the window and fast. My tongue begs for hers and when they meet the combustion is almost too much for me to handle. I pull the scarf from her eyes. I need to see her. "Merry Christmas, my girl," I say as I pick her up and lay her on my bed. Josie reaches for me, but I shake my head.

I sit back on my knees and look around my room, proud of myself. I motion toward the tree that is twinkling with white lights and color ornaments. "Which do you want to open first?

"You," she says, pulling me down on top of her. Her hands fist at my shirt, pulling it over my head. Her nails dig into my back as I grind against her. "I want you all of you, Liam."

"You can have me, but I have something for you first." I pull away reluctantly and eye my girl lying on my bed. It's a sight to behold that's for sure and it's making it hard to concentrate on anything other than the raging hard on in my pants. I kiss her once and fight her attempt to pull me down on top of her. I smile, winking as I move away from her.

My heart is racing as I reach for my guitar. I chance a look at Josie, who sits up when she sees me sit down with it resting on my leg. She looks at me questioningly with her eyebrow raised. She's not expecting this. I close my eyes and hope she likes what I'm about to do.

I strum the strings and let the melody fill the room. I can't look at her while I'm doing this. Call it stage fright or whatever, but I need to hear the acceptance in her voice and not see her expression.

I know my voice isn't that great, it probably sucks and I'm likely tone deaf, but I sing for her and from my heart. I belt out the lyrics I've spent months on. They're meant to tell her how much I love her and what she means to me. But now that she's in my room, I think they sound like shit and they're not telling her exactly how I feel.

I stop and switch songs to something she'll know. I've

learned a few riffs of *Never Say Goodbye*, but I don't sing. I can't. I've lost my nerve. I set my guitar down and take a deep breath before looking at her.

Her blue eyes are staring not at me, but my guitar. Her mouth is slightly open. I rub my hands down the front of my jeans before getting up and putting my guitar away in my closet where my secret should probably stay.

"Um… Merry Christmas," I say as I sit on the edge of my bed, close enough to touch her. She looks up at me and smiles, but it doesn't reach her eyes. She doesn't have to tell me she didn't like it because I can see it written all over her face.

"That was for me?"

I nod and pick at a piece of lint on my comforter.

"Wow that was… when did you learn to do that?"

I shrug and clear my tightening throat. I so needed her to accept this… this part of me. "I've been teaching myself. I wrote… never mind."

Josie laughs lightly. "Sterling must love that."

She's right, I made a mistake. I should've told her when I bought the guitar what I was doing. I've surprised her and like everything else in my life, she's worried about what Sterling is going to think.

"He doesn't know."

"That's because he'd never approve." Her hand finds mine and she rubs her thumb across the top of it. "Are you ready for signing day?"

I nod as I downcast my eyes. I can't blame her for changing the topic so quickly, it's all she knows. Sterling has expectations and I've shared those with her and we've created a path that we can't deviate from.

I'm trying not to let my emotions get the best of me,

but it's hard. I needed her to like this, like me, for what I was doing. I swallow hard and bite the inside of cheek to keep everything in check. I reach for one of her presents that are sitting under the tree and hand it to her. "I love you, Jojo," I say, pressing my lips to her hand.

"I love you too, Liam." She takes the present and sets it aside and crawls into my lap. I could hold her like this all night and I know she'd let me, but right now she has other ideas in mind. I want to tell her that sex can't fix this, but I love her too much.

CHAPTER 16

THINGS with Josie have never been better. Not that we've been fighting, but my Christmas fiasco could've caused us a lot of damage. I had reservations about showing her to begin with. I wasn't ready. If anything I should've waited until I could perfect the words I was trying to express to her. I'm not giving up though. If I can only play music to clear my head, so be it.

Today's the big day, at least in Sterling's eyes. I'm nervous and still unsure. I don't know where I want to go to college. I've narrowed it down to five schools, Auburn included, but am no closer to making a decision now than I was last month or even last night. I'm going to ask Josie to come with me though, so my decision needs to be made with her in mind. When we're away at college everything will be perfect because we'll be together. My parents won't be around to bring her down and I'll have my girl in the stands for each game.

The camps are all done. No more showcasing my talent for the scouts. They've seen me play and the offers are on the table. I just have to pick. I can go with what I consider the safe school. The one that will cater to my every need regardless of what those may be, or I can go with what I want and have to work my ass off to make a name for myself.

The door to my hotel room swings open, crashing against my wall. I sit up quickly and find Mason standing in my doorway.

"What's up?" I ask confused as how he got into my room. While my dad tolerates Mason, he was none too happy when Mason and Mr. Powell made the trip to New York for National Signing Day. According to my father, Mason is beneath me. Being away from my father is probably the only reason I'm looking forward to college.

"I can't believe it's signing day," he says, shutting my door. He pulls out the desk chair, spins it around and sits down. "We're going to college in a few months."

"I know." I adjust so I can sit against the wall. "What's going on, Mase? How'd you get a key to my room?" I ask, needing to know why he's here. When I look back on my childhood I'll never be able to say I had fabulous parties at my house or that Spiderman birthday cake that I wanted when I was ten. My parents didn't get it. Not like Mason's. Not like Josie's who let me sneak into her room at night because they know what kind of asshole Sterling is and they know how non-existent Bianca is. So to have Mason in my room, on signing day, only means one thing. He has a good offer.

"Have you decided?" he asks, avoiding my question about the room key.

I shake my head slowly. "That's what I've been trying to do all morning."

Mason leans back and rests against the particleboard desk. "So you know I have a lot of DII offers, but last week the University of Texas made an offer and I think I'm going to take it."

"Yeah?" I answer, happy for him. "That's good, man. They have a solid program." I know this because I took a tour there and watched a team practice. They're up and coming and going to be a contender for the national title soon. They've been talking to me for a year and I have them shortlisted, but haven't paid much attention to them.

"How come you're just telling me this now?" I'm curious as to why he didn't say something last week. We're supposed to be best friends.

He shrugs. "I don't know. It seems like nothing compares to what you have sitting in front of you."

"That's bullshit, Mason. You worked hard. You deserve this. Are you signing today?"

He nods. "I'm nervous though," he admits which causes me to sit up a bit straighter.

I nod. "Me too." I pick at the hem on my jeans before looking at him. "Do you ever want to quit and do something different?" Because I do, every day, but I don't tell him that.

"Nah. I don't see the NFL in my future like you do, but I want to coach and give back to the community. I want to do my four years, get an education and come back here and marry Katelyn."

"Yeah that sounds good."

"Why? Do you think about quitting?" he asks.

Out of habit I look at the bottom of the door for the tell-tale sign of someone standing there. When I don't see anyone I look back at Mason and nod. "All the time, man. I don't love the game like I used to. The pressure has been too much and I feel like I'm a bomb about to detonate. I hate all this school bullshit. In two hours I have to decide what school I want to play for and if I don't pick Auburn, Sterling is going to freak out."

"So just pick Auburn."

I roll my eyes. He makes it sound so simple when it's not. "I don't know."

"Dude, you have it so easy. You have all these colleges coming after you. I would've given my left nut to be in your position. Stop bitching. Pick a school and say 'fuck you, dad'. Hell, come with me that will really piss him off."

He's right. If I was to pick a school that isn't in Sterling's top five, he'd be livid. Doing so means he could cut off my trust fund and even though my schooling will be paid, for I could use that money for Josie.

But Mason's wrong. I don't have it easy. He doesn't remember how much he depended on me to make sure he broke the rushing record this year. He didn't have a team to lead. He didn't have multiple players waiting and hoping that my actions each game night didn't screw up their chances at playing college ball someplace. He doesn't have the parents I do and the expectations. Even the college coaches add pressure.

"I should probably go before your old man gets back. See ya down there." Mason leaves without me even acknowledging him. He doesn't know that his little chat, while I'm sure it helped him, did nothing for me. I just want someone to sit down with me and go over the pros and cons of each school. My father will only discuss Auburn and isn't helping me make an informed decision.

I'm probably the only quarterback signing today that doesn't have a clue about which school they're picking. I've made no verbal commitments to any of the schools and right now I don't even want to put my name down on the dotted line.

I want to run.

THE lights are bright and blinding as I take a seat next to another top recruit. There are ten of us sitting at table, five on each side and we're separated by a podium. We're the top recruits of our senior class and we're all about to make some team very happy and others very upset. But those teams will move on and hope their next pick will come forward and say they'll play for them.

The Master of Ceremonies is full of joy and overly enthusiastic. This is like the pre-NFL draft, only we're not about to make millions of dollars. At least *we* won't, but the schools will definitely benefit financially from us.

Cameras start clicking and it's then that I realize someone has chosen a school. I give the obligatory clap and wait for my name to be called. My dad is sitting in the crowd with his blue and orange colors on, waiting for me to make *his* right decision.

"Liam Westbury," the commentator says my name. I stand and listen to him rattle off my stats earning some heaving clapping from the galley. Someone whistles and I smile knowing it's Mason.

"Mr. Westbury, please tell us where we'll be watching you play in the fall?"

I look out my dad who nods. It's now or never, and in

the next few seconds, I'll be making a decision that will either make or break me. I take a deep breath, closing my eyes and imagine my girl out there waiting for me to tell her where we're going.

"This fall I'll be playing along the side of my running back, Mason Powell, at the University of Texas. Hook 'em horns," I shout out to the crowd. I don't know what came over me, but I feel good about my decision. Playing next to Mason for an additional four years is worth it. We can bring the girls to Texas with us, rent a place off campus and just live our lives.

I don't chance a look at my dad. I know he's beyond pissed. I mentally prepare myself for whatever he's going to do to me. It won't be pretty. I may need to call the Prestons tonight and ask if I can move in because I'm fairly certain that Sterling Westbury is going to kick me out of the house.

I just chose the one school that was at the bottom of my list and that's completely unheard of. I sit back down as a hush rolls over the crowd. I chance a look at the Texas coach. He's stunned and when he makes eye contact with me I see nothing but pure elation. I don't have a clue what my role will be there, but that doesn't matter. I'm going to school with my best friend and right now that seems more important than anything.

The last kid commits and we're all ushered off the stage. I want to hide, but it'll be no use. Sterling's going to have my ass no matter what. I mingle, waiting for my dad to get backstage. I don't even want to know what he's talking to his buddy Hal about. If I was to guess he's devising a plan to make everything null and void and forge my name for Auburn. Knowing Sterling, he's writing a check to make sure today never happened.

"Liam," he commands sternly. I don't turn around to face him. I stand still and wait. He won't make a scene, not in front of all these other athletes, parents and alumni. "We need to talk. Now!" he growls into my ear. "If you'll excuse us gentlemen we have some business to take care of."

My dad all but pushes me out of the room and directs me into a conference room that isn't being used. I jump when he slams the door. The wall shakes, not because of the force, but because of the flimsy material they use to make these rooms. Everyone's going to hear what he says to me. I'll never be able to face my peers or the coach from Texas again. He'll know this wasn't a school that we even considered.

"What the fuck are you thinking?"

How does one answer that question without sounding like an idiot? It's not going to matter what I say, the answer is wrong. Either I wasn't thinking or I was thinking with the wrong part of my brain.

"I was thinking that it'd be nice to play another four years with Mason."

"Are you shitting me here, Liam? Because if so, this isn't funny. University of Texas, *really*? Since when did they matter? When did they even move into the top five?"

I stand there listening to him. Right now he's calm, but that won't last I'm sure. He pushes my shoulder when I don't answer.

"Answer me smart ass. I didn't bust your balls since fucking pee-wee football so you could half ass it at some school that doesn't deserve you."

"Texas is a good program. They're building."

"They're *building*?" he starts to pace, pulling at his already receding hair. "They're building and what, you think you're the answer? Are you going to help them build their program and then in five or six years when you're gone they can win a national championship? Jesus Christ, Liam, do you ever fucking think with your head?"

"I was thinking with my heart!" I bellow out. "I was thinking that Mason and I have great chemistry on the field, and how easy that can transfer to a new school. I was thinking that I didn't want to pick a fucking school today, and that I wish this shit would just all go away. I picked Texas because I'm going to have a friend there, someone familiar. Someone that is going to help me get through not having anyone around or being someplace that I don't want to be. I don't want to go to Auburn or Alabama or even Ole Miss. I don't even want to play football anymore!" I yell at him causing him to step back. I cover my face in frustration and try to catch my breath.

Sterling pauses and fixes me with his steely gaze. "You're unbelievable and completely selfish, Liam. This is not how I raised you." With that he walks out, slamming the door.

CHAPTER 17

I HAD always wondered what it would be like to piss my dad off so severely that he'd never speak to me again. I accomplished that task satisfactorily and haven't heard a word from him in months. In fact, family life in the Westbury household has pretty much ceased to exist. Dinner isn't made. The TV isn't turned on. I haven't seen my mother in weeks. If this is their form of punishment, I don't know whether I'm supposed to feel hurt or thankful that they're aren't trying to tear me down with my decision.

My decision to attend the University of Texas hasn't been without complications. In the days after I made my choice, my father fielded call after call asking about my decision while I sat in his office, stoically, wondering if I had made the wrong decision. It didn't matter if I did. I was going to Texas and there wasn't anything I nor anyone else could do about it. Worse case, I transfer, but that will mean I'll likely miss my freshman year. I can't do that to Mason though. He's excited that we'll be taking the field together; at least I have his support if no one else's.

Baseball is over. Nick Ashford was the hero of the season. I didn't even care, not about him nor the season. I want high school to be over. We won the state title with Ashford getting the most valuable player of the season. It didn't escape my attention when I saw him eying Josie either. I don't know where he's going to college, but for the sake of his kneecaps it better be at least a plane ride away from Beaumont. I don't want him anywhere near my girl.

As Mason and I will now be together, I've decided not to ask Josie to go to school with me. The thought of Katelyn being alone didn't sit too well. I wouldn't want Josie alone, so taking her away from Katelyn is the wrong thing to do. They can go to college together, while Mason and I destroy defense in Texas. We'll make sure we see the girls as much as possible. Josie knows that during football it will be almost impossible, but I'm going to make the time. Texas is within a day's drive so it shouldn't be too bad.

I have two more rites of passages before I'm free from the confines of teenage life: prom and graduation. The latter of which can't happen fast enough. I'm ready to get the hell out of this house. I need to talk to the Prestons and ask if I can stay at their place while I'm on vacation. Once I leave I'm never coming back to this house. There's nothing here for me except memories that I want to forget. It's time to create new memories with Josie and prepare our life together.

Tonight can be the beginning. It's our last dance

together. Senior prom is upon us and I've gone all out just for her. That's the one thing I'm surprised about – Sterling hasn't cut off my funds. I keep spending and the money seems to be there. I'm not complaining. He's making prom as special as it can be for Josie. I've rented a limo and we'll pick up Mason and Katelyn, but once we leave the dance, it's just us. After, we're hitting the hotel. I have no intentions of leaving her tonight. I want to hold her in my arms until the sunlight is peering through the floral drapes that hang over the sliding glass door. We're going to stay there until the housekeeper knocks and tells us it's time to leave. Only then will we untangle and journey back into real life.

I just want one night – one glimpse – of what our wedding reception will be like. The dancing, the drinking and the nightcap that only adults think they're permitted to enjoy. I'm allowed to have that fantasy, even if I'm just eighteen and ridiculously in love. No one needs to know what I'm thinking. The guys will know exactly what's going on when I take Josie by her hand and lead her out of the country club and into the waiting limo.

The buttons on my crisp white shirt slide into their designated spots with ease. Sitting on my dresser are a set of cuff links that my grandfather left me. I don't remember him much, but in my mind he's nothing like Sterling. I slide the links through and bend the clasp. My slacks go on next, tucking my shirt in. I stand in the mirror and adjust my bow tie. My hair is short and I run my hand over the top of head just to give my hair a little bit of life. My vest is next, buttoning it before I step into my shoes. Once they're tied I look at myself, taking a mental picture. This will be my last time in a tux until Mason's wedding or mine, which ever will happen first. With one last look I slide my arms into my jacket and button my coat.

Josie's corsage is already sitting on my dresser. I picked it up this morning, fearful that if I kept it in the refrigerator something would happen to it. I shouldn't have to live with that fear, but I do. I don't know what Sterling is capable of and Bianca, well she just doesn't engage. She doesn't care. I can't imagine being a parent and not caring about your child. They're a product of you and your partner, isn't that supposed to be best of both worlds in your eyes?

I walk out the front door, slamming it as I leave. I hope they're staring at each other ticking off each and every mistake they made with me. Eighteen years of raising someone and it'll all be for nothing.

At the end of my driveway is a black stretch limousine. The driver is at back door, waiting for me. Josie has no idea about this or my plans for tonight. I like that I'm going to surprise her or maybe she expects it. It doesn't matter because the look on her beautiful face will be worth it. In the back there's a dozen long stem roses and a bottle of champagne. We'll go to dinner first before picking up Katelyn and Mason. As fun as double dates are, I want to be alone with my girl for a bit.

The car pulls up to the Prestons and I'm out and hurrying up their walk way before the driver can get out. It's not protocol, I get that, but I'm eager to see her. I knock once and Mr. Preston opens the door, allowing me in.

He pats me on the shoulder. "She'll be right out. You know how she likes to make you wait."

"Yeah I do," I acknowledge. He stands next to me, waiting for a different reason. I try to put myself in his shoes and can't. I can't imagine my teenage daughter about to walk out of her room for prom for the last time.

I look up when her bedroom door opens. She steps out into the hallway and I swear there's a halo over her head because she looks like an angel. I swallow hard as she gets closer and quickly change my assessment. She's no angel. She's like Athena, the Greek Goddess of war, dressed to take any man that looks at her to slaughter.

"Holy…" I shake the cobwebs from my eyes and refocus. Her dress is white, contrasting perfectly with her tan skin and hangs from her body in all the right places. My eyes wander over her body, noticing the slit up the side much like her homecoming dress. The sides of her dress are missing giving me a clear shot of her boobs.

"Turn around?" I say huskily, afraid to look at Mr. Preston. He has to know I'm eye fucking his daughter into oblivion. Screw prom, we're going straight to the hotel so I can put her on the table and just stare at her all night. Josie turns slowly showing me the back of her dress. It swoops down, leaving her back fully exposed. I discretely adjust myself when she turns back to face me. I step forward and wrap one her of her curls around my finger.

"Holy fuck, Jojo. I don't know how I'm going to keep it PG," I whisper to her, hoping her parents can't hear me.

"Who says you have to?"

I shake my head. "Damn girl you're a walking textbook of sins and I'm about to commit each and every one of them." She laughs, throwing her head back. I pull her white and gold corsage from it sits box. Now I know why she said gold. It's perfect.

"Pictures?" her mom requests. I take her hand and bring it to my lips and kiss her. We turn and face her mom and smile, making a memory that I'm sure I'll never forget. "You guys look so beautiful together," she says as her camera clicks. We pose for various photos before we head to the car.

With her hand in mine, I open the front door and pull her behind me. She freezes, letting out a gasp. "What's wrong, Josie?"

"You rented a limo?"

"Of course, it's our last prom. We have to go out in style."

"You're crazy, Liam Westbury."

"Crazy about you." I pull her to my lips quickly. "Come on babe, we have memories to make."

"LET the party begin," I yell, walking into the country club. After dinner we stopped and picked up Mason and Katelyn, who had their own provisions and we proceeded to drink as much as we could before we arrived.

Katelyn and Josie are giggling at me, which is fine. I'm feeling fantastic and am about to dance with my girl until they tell me it's over. I've never been a fan of staying at these dances for very long, but when you have someone as hot as Josie on your arm, you have to stay and show her off. I want every guy in the room to be jealous of me tonight.

I pull her into the middle of the floor and hold her in my arms. We sway back and forth to the music as people around us dance with their arms flailing around. We could dance like that, but then I'd have to let her go and that's just not happening.

"You're so fucking beautiful, Josie. I stand here and hold you in my hands with your body pressed against me. All I can think about is taking you out of here. I had plans to take things slow, to make love to you like you deserve. Not in my truck or when you're parents aren't home. I want to ravage your body and make you come undone by a simple touch, but I don't know if I'm going to be able to do that. The way you're dressed… you're begging me to take you up against the wall with your legs wrapped around my waist."

I brush my fingers along her exposed shoulder and watch pebbles follow in my path. Her reaction to me matches the way I feel about her. The simplest of touches from her can weaken me in a heartbeat. That can't be normal, but I'm not willing to test the theory. I hope that we always make each other feel like this down the road. I don't want her to become robotic like my mother, and I definitely can't stomach the thought of me being like my father.

Our night continues with our friends. We dance, laugh and enjoy each other's company. It's nice to see everyone sticking around for this dance, knowing that it's our last and in a few short weeks we'll be graduating. I don't want to think about that, at least not tonight.

After Josie and I are announced as prom king and queen we take our exit. I've been a patient man, but even my resolve is starting to waver. Too many times to count, my hands have found their way into the side of her dress and it's taking every ounce of self-control to not find out how her dress is covering her breasts. However, when we get to the hotel, I'll be finding out.

THE limo drops us at the hotel. I hold her hand in mind, but feel her jitter. Is she nervous? This isn't our first time, but it will be a night with no interruptions. No rushing. The first time we had sex with each other, we were both virgins. Our relationship was progressing and my horny teenaged self couldn't keep my hands to myself or out of her pants. I rented a hotel room because I didn't know where we could try and do it without getting caught. I was a nervous wreck and heaved my lunch before I picked her up. She brought her backpack with her and the whole time we were driving to the hotel I thought we were going to end up studying. I was pleasantly surprised when she took her bag into the bathroom and came out wearing lingerie. I knew in that moment we'd fumble through the motions, but figure it out soon enough.

We walk into the lobby hand in hand, not surprised to see other classmates here. A few offer us a chance to party with them, but we politely decline. I checked in earlier and set up the room. I don't want prom to be a cliché, I just want the opportunity to peel this dress off of her. Had I known about it, we would've ditched slow dancing and went right to the Tango.

I open our room and allow her to enter first. The lamp is on in the corner, giving the room a soft glow. There are rose petals on the floor and bed with a bottle of champagne sitting on the nightstand.

The door shuts, the loud bang causing her to jump. I step behind her, my fingers dancing along her skin. I press my lips to her bare back before wrapping my arms around her.

"I know it's not the Hilton, but I wanted to be alone with you for one night. I want us to be together without any interruptions or just some quick fuck in my truck. I don't want to sneak around or have to muffle your cries with my mouth."

Josie turns in my arms, her hands resting on my lapels. "You thought of everything."

I shake my head. "I didn't think about a change of clothes for the morning so we'll be doing the walk of shame."

"I'm not ashamed to be with you, Liam."

I lean forward and ever so softly press my lips to hers. Her mouth parts and move with mine. Our tongues meet in a slow and tortured dance. My hand moves up and down her arms, to her neck and down her back. I can't touch her enough. I pull away, hesitantly, and move into the room. I press play on the radio and music echoes throughout the room. I slip off my bow-tie and my jacket, resting them on the table. I undo my cuff links, followed by the buttons on my shirt. Josie stands there and watches, which is exactly what I want. I remove my shirt, leaving my pants on, but unbuttoned. I beckon her forward, she saunters as if she's on a tether that I'm pulling.

"I want to take things slow, but I'm not sure if I can. Lately, I've felt like there's a distance between us and I don't know if it's from me leaving soon or if it's all in my head. Sometimes I feel like my world is going to blow up and I'm going to lose everything. But then I'm with you everything feels right. I can't lose you, Jojo."

She runs her fingers up and down my back before they rest on the waistband of my pants. "I'm not going anywhere, Liam. I know you're under a lot of strain from your father about school, but I'm here, always. We can try to go slow."

"I want to savor you."

Josie nods, biting her lower lip. I run my thumb over her mouth before cupping her face and bringing her to me. My hands travel down her neck and to her shoulders. My mouth follows, blazing a trail on her skin.

"Jojo, how on earth is this dress staying in place?" I ask as I kiss the valley of her chest.

"Tape," she says. I straighten and look at her. A smile creeps across my face. I bite my lip as I shake my head.

"Well then, by all means, let me unwrap my present."

CHAPTER 18

IN all my years at Beaumont High, I've never attended a party at the Appleton house. From what I've heard, they're legendary. Candy Appleton is the youngest of four. Her older brothers are all off at college and have maybe even graduated by now. Growing up, the stories that have been told would put the stories in *Playboy* to shame. Most were told to me as a form of punishment. If you end up at their house you can kiss – insert whatever my prized possession is at the time - goodbye. I stayed away, mostly for fear that something would happen and I'd lose my scholarship. It also doesn't help that Josie doesn't like Candy, but I don't like Nick and that doesn't seem to stop Josie from talking to him.

Candy graduated with me a few short hours ago and while most of our classmates are still with their family, her house is bustling with action. I have a feeling it's not just our classmates that are here. If her older brothers are home, it means the booze will be plenty and I for one, am eager to tie one on. It'll be interesting to see whom I run into tonight and how much they've changed after a year or two in college. Maybe they can shed some light on the way I'm feeling.

I meander through her house, nodding at people I know. Bodies are pressed against each other; some are dancing and others are getting to know each other without talking. As I look around I notice that the people here aren't my usual crowd. Only a few of my teammates are here, everybody else are people I've known for years, but haven't really hung out with. Looking at them now, it makes me wonder why that was. I shake my head, knowing exactly why – Sterling. If it weren't for Mason, I'd have no friends. Who the hell would want to be my friend anyway? I have nothing to offer them. You can't party at my house or even come over. Why would anyone want to be friends with that kind of loser?

When I think about it, they don't. Sure people are saying hi, they'll talk to me and hang around me and according to some popularity vote with the yearbook, I'm the most popular guy in school, but I have no friends. I have Josie, Mason and Katelyn. That's it.

I stand against the wall with a beer in my hand. I'm people watching. Looking to see how everyone interacts. Nick is in the corner talking to a brunette. Maybe that's his Josie replacement. Short of actually kicking his ass, I've threatened him one too many times. I don't think it's too much to ask that he stays away from my girl, but apparently it is. He can't seem to get it through his head that she's mine. It's not like we just started dating or we're just having some type of fling. Two plus years together ought to stand for something. Nick claims he just wants to be her friend, but I'm not buying it.

I walk outside and check out the Appletons' yard. Their set up is party central with a built in pool, pool house and trees offering privacy. I can only imagine what goes on back here. Rumor has it that Candy is a sure thing. I wouldn't know. I've never been interested in her. I set my sights on one girl and she was receptive. I don't regret spending all my high school years with her. Every single moment has been worth it.

The wind blows, but doesn't cool down the air. Earlier today a storm rolled through making it impossible for us to have graduation outside. Instead, they packed us into the gym like sardines and forgot to turn on the air conditioner. It was stifling up on the stage with the bright lights shining down on us. I wanted to drop down behind the stage and leave. No one would've missed me, except for Josie.

Garbage cans are strategically placed every few feet, making the clean-up easy. I take a long pull of my beer and toss the empty bottle into the nearest can. I have no excuse not to get drunk tonight. I just had my last monumental high school occasion and my parents couldn't be bothered to show up. To add to that my girlfriend is out with her family for what was deemed "Preston" only time. I think that's what pisses me off the most, not being invited. I was just thinking about asking Mr. Preston if I can stay with them when I come home on breaks, but clearly this was a "you're not welcome" memo.

I find a cooler and pull out another beer. The cold liquid does nothing to ease my anger. I'm pissed about graduation and everything that happened after. Josie and

I weren't able to sit together because the seating was done in alphabetical order, but I could see Josie from where I was. When her name was called, I stood and whistled, clapping loudly for her. She did the same for me and just like that we were free. Four years of high school and it was over with the calling of your name.

After all the pomp and circumstance was over, I found Josie outside with her family. Flashes of a fun-filled night sitting around a table with her parents, aunt, uncle and cousins ran through my mind. This was going to be the best night even if we're doing the mundane family thing. We'd be together and that's all that matters. Except that's not what happened. Mr. Preston, while apologetic, informed me in a roundabout way that this was a family event.

I walk around aimlessly. I could stop and talk but I don't want to answer the questions asking where Josie is. We've never not attended a party together and I can only imagine what this looks like. Honestly, I don't care right now. Why didn't she speak up and invite me? It's not like we've just started dating.

"Hey Liam," the voice startles me, coming from behind. I turn and see Candy sitting on her bench swing with one of her legs tucked underneath her. A cooler rests by her other foot with a beer in her hand. It's crazy to think her parents are okay with this.

"Candy," I say, cordially. We aren't friends, but we used to be back in middle school. We just grew up and went in different directions.

"Wanna sit? It can get claustrophobic in there." She nods toward her house. I turn and look as if I need confirmation.

Against my better judgment I sit down next to her. She doesn't move or adjust the way she's sitting, so her knee is resting against my thigh. We sit without talking, and drink. I don't know if it's five or six beers that I share with her, but they're starting to pile up in front of us. The buzz is working, it's numbing my anger.

"Where's your ball and chain?"

I chuckle, not at what Candy calls Josie, but the fact that Josie isn't here. I shake my head and start to peel off the label on my bottle. "Don't know, family shit."

"Aren't you guys all but married now?"

"Nah, that's Mason and Katelyn."

Candy laughs. "Yeah I heard he proposed the other day. What'd she say?"

"Same thing she's been saying for a year, yes, but not yet."

"Do you think they'll get married?"

I look at Candy and see hopelessness. I see a girl who just wants to be loved, but went about it the wrong way. "Yeah, they'll get married and have a shit ton of kids."

We grow silent again. It's peaceful aside from the music and noise coming from the people in her pool. I watch Candy from the corner of my eye. Her leg swings back and forth, but she's too tiny to move us. It's me moving the swing, keeping us going. Candy fumbles with something from her pocket and I watch as she takes out a cigarette and lights it. She blows smoke into the night sky, closing her eyes while she does it.

"Want some?"

"No thanks," I reply.

She hands it to me anyway. The brown stick burns a sweet smelling fragrance into the air. I'm intrigued to try it, but know I shouldn't.

"Go on, it won't hurt you," she says, closer than she should be. I bring the cigarette to my lips and inhale. Immediately, I start coughing, but Candy doesn't laugh. She takes it from me.

"Like this," she says, smiling. She shows me how to inhale and exhale properly. Honestly it makes me feel like a bit of a dweeb not knowing the basics. Candy leans forward, one of her hands rests on my shoulder and the other holds the cigarette to my lips. I know I should move away, but I'm enticed.

I purse my lips and let the cigarette rest inside, inhaling until my lungs are burning. She pulls it away, but not before I hear a gasp. I look up and see Josie standing a few feet away from us, shaking her head.

"Josie," I gasp, though another coughing fit, but it's too late. She's gone.

CHAPTER 19

JOSIE runs from Candy's yard before I can really comprehend what's going on. I stand, knocking Candy away from me. Her cigarette falls onto my shoe. I kick it off, frustrated that I allowed myself to get into this situation.

"Well that was unlucky," Candy says as she bends down to pick up her cigarette.

"You have no idea," I mutter. "I have to go," I look at Candy. She half smiles and nods before looking down at her hands. I don't know why I feel the need to tell her, but I do.

"You know, Liam, I've known you for a long time and even though we haven't been friends, I do care about you. It's hard to believe, I know," she chuckles, taking a deep breath and continues. "I made one mistake in high school and that was being with the wrong guy. My classmates gave me a reputation that I didn't earn. It's funny how everyone knows that you and Josie have sex, but she's not labeled a whore. I've been with one guy and I am."

"What's your point?"

Candy shakes her head. "I guess I don't have one. I don't know. I just wish things were different."

I stand next to Candy and let her last few words soak in. She doesn't know how much those words hit home for me. Every day I wish things were different and hate that I can't change anything. It's too late. My path has been laid out for me for years and my girl is right there behind me, pushing me along. Why? Because she doesn't know any better. Because it's what I told her I wanted and I can't seem to find the words to tell her that I want something different. How do I know if I want something different or just want out of Beaumont?

"I know what you mean. Listen I gotta go. We've never fought before and…" I look at her and try to grin, but can't.

"See ya later, Liam Westbury."

I nod and walk down the same path Josie just took when she ran out of here. I stuff my hands deep into my pockets and walk past my truck. I'm in no shape to drive and I need to think about what I'm going to say to Josie to explain what she saw. Thoughts of breaking up creep into my mind. Was today a sign that she's ready to end things? I don't want to think about that, but the truth of the matter is it could happen. I'm leaving for school sooner than she'll have to check into her dorm. I thought about asking her to go with me, but nixed the idea when I signed with the University of Texas using Katelyn as an excuse. I shouldn't care about Katelyn's feelings, but mine and Josie's. Everything with us is changing and there's no stopping it so maybe breaking up is the next step. I want to marry her though. At least I think I do. I see her in my future, by my side.

What if she doesn't see me in her future?

I stop and bend over. My hands are clutching my head as I scream loudly into the night air. I hate having so much doubt in my life. I'm eighteen, everything should be simple. I should be happy and relieved that I'm done with high school, but I'm not. I want to start over. I want to go back and tell Sterling that football isn't everything. I want to tell him that I want to have football and music… I place my hands on my knees and breathe in and out, trying to catch my breath. Music - I don't know where that came from. I haven't touched my guitar in months. Not since that fateful day in my room. I should've told Josie about what I was doing then maybe her reaction would've been better. But I kept the secret. Just like I'm keeping the secret that I don't want to play football anymore.

I will though because it's what's expected of me and God forbid I let anyone down.

JOSIE'S house is dark and has never felt more unwelcoming than it does now. I stagger to her window, drunker then I'd hope to be by the time I arrived. My hands try to lift the windowpane, but it doesn't budge. I try again with the same results. She's locked me out. I rest my head against the cold glass and sigh. I could scream and yell, but right now I really just want to cry for what I've done to her tonight.

"Josie," I say loud enough for her to hear me. My knuckle taps on her window. The annoying ping grates my nerves. She's never done this to me before. I haven't either. "Josie please open the window." Tap… tap… tap. "Josie, please."

"Go away, Liam."

I straighten and cup my hands trying to see in through her blinds. "Josie come on, let me explain."

I wait and listen for any movement, but hear nothing. She's not coming to the window and that pisses me off. I knock a little harder on her window. "Josie, open up and talk to me."

"Go home, Liam."

"I don't have a home, Josie. Come on babe, open your window before someone wakes up." As upset as I am with Mr. Preston, I don't want him waking up to hear us talking. "Baby, come on."

Her blinds spring up and facing me is one angry Josie with make-up running down her face. She's been crying and I don't blame her but she's reading too much into what she saw earlier. If she'd just talk to me, she'd understand.

Josie raises her window and leans out. I don't move, holding my spot against the side of her house. "Go home, Liam. I don't want you here."

"What?" I choke out.

"Leave." She points out toward the road. I follow her arm, shaking my head. I reach forward and try to touch her before she pulls back. "Don't touch me."

"What the hell is wrong with you?" I'm angry and drunk, not a good combination. "Get out here and talk to me because if I leave, I'm not coming back. Is that what you want?"

My words make her pause. She looks at me briefly

before stepping back into her room. I hear her door open and close and can only assume she's on her way out here. With my luck today she's gone and gotten her father to come out and kick my ass. Maybe that's what I need, my ass kicked.

Josie comes around the corner, dressed in her stupid tiny shorts and one of my t-shirts. In this moment I don't care that she's mad, I want to drag her ass behind the tree and do things to her that will make her dig her nails into my back.

She stomps toward me, her finger poking me in the chest. She continues to do this until we're closer to the aforementioned tree and almost far enough from the house where her parents won't hear us clearly.

"You don't get to come over here drunk and demanding shit from me Liam Westbury. I don't know who the hell you think you are, but I'm done with whatever is going on in your head."

I put my hands back into my pocket and bite the inside of cheek. "You're done, huh?"

"I will be."

I nod. "I see and why's that?"

Josie crosses her arms, which does nothing for my resolve. "I saw you with Candy."

"You didn't see shit, Josie. You saw us sitting on her fucking bench talking. That's it."

"You were smoking."

I throw my hands up. "Oh man, you better call Sterling and tell him Beaumont's golden boy was smoking. Better sound the sirens because Liam Westbury is going off the deep end here. I had my reasons for doing that tonight."

"Oh yeah, like what?" She challenges. I shake my

head and step away from her, only for her to step back in front of me so I can see her.

"Never mind. I'm going."

"Don't you dare leave," she cries, pulling on my arm. "You were cheating on me."

"The fuck I was," I roar. "I've never even looked at another girl, unlike you and your touchy-feely bullshit with Ashford." Josie drops her hands and steps back. I laugh to myself and groan. "You don't think I see you in the hallway but I do. I see you touch his arm when you're talking to him. I see the way you smile at him."

"He's a friend," she says, quietly.

"Yeah well so is Candy, so there, we're even."

"Is that what this was? Are you trying to get even with me because of Nick?"

"No, Josie. I'm trying to numb the fucking pain of not having anyone in my life that gives a shit. My parents didn't even show up for my own fucking graduation, and when I thought I'd be with you, your father tells me I'm not welcome. So I did what I needed to do and if that means I went the Appleton's to get drunk so be it, and I happened to smoke with Candy, so fucking what? After today, who really gives a God damn shit how I feel or what I do?" I realize I'm yelling and pointing at her and I don't like that. We've never been down this path before and it's not someplace I want to be with her. I put my hands back in my pockets and turn away from her.

"I do," she whispers, weakly. She reaches for me, but I shy away. I don't want her to touch me out of pity and that's exactly what she's doing. Earlier, she should've pitied me, spoke up to her father, but she didn't.

"It doesn't matter anymore, Josie."

"Of course it does."

I shake my head and wish I were back on that swing getting drunk with Candy because she didn't care about anything. She just wanted someone to drink with.

"I'll see ya around." Only after I say those words do I understand the magnitude behind them. I don't wait for her response. I walk away. Nothing good is going to come from talking to her tonight or even tomorrow.

CHAPTER 20

THERE'S only been one other time in my life, well the life I've shared with Josie, that I've gone longer than two days without talking to her. Those days were unavoidable since I was with Sterling touring colleges. But at night, I'd sneak out and call her and just say hi so I could hear her voice. But as I lay here now, with my arms behind my head and staring at the ceiling she painted, I can't bring myself to call her or even muster enough courage to get out of bed to go to her.

I'm a dick, an ass, a piece of shit boyfriend. I'm whatever names I can conjure up in my head to describe the feelings I'm having about myself. I don't know if I'm right or wrong about what happened the other night. I do know that I'm confused. I'm hurt and angry and I'm counting the days until my feet land on campus so I can put Beaumont behind me. Graduation wasn't what I thought it was going to be and by the end of the night, everything was nothing but a fucking blur. Worst of all, my girl and I walked away from each other not speaking.

I keep thinking that life is supposed to be easy, simple even. I don't see Mason having all these problems. I know Katelyn's mom is uptight and not a fan of Mason's, but she doesn't tell Katelyn to stop seeing him. Mason's dad has been to all our games and yeah, my dad shows up, but he's not there to watch me play. He's there to make sure I don't do anything to embarrass him, like ask for a sub when I'm tackled and can't breathe. No, Liam Westbury would never ask for a sub. "Suck it up, son," he has said so many times over and over again.

I'm selfish. I know this. I have the life most guys my age want. I'm going to college to play football for free. I have a hot ass girlfriend and my parents don't give a shit if I come home at night. What more could an eighteen year old ask for?

I want someone to care. I don't think that's too much to ask, but maybe it is and I should just give up the notion that someone will someday and just go with the flow of having a shitty life the rich way.

My door opens and I don't even lift my head to see why my mom is in my room. She has no business being in here. It's not like she's having a sudden change of heart and is going to invite me to join her for lunch. She probably doesn't have permission to even be in my room. Sterling would never allow it. I have no doubt he hides her vodka to get her to comply with his demands. I'll never be like him. I'd rather be alone and living in a cardboard box before I act like that prick.

"Liam," she says only it's not my mom it's Josie. I lift my head slightly just to confirm that my ears aren't bullshitting me. I've been in my room since the night of graduation, for all I know I'm hallucinating because there's no way in hell Josie Preston would set foot in this house unless she knows for sure that no one is home.

"What are you doing here?" I ask, laying my head back down. I can't look at her knowing that we're through. These past few days have been the worst of my life, and a glimpse of what college will be like. I knew I wouldn't have her with me, but at least we'd talk. Now we're not even doing that.

The foot of my bed dips as she sits down. I stay in the same position. I'm not going to look at her knowing that she's here to make sure we're finished. I know how town gossip works, I'm sure Ashford drove her over to make sure she tells me were done. It's okay, they can have a long happy life together while I bust my ass playing a game I'm starting to fucking despise. Hell, maybe I'll finally start listening to Sterling and take advantage of what all those girls at college are willing to give me.

"Liam, can you look at me?" I close my eyes and shake my head. She has to know how much it pains me. I can already hear the disconnect in her voice. It's really better this way, especially for me.

"Liam?"

"What, Josie?" saying her name out loud feels like I'm pressing a sharp blade to my skin, just waiting for it to pierce me and draw first blood.

"I'm here to talk to you. Can you at least look at me?"

I sit up quickly, startling her. "Well go on then, tell me that you're done with me and get out of my room. I'm not in the mood."

She balks, shaking her head. "What is wrong with

you? I came here —"

"And I'm still trying to figure out why?"

"To see you," she says quietly. She's trying to maintain eye contact with me, but can't. Not that I can blame her, I'm not exactly smiling at her right now. I move to the side of my bed and rest my elbows on my knees. My heart is breaking and staring at her is only making it worse.

"I'm sorry for being a dick, Josie. But you really shouldn't be here. Sterling will probably show up and find you and it'll be ugly."

"I'm not leaving until we figure this out. If your dad wants to toss me out on my ass, so be it. But until that happens you and I are talking."

I look at her over my shoulder and see tears pooling in her eyes. I knew this wouldn't be easy, but I was hoping tears would be avoidable. We've had a few days to figure shit out and what we're going to say to each other. She thinks I cheated. I think she likes Ashford a bit too much. It's jealousy that's going to drive us apart and there's nothing I can do about it. Hell, I don't even know what to do about it. I don't know how to change it either.

"I don't like to see you cry, Jojo, so say what you have to say. I can take it."

Josie takes a deep breath and I focus on a spot on my floor, hoping that it can keep my attention because looking at her will break me.

"I love you, Liam Page Westbury, and I don't know why we ended up like this for the past two days, but I don't like it. I don't like not seeing you every day or even hearing your voice. We had a fight… our first fight and it was a big one. We've never even argued before and that fight was huge. I don't know how we're supposed to fix it, but we have to because I love you too much and I can't live if you're not in my life."

Against my better judgment I turn and look at her. Tears are falling down her face. I want to reach for her and hold her against me, taking away all the pain I've caused. This only proves my point – I'm a piece of shit boyfriend.

"Josie —" she puts her hand up to stop me.

"Let me finish." I nod. "You're leaving for school soon. We only have weeks, Liam, and the last thing I want is to spend the rest of our time together with this hanging over our heads. I won't be able to handle being away from you knowing that things weren't perfect when you left. Until football is over, I'll hardly see you and I hate to think that you'll be unsure about us while you're in Texas," she sobs. Josie covers her face with her hands and hiccups. It only takes me seconds before I have her pulled into my arms. I'm stroking her back, her shoulders and arms, anything I can to soothe the pain I've caused her.

"I love you, Josie. I hope you know that. The other night – I was drunk and hurt – it's no excuse, but it's all I can offer."

"I'm sorry about my dad, Liam. I didn't know he was going to do that and when I asked him why, he said something stupid about my cousin and family and I was pissed. I ditched as soon as I could, but then I found you and Candy."

"We were talking, Jojo."

She shakes her head. I shouldn't have to defend my actions. It's not like I was doing something bad.

"You were smoking."

I tense briefly in her arms. "I was trying something

new. That's what we're supposed to do, right? How are we supposed to grow as people if we don't try new things or test limits? I'd never do anything to disrespect you, babe. I wouldn't. Nothing is worth that."

Josie nods and snuggles into my chest. I lay us back onto my bed and curl her into me. "Are we breaking up?" I ask, stupidly.

"I don't want to, ever."

"Me neither, Jojo. I love you more than anything."

"More than smoking with Candy?"

I nod, unable to answer. I do love Josie, but smoking with Candy was peaceful and relaxing. There was no talk about expectations or life. I look into Josie's blue eyes and smile. "Yes, baby." I say as I bring my lips down onto hers. I pull her to me, sliding my leg in between hers. Her leg hitches over my hip as she moans into my mouth. I've heard make-up sex is the best ever invention, but I don't know what's going on downstairs and the last thing I need is for my father to bust open my door when my robotic mother tells him Josie's in here and have him find us in a compromising position. So right now I'll make out with my girl before she slips away from me.

CHAPTER 21

'M packing the last bit of camping gear into my truck when I hear the screen door open and shut. There's a squeak, something that I'm surprised hasn't been fixed yet, but I guess if you never come out here you don't know about it. I know about it, but refuse to oil the hinges. Personally, I like the noise. It's somewhat soothing in what is otherwise a rather quiet house.

I don't have to turn around to know that Sterling is approaching me. It's the stench of his cologne that wafts through the air that alerts me to his location. I move the storage totes full of camping supplies around in my truck, tying them down with bungee cords just to keep myself busy. I really have no inclination to turn around and see what he wants. It's funny, really. He hasn't spoken to me in months and now he's standing out here watching me. Maybe he thinks I'm moving out or leaving early for college. The thought has crossed my mind. I can check in anytime, but next week is the *official* day to report. I'll have one day to acclimatize myself before football starts.

Sterling clears his throat causing me to stiffen. I was so close, yet still couldn't get out of here before he decided that today of all days he would talk to me. Mason and I are taking the girls camping for a week. Next Monday we leave for the University of Texas and won't see them for a few weeks. I've already looked at our game schedule to figure out when I can sneak back to see Josie. Even if I can only see her for a few hours, the drive will be worth it. I also have to find a way to get her to campus for a weekend. The college football season is much longer than high school and there's definitely no way I'm going the whole time without seeing my girl.

I adjust the tote in front of me simply because I don't want to turn around. I have nothing to say to him.

"I thought we could talk." I ignore him and move to the side of my truck and start tying down the tarp. I was going to do this when I stopped at Josie's, but right now the distraction affords me the opportunity to zone him out. "Son." I stop and raise my eyes slowly to meet his. He looks like he's aged at least ten years since we went on the college visits.

"You lost the right to call me son a long time ago," I inform him through gritted teeth. I pull on the rope and thread it through the side of my truck.

"We should talk."

"We have nothing to talk about and I'm going to be late."

"Look, you're leaving soon—"

"So what, this is your "let's make amends for being a douche" moment?" I state, not making eye contact with him. "I'm not interested in anything you or your wife has to say."

"She's your mother."

My actions are so fast they surprise me. I'm in front of Sterling with my finger in his face. "She's not my mother any more than you're my father. Parents don't treat their children like scum and that's what you do. You couldn't even be bothered to show up for my graduation. My high school graduation for God sakes. Who misses their child's graduation?" I shake my head. "The time for you to be parents is over. I'm leaving in a week."

"That's what I want to talk to you about."

I scoff. "Whatever. I'm going to be late."

"Five minutes." I roll my eyes and start working on the other side of my truck to tie down the tarp. "Your mother and I decided we've been wrong and we're going to make it up to you."

"No thanks." I finish doing all I can on my truck. I'm out of avoidance tactics. I look at him for the first time in a long time and notice that he's aged since that fateful day in February. I shake my head as I look down at the ground and kick an imaginary rock. I wish things were different – that he was more like Mason's dad – but he's not. I should've swallowed that knowledge long ago, that I'd never have the kind of father most kids dream about. He's about structure and social status.

Sterling sighs. "We'll financially support you while you're away at college as long as you maintain your GPA and position on the team. I'm not thrilled with your choice of college, but what's done is done. If you thrive, like I know you can, you'll be in the NFL draft in four years."

He makes me want to yell and pound my fist into my truck. They're going to support me… financially. But when I need the emotional support they're nowhere to be found. It's a little too late for him to come at me with this now.

"Whatever," I say again as I hop in my truck and start it. I don't look in the rear view mirror as I'm pulling out of the driveway to see if he's watching. I can't bring myself to care.

WHAT if a bear comes and tries to eat me?" I roll my eyes and shake my head slightly at her remark.

"Seriously Josie, a bear isn't going to come around here. He'll hear you and Katelyn complaining all the time and think better of it."

Josie hits me, causing me to laugh. The drive here all she did was talk *what if's* and it doesn't matter how must assurance I gave her, she's still scared.

I pound the last stake into the ground and pull her into my arms. Tonight, and for the next five nights, we'll be in each other's arms. No parents, no curfew, no rules. It sounds just about perfect.

"You'll be fine, I'm here," I reassure her, pecking her on the nose. I pull her hand into mine and walk the short path back to our campground. There are four chairs set up around the fire pit and a fire is already going.

I go to the cooler and pull out a beer, taking one of the seats. I twist the top, throw it into the burning flames and watch the metal change colors. Josie moves her chair closer to me, putting her arm through mine and resting her head on my shoulder. Katelyn and Mason sit down opposite us and mirror our positions.

"I can't believe this is it. Our last hurrah," I say, pointing my bottle toward Mason as a nod to what's about to come for us.

"I'm going to miss you," Josie whispers in my ear. I notice Katelyn looking at Mason like she's hiding something and truth be told, they haven't spent much time with us this summer. It makes me wonder if they're pregnant. Honestly, I wouldn't be surprised. He's been asking her to marry him for a while now. It would suck though.

Mason clears his throat and kicks the dirt in front of him. He's looking everywhere but at me and I'm not sure what to think.

"What's up, man?" I ask, as I empty my bottle. I set it on the ground and place my hand on Josie's leg. My thumb rubs circles on her thigh.

Mason shrugs. "I have something to tell you."

Josie's grip on my arm gets a little tighter as I adjust in my seat. What on earth could he possibly need to tell me in the middle of the forest? "What's up?"

He looks at Katelyn who nods and kisses him on the shoulder. When Mason looks back at me, he's not making eye contact. Whatever he's about to tell me is bad, but unless he's told me that he's slept with my girl, it can't be that bad.

"I've decided to stay and go to school with Katelyn."

I stiffen. I take everything back. This is right up there with sleeping my girl. "What do you mean?" It's a stupid question. I know what he means.

"I don't want to leave Katelyn."

"So you just…" I have to close my eyes and count to ten. I lean forward and Josie starts to rub my back.

"Did you know?" I ask her, quietly. She shakes her head. There are tears in her eyes and for the life of me I can't understand why. Are they for me or for the friendship I've shared with Mason?

"Liam —"

I hold my hand up, not ready to hear what he has to say. My eyes burn an imaginary hole into the ground. I'm biting my lips so hard I can taste the iron seeping into my mouth. He's not going and I am. Everything I've done, every decision I've made has been for nothing.

"I chose the University of Texas because of you and now you're not going?" My voice is sharp, the anger rushing forward. I can't hold it back.

"I'm in love." His answer is weak and not good enough.

"And you don't think I am? I was going to ask Josie to go to school with me until you told me about Texas. I had an offer from them and thought you'd appreciate us playing together. I wanted to take her out of Beaumont and never return, but didn't ask her because I didn't want Katelyn to be alone."

"Thanks —"

"Just stop, both of you. Why couldn't you tell me this before we got here? Afraid I'd bail?"

I stand and stare down my friend, who right now I wish wasn't my friend. He's someone who has just turned my last camping trip into a fucking nightmare. I'm stuck here for five days with him when all I want to do is fucking leave.

"Liam —"

"What, Mason? What on earth do you have to say? Is it that you didn't want me to go to college with you?

Because if that's the case you should've fucking said something when you barged into my hotel room. Do you really think I want to go to Texas? Fuck no. I did it for you, so you wouldn't be alone because you kept going on and on about your damn scholarship and I thought if I were there to help and support you, things would be okay. Boy was I fucking wrong." I grab my hair and pull it, letting out a loud yell. I bend over and try to catch my breath. I want to fucking cry I'm so frustrated. I feel Josie's hand on my shoulder, trying to comfort me. Unfortunately it's not going to work, not this time.

"And to think I could've had a decent fucking home life these past few months had I chosen the right school, but who the hell gives a shit about that?"

I kick my chair into the fire, startling Josie. I glance in her direction before heading off into the woods. There's nothing they can say, what's done is done. I was stupid for trying to do what's right for my friend when I should've just thought about myself. Josie and I could be packing and getting ready for school, instead we're getting ready to say goodbye. She'll be with her friends and I'll be alone.

Just the way Sterling prefers it.

CHAPTER 22

I HOLD Josie in my arms. I know she's trying not to cry but her tears dampen my shirt. I don't push her away. My bags are packed and strapped down in the back of my truck. The next stop is the University of Texas. We've had a rough week and it definitely hasn't gone like we had planned. They say plans are supposed to change. I don't know who *they* are but their theory is spot on.

My dad got wind of Mason backing out of his scholarship and did everything he could to get me into one of the five I had shortlisted, but he couldn't. I was actually thankful for his attempt and it was nice to see him step up, but in the end it was all for nothing. He's disappointed in me and so am I. I'm off to a college that I don't really want to be at and it's my own fault for putting others in front of me. Sterling's incredibly selfish and says I need to learn to be this way too.

The sun is rising over the valley now. We've been out

here for an hour or so. I'm not supposed to leave until tomorrow, but there's a party tonight at the tower and I can't bring myself to be there. I thought it best, under the circumstances that I leave early. I can take my time and maybe figure out my life while I'm driving solo on the highway.

I bury my nose in Josie's hair, determined not to forget what she smells like. I don't care if I'm going to be gone for a day, a week or a month. I need to make sure every sense that I have has her memorized. I'm kicking myself for leaving her behind but she hasn't asked if she can come, which tells me that she wants to stay and go to school with Katelyn. That's what girls do, they go to school with their girlfriends and join sororities and do girly shit. She wouldn't have fun in Texas. She wouldn't know anyone and she'd spend most of her time waiting for me to be done with football. That's no way to start your college education. I need her to be happy. If she's happy, I'm happy… even though I'm not.

"I'm going to miss this," I say into her hair. My throat is tight. It's painful to speak. I'm fighting back the tears that are threatening my manly existence. She's never seen me cry, even while we were camping. I held it in. I couldn't do it even though I wanted to unleash a fury on everything around me. Instead, I let her hold me. Console me. I berated her when she apologized. This wasn't her fault. It was mine and mine alone. I tried to do what I felt was right.

"I wish things were different, Jojo."

She clutches my shirt in her hands as she pulls me closer. "How so?"

"I wish you were going with me or we had chosen a

school together."

"Me too," she whispers, breaking another piece of my already crumbling heart. Everything could've been so different and it should've been.

I have to squint when the sun comes up. It's going to be a hot day in Beaumont and that means I'll miss my girl in her bikini lounging by Katelyn's pool. We didn't do nearly half the stuff I wanted to and now that I think about it, it all seems so trivial and mundane. I should've taken us on a trip across country, just the open road and us. We had nothing holding us back in Beaumont, at least nothing that couldn't wait.

Instead we're sitting in my truck with the sun telling me it's time to go and say goodbye. In a few days, I'll be busting my balls in the hot Texas sun, trying to impress a coach who hasn't spoken to me since I said I was going there. Maybe it's a sign. If it is, I don't have a fucking clue what it means.

The next song on my mixed tape starts to play. I try not to let on my excitement, but it's there, sitting on the edge ready to burst out. Josie shifts in my arms and I know this is it. She's going to tell me that she loves this song. I can feel it.

"Who's singing?"

I wrap my arm around her a little tighter and nuzzle her ear. "Me." I listen to the words that I wrote her play out over the speakers.

Can't take my eyes off of you
I'm a man that's speakin' the truth
This love could make mountains move
Hope you feel the same way I do

I wanna be holdin' you
When the dawn is breakin' through
As yesterday fades with the moon
And forever fills up this room
I wanna wake up with you

I wait for her to say something, to acknowledge what I'm doing on the stereo, but she doesn't. She holds me the same way as she did before the song came on. I can't win for trying here and I don't know how to get through to her. Right now, there's no point in prolonging the inevitable.

"How did you get your song on there?"

I lean back into the seat and pull her a little closer. This is the first time she's asked and maybe I can find a way to express myself a little better now. "It's a crappy recording, but the player did an okay job."

Josie leans into me and I use this moment to remember the scent of her hair.

"You're going to move mountains at Texas, Liam. You'll break all their records and win the Heisman." Her fingers rub up and down along my t-shirt, giving me the chills.

"There's more to life than football, Jojo."

She chuckles. "Sure there is."

There could be, I want to add, but she's right. My path is football and she'll follow me no matter what. It's what we agreed to do a year ago when we laid out under the stars in the bed of my truck. The American Dream and I'm at the helm.

I have to drive her back home and hit the road. I lean forward and start my truck, letting the engine roar to life.

Every step is now methodical and slow. Shifting out of park I wait for her to move off my lap. It's all happening and there's nothing I can do to stop it.

I hold her to me on our way back to her house. Her parents will just be waking. Their coffee pot will start and her dad will come outside to get the paper. Tomorrow at this time, she'll be sleeping in her bed and I'll be in some dorm room staring at a white ceiling wondering how the fuck I got there. I pull up in front of her house and put my truck in park. I don't shut it off. I can't stall any longer.

"I love you Josie Preston. You own my heart. You stole a little piece of it the moment I saw you and you've taken the rest every day since," I tell her. Before she can respond I disengage and step out, afraid to look at her. The tears will do me in. Destroy me like a dagger to my heart. I need her to be strong, but that's a lot to ask of her. Our lives will be changing in a matter of minutes and all I can think about is that it could've been preventable.

Josie follows me out and right into my arms. I hold her, pressing her against my idling truck. My hands roam, cupping her ass. "God I'm going to miss you," I say as my lips crash down on hers. She whimpers into my mouth as she cups my face with her hands. Her tears stain my cheeks. We part and I press my lips to her forehead. I swallow hard and clear my throat. "I gotta go, babe."

She nods, but doesn't let go. I bring my hands over the top of hers and kiss her one more time. "I love you, Jojo. You're forever my girl."

I pull her hands away from my face and jump into my truck without looking at her. I pull away, knowing she's standing in the road watching me drive away. Everything in my heart is telling me to go back, but I don't. I can't.

TWO weeks.

It's been two weeks since I left Josie and Beaumont. Fourteen days since I set foot in the hot Texas sun in the middle of summer. This is not how football should be played, but I'm here, trying to learn. My dad has called a few times, but I don't return his calls. He wants to know how things are going and honestly, I'm too afraid to tell him. I'm not seeing any field time and the coach has barely said two words to me. I suit up with my pads on, ready to take the field, but nothing. No snaps for Westbury. I know I need to talk to him, but I'm at a loss as what to say. This should've been a sign. Actually, it was and I ignored it. When the coach didn't make contact with me after signing day, I should've known. He doesn't want me here.

It's not even football that I care about right now. It's the student pub on campus that I've started frequenting. They have open mic in the evening and I've been there every night. The first couple of days, it was just me and the kid behind the pretend bar, but as students started filtering back to school the crowd has grown. I'm not being heckled or having rotten fruit thrown at me so I take that as a plus.

Practice today sucked. That is the only way to sum it up. All I do is stand on the sidelines, in the same pose for the entire practice – me with my helmet on and my hands cinched tightly the collar of my jersey – waiting for my name to be called.

It's being called now. One of the students calls my name and I walk up on the small stage and sit on a stool with my guitar resting on my knee. It's hard to think back to when I was packing to leave that I almost threw it out, but thought better of it. If anything, I thought, I'd be able to play it in my room at night. It's not like I have a roommate that would be put off with my playing. Being up on the stage, in front of my peers, pouring my heart out gives me a different kind of satisfaction. It's knowing that I'm entertaining them, affording them the opportunity to put their worries aside for a brief moment and just relax. At least that's how I feel about music while I'm playing. Strumming my guitar and creating a melody, even if the words aren't mine, makes me feel like I'm accomplishing something great. Hearing them clap for me, before I even start playing, makes me feel like this is my path.

But how do I change my path, one that has been set out for me for as long as I can remember? I can't. I'm here on scholarship to play football, not play guitar and cover other peoples' songs. At best, this is a hobby.

Tonight, after performing, I'm relieved. The stress from the day is gone at least for the time being. I like walking across campus with my guitar on my back and hearing people ask me when I'm going to play again. No one knows me as a member of the Longhorn football team, they know me as the guy who gets on stage and sings for them and I think I like that.

Each step I climb that takes me to the third floor where my dorm room is, brings me closer to feeling the same anxiety I feel when I'm on the football field. I'm supposed to have a roommate, but he backed out, telling me that he was staying behind and attending college with his girlfriend. It's when I get back to my empty dorm room and I'm lying on my bed that my mind starts working in overdrive. What's Josie doing? Was I a bad friend to Mason? Is that why he's not here? So many questions and not enough answers run through my mind.

The one thing I do know is that I'm desperate for acceptance and the only time I'm getting that is while I'm playing my guitar. On the field, I'm a nobody and I'm not prepared to be that person. As much as I hated the image of being Beaumont's golden boy, this is far worse. This is painful and unwarranted. Thing is, I don't know how to fix it or even if I want to. Maybe I can be content sitting on the sidelines for the next four years.

As I play those words over and over again in my head. I know that's not the case. I'm here to play football and if the coach is not going to let me play, I need to transfer. I'll have to sit out a year, but I can't sit by and watch as a coach alters the plan. Josie's counting on me.

CHAPTER 23

"HEY baby," I say as soon as she answers the phone. I know I've awakened her, but I can't sleep. It's three a.m. and my anxiety is building. "I'm sorry I woke you."

"It's okay," she slurs into the phone. I know she's not that coherent, so maybe if I just talk she can listen. "What's going on?"

"Nothing… I just," I can't spit the words out of my mouth. They're there, sitting on the edge of my tongue, but are too thick to leave my mouth. "I can't —"

"Are you okay?"

"No," I say weakly. "I need to come see you."

"What about, football practice?"

I close my eyes and wish she hadn't brought it up. I'm not living her dream right now. I'm treated like the child that was produced from a torrid affair. At best, I'm third string and standing in front of me is a walk on who hasn't won a high school game. I'm being punished and for what, I don't know.

"Josie, I need to see you. It's been six weeks and I can't… you don't… I need you Jojo. I'm leaving now." I hang up before she has a chance to respond. It's selfish I know, but I need her. I need the comfort that she can provide and I need to talk to her about school. I have to know what our future will be like if I leave Texas, because honestly I don't know if I'm going to make it a full semester at this rate.

I drive all day and night, exceeding the speed limit until I hit the Beaumont town line. Josie leaves for school in a few days and the fact that she's going to school with our friends makes me envious. I need that connection and I don't have it. I don't have one friend on the football team where I have to spend a majority of my time. I have no friends in class because I haven't made an effort and at best I have a few people who I could call my friends from the student pub if I was to ever hang out with them. But I don't. I spend any free time locked up tight in my room contemplating my life. This is not what I wanted. My life is not going according to plan.

Josie's house is dark when I arrive. I don't know if she's waiting up for me or not. I haven't spoken to her since I left my dorm room, only stopping for gas and coffee to keep me awake. I park and barely have the truck shut off before I'm out the door and jogging to the back side of the house where her window is. I rest my head on the cool glass and pray that she's left her window open for me.

My hands push gently on the window sill and relief washes over me when it slides up. I heave myself in, mindful of the noise I make. I don't want to wake her parents. I don't want to have to explain myself or my appearance. I close it behind me, all the while never taking my eyes off my girl. I stand in the middle of her room, like a midnight stalker, and watch her sleep. She shows no sign of having any demons in her life and why should she? I'm supposed to be taking care of everything for her. I could stand here and stare, but the urge to touch her, hold her, is too great and overpowering. I quickly shed my shoes and clothes and crawl into bed with her. I don't know what her reaction to me is going to be, but I'm excited and nervous to find out.

"Josie," I whisper against her skin, skin that I've missed desperately. I rub my stubble along her face. She twitches and that tells me she's been awake this whole time. "Are you pretending to be asleep, my girl?"

She giggles, turns and wraps her arms around me. Her lips find mine, her tongue making its presence known. This is what happiness is. She's what makes me happy, content. Her fingers trail down my face and into my scruff. I haven't shaved in weeks and I didn't know how she'd like it. It's a Longhorn thing – we don't shave until we win – but at this rate with the QB we have, I'll be a Sasquatch by the end of the season.

She pulls away against my wishes. I don't want to stop. "What's all this?" she asks as her fingers move in and out of my beard.

"Some tradition," I say, as I pepper her with kisses. "I'll shave as soon as we win."

"Well you won't win if you're not QB1."

I bring my lips down to silence her. I don't want to talk football. I don't want to talk about anything but her and me and how much we've missed each other. I move and settle between her legs, my mouth leaving a path of delight as I move down her body. I lift her tank top, exposing her darkened skin. The image of her poolside flashes before my mind only to remind me of something else football has taken from me. I kiss her exposed skin, every inch until I pull her up to remove her shirt. Her hands roam my body until I gently push her back down so I can continue my ravaging of her body. I sit back and look at the beauty in front of me. As much as I want to stare at her, my need for her is far greater. I bend forward and latch onto her breast. Her back arches, encouraging me, her other breast is being cupped and fondled by my hand. My body shakes with anticipation.

Josie shimmies closer to me, bringing her hips up to meet mine. She grinds against me, creating the much needed friction. The absence we've had is evident in her movements. She wants me just as much as I want her. She grabs at my briefs, pulling them down just enough to take hold of my erection. I close my eyes and hiss at the contact of her hand.

"Liam," her voice is full of lust, full of need.

"Yeah, Jojo?"

She doesn't answer. She pushes her panties down, her legs working to remove them. Her hands grip the sides of my briefs, yanking them down until I'm free. Her movements are rushed. The longing is there as her hands land on my backside, pulling me forward. The moment I enter her, time all but stops. Everything slows down, our breathing, our actions. I look at her, as I move in and out of her slowly. Nothing excites me more than to see her mouth open in ecstasy. I kiss her deeply to muffle her oncoming cries. I wish, in this moment, we were back in my dorm room where she could be herself and cry out in euphoria instead of having to try and stay quiet.

Josie's hands roam from my back to my chest and down my arms. Her hands cup my face, her fingers thread into my hair, anything to keep me going. I know her body well, I know she's close. As much as I'd love to go faster, to be able to watch her come undone, I don't want to wake her parents. I grip her headboard with my hands when she tightens around me. She bites my chest to stifle her cry causing me to groan heavily into her pillow. I'm close and won't last much longer.

"Liam, condom," she says because she knows I'm there.

"I'll pull-out," I reassure her as I take hold of her hips and thrust into her.

"I love you," she whispers against my mouth. "I miss you so much. I need you, baby," she says over and over against me effectively breaking my heart.

I try to slow down to make this last but she has other ideas. Her legs lock behind my back, giving me a different angle and that's when I lose it completely and spill into her.

"Shit, Liam," she whisper screams, throwing me off of her. I slam my face into her pillow, but pull her into my arms. I fucked up, I know this.

"I'm sorry. I'm so sorry." I repeat over and over again in her ear.

"We have to be careful, Liam, we can't get pregnant."

"I know, I'm sorry," I say, again. She gets up and goes to the bathroom while I use the tissues from her nightstand to clean up. I lie back in her bed and think about her, plump with my child and smile. It would be a good thing and if it happened tonight, I wouldn't care. It would be my excuse to get out of Texas and come home to Beaumont. As much as I hate saying it, I hope that we did the unthinkable and created a child because then I'd have no excuse.

Josie comes back and crawls into my arms. I hold her against my chest, my fingers running up and down her bare back. My hand rests on her hip, my fingers splayed out over her abdomen and all I can think about is that I got her pregnant and that thought excites me. Maybe in the back of my mind I knew this was the answer, the solution to my problems. Selfish, yes, but I'd marry her in a heartbeat. She wouldn't be alone, raising a baby. We'd be a family. I can go to school here and work to support her. I'd make it work.

"What's going on, Liam?"

I sigh and know I have to tell her. She needs to know that I hate school and it's when I'm on the stage that, for the first time in a month, I've felt really at peace with my life. How can the two things that keep me calm be something she doesn't understand? I don't even know if I'll be able to make her or show her how to grasp what it feels like to play the guitar and sing in front of twenty people or so.

"I hate school, Jojo. I hate the team, the coach, everything. I hate that you're not there. That Mason's not there. Everything about the place is sterile and uninviting. It's a great campus, but I don't belong there. I made a mistake and now I'm paying the price. Beaumont's *golden boy* has fucked up and there ain't shit I can do about it."

Josie sits up, resting her head on her hand. Her fingers

play with my scruff and if I didn't know better I'd think she likes it.

"You're one of the best quarterbacks in the country, Liam. Talk to the coach and find out why you're not playing."

I nod, but say nothing. Those aren't the words that I want to hear from her. Of everything I just said to her she picks up on the football part. I want her to tell me to quit and come home. I want her to tell me that she'll come back with me because having her there will ease the fucking anxiety I'm feeling every night when I'm alone.

She's not alone; she doesn't know what it feels like. She has our crew, our friends. I have nothing but an empty dorm room with bare white walls because I haven't found an ounce of energy to decorate it. Because decorating makes everything final and this can't be what I'm destined for. This was not the path and the great American dream. I'm on the high road to Loserville and she'll be watching me from the sidelines, shaking her head because I fucked up.

"I don't know, babe."

"What don't you know? They recruited you. They wanted you to play. Yes it sucks that Mason pulled a fast one, but it's not like you guys were a package deal."

"Yeah, I guess," I say to appease her. "It's just not what I thought it would be. I don't know, high school doesn't really prepare you to be hundreds of miles away from the one you love, does it?"

"No, I suppose it doesn't. But I'm here, you know that and I'll be coming down soon."

That's right, I invited her down for a game, but I don't want her there, not now. The last thing I want is for her to see me sitting on the sidelines like some has-been. It pains me enough to be there, watching the game unfold in front of me and not be a part of it. I don't know how I'd cope knowing my girl is in the stands, watching me watch something I can't be a part of.

I pull her back into my arms and rest my chin on top of her head. I love her so damn much it's going to be the death of me. I can't tell her this, of course, because she won't understand. She's not under the pressure I am, she only adds to it.

CHAPTER 24

JOSIE'S in college now and loving it. I'm resentful. She's going to parties and having fun while I'm stuck here, sleep walking my way through life. If I didn't love her so much, I'd tell her to shut up when we're on the phone because the constant yammering about how much fun she's having and how she wishes I were there, is too much to take.

I know I shouldn't feel this way toward her, but I do. I don't want to hear about all the great friends she's making or how last night Mason ran for his first collegiate touchdown. That's all supposed to be me. *I'm* supposed to be the one she raves about. It's me who should be having fun and be completely exhausted when we talk. I should be the one having to return her phone calls, not the other way around. When I call her, I want her to answer. I don't want to leave a message and wait for hours and hours only for me to call back because she hasn't called.

None of this college experience is going like I thought. My only solace is the open mic nights. I've been promoted, if you will, from the five p.m. to the nine p.m. slot. I don't mind as it gives me a bigger audience to play in front of. Most of these people don't even know I'm on the football team. How sad is that? I'm here, for the benefit of the Longhorns, and I'm more of a hit in the pub than I am on the football field. Isn't life grand?

Open mic nights have become my lifeline. I don't care about my grades or the football team. Hell, I'm not even traveling to away games. I refuse to answer any calls from my dad and the coach won't take a meeting with me. I'm sitting here wasting away and frankly, I don't give one shit. Except I hate *here*. I don't hate the University of Texas, but here in general. I don't know anyone and I'm not putting myself out there to make any friends. I can't be bothered. I wake up, go to class, go to practice, hit the weight room and return to my room where I practice my guitar instead of doing homework. When eight o'clock rolls around I trudge across campus with my guitar on my back and into the student pub where I'll put on a show. Most of my songs are covers, but I do play one that I wrote, the one for Josie that she didn't understand.

Girls dance while I play. They don't just sit around and talk to their friends. They get up and dance in front of me, sometimes with other guys or just with a group of them. I know they're flirting but I don't care. The only girl I want to look at me like this is in college hundreds of miles away, not giving a shit about whether or not I'm going to fall apart.

My phone rings and I roll my eyes thinking it's my father. I should give him credit; at least he's checking on me, but I have nothing to tell him. He sees the television. He knows I'm not playing. He'll want to try to fix things and honestly, I don't know if I want him to. I can get a free education while I'm here. I'm going to need it since the NFL is definitely not in my future now.

I look at the screen and don't recognize the number. It's probably a prank or it could be my dad calling from some far off location. This is like buying a scratch-off lottery ticket. You have a fifty/fifty chance that you're going to win at least something. More often than not, you lose and you go on with your day. I can answer and win a million dollars or it could be my father. Either way, it's worth the risk.

"Hello?"

"Liam?" I pull my phone away from ear and look again to see if I recognize the number. I don't, but the woman on the other end sure says my name in a familiar tone.

"Yeah, who's this?"

"This is Betty Addison," she sighs, taking a deep breath. "There's no easy way to say this so I'm just going to be blunt. I'm your grandmother."

I pull my phone away again and look at the screen. I don't think I heard her properly, but I swear she said grandmother. I only know my father's side of the family and his mother died when I was young. When my Gram passed, I cried for days, she was like a mom to me. My mother never talks about her parents.

"Um… okay."

"I'm in town this week and I thought we could have lunch. There's a nice little café by your campus."

"You're here?"

"Yes, you go to the University of Texas, right?"

"Yes, but how did you find me?"

"I have my ways Liam. I'd really like to meet you, buy you lunch and just talk."

What do I have to lose and it's free food away from the cafeteria. "Sure," I say and before I know it I'm agreeing to meet her tomorrow at noon. It dawns on me that she's been absent all my life and that irritates me some. Does she know what kind of man Sterling Westbury is?

'M nervous as I wait for her... do I call her grandma? My leg bounces, causing the table to jiggle back and forth. When the chair in front of me pulls out and she sits down, I see an older version of my mother. Or what I envision my mom will look like if she doesn't die from alcohol poisoning first.

"It's so nice to finally meet you," she tells me while studying my face. I don't return the sentiment because I haven't known she's existed for more than twelve hours.

Conversation is awkward at first as we get to know each other, but half an hour in it's like I've known her my entire life. We sit and talk for hours. My grandma tells me she's an actress, but hasn't acted in years. When I ask about my mom and why they don't talk, she shows me a picture of Bianca. She's dressed as a starlet, holding a trophy. Betty says it's her Rising Star Award. She won it at sixteen.

"She never told me," I admit quietly, complete enamored with the beauty that was my mother. An actress – that's what she wanted to be.

"When she met your father she gave up her dreams for his. I fought hard to make her see what she was doing, but your father was determined to have a trophy wife on his arm and your mother would do anything to please him."

"That's how she is, or was," I add. "My mom, she drinks a lot and doesn't really have any emotions. My parents..." I shake my head, but something inside of me tells me I can trust her. "They're not good parents."

"Why are you here at the University of Texas?"

I smile and lean forward to tell my grandma my story. It flows freely, starting in the eighth grade and until I graduated. I tell her all about Josie, Mason and Katelyn and even playing my guitar at open mic nights. She in turns tells me about my mom and I sit and listen to her stories, each more fascinating than the one before.

Betty reaches across the table and takes my hand in hers. Her smile in infectious and I can see why she's an actress. I make a mental note to find some of her movies so I can watch her perform.

"You remind me of your grandfather."

My ears perk up. Half of me wants to ask her everything that I've missed, but the other half doesn't want to know because I've missed so much and I don't know if I can bear the heartbreak of knowing that someone out there actually cares about me.

"He was a jazz musician, played the trumpet. We were married for five years." She waves her hands as if wiping away a memory. "He liked his booze and women a little too much, but was a good dad to Bianca."

"I hate that she has never talked about her family. I feel like I'm in the Twilight Zone here."

"I know how you feel, but I'm here now, for whatever you need Liam, whether it's football or singing. I want you to be able to count on me."

I move my coffee cup back and forth. "I don't like football anymore and..." I shake my head and lean toward her. "No one back home understands this music thing, but I feel —"

"At peace when you're playing?"

I nod. "How do you know?"

"Your grandfather was the same way. He'd play for hours in the garage just blowing that old horn and when I asked him once why, he said because it's the only time when the voices aren't telling him what to do."

I smile and agree. "That's exactly how I feel. I lay in bed at night and the anxiety is so much I feel like it's trying to drown me. What was his name, my grandfather?"

Betty lights up. "Charlie Page."

"Page is my middle name," I say and she nods. "At least my mom gave me that."

"If you don't like football, why do you do it?"

I shrug. "It's hard to stop something you've been doing for so long, but my heart isn't in it."

"What's your heart telling you, Mr. Liam Page?"

I like the way she says my name. I say it a few times in my head. "It's telling me to try music."

"I think you should listen."

Before we know it, it's dark and the café is closing. Betty follows me back to campus and sits front row while I perform. She beams with pride and claps wildly when I finish my five-song set. I walk her to the door, happier than I've been in a long time and thankful that I finally have someone who understands the pressure that my father has put me under. I hate that he did the same thing to my mom.

"Thank you for everything, Betty," I say, as I'm holding her hands in mine.

"Would it be too much to hear you call me grandma just one time. I'm an old lady and I've dreamt of this moment for so many years."

I lean forward and peck her cheek. "Thank you for a fabulous day, Grandma."

She beams, lighting the room with her infectious smile. "If you ever find yourself in Los Angeles, you give me a call. I have a house on the hill that overlooks Hollywood and a room with your name on the door just waiting for you."

"I will, Grandma."

She pulls me close and whispers. "Follow only your dreams, Liam."

LIE in bed, unable to sleep. I'm antsy and on edge. I slip on my shoes and leave my dorm, walking across campus to my coach's house. I know it's late, but I don't care. I need answers and I want them today.

I knock three times before he answers. He's still in his burnt orange polo and khaki pants. Always dressed like it's game day.

"Westbury, it's late. Whatever you have to say it can wait until tomorrow." His arm rests on the doorjamb as he hunches over. He's not a man of authority, at least not right now, but the smirk on his face tells me that he's not pleased to see me. I stand tall and square my shoulders. This moment is going to be the catalyst for what comes next in my life. I have to do it with conviction or he won't take me seriously.

"Actually it can't. I've been doing a lot of thinking and I'm stumped. You haven't won a game all year. You've only scored three touchdowns in five games and yet I'm still on the bench. Why is that?"

He folds his arms across his chest. "Do you think you're better then Rogers?"

"I know I am, but you won't play me." My words are matter-of-fact. I know I'm the best on the field, yet game after game I sit there watching us lose. I watch the game recap. I read the articles. Everyone's asking why I'm on the bench and now I want to know. His answer may change my mind. Deep down, I'm hoping that it does. I want him to tell me that he's going to start me on Saturday. If he does, I'll stay. If he does, I go back to my dorm, call my girl and wish her a goodnight. If he does, the dream is still intact and no one has to know how close I am to breaking.

"And you're asking me why?"

"Yes sir, I am."

"It's simple. You don't want to be here, you said so yourself. I heard you that day, in the hall. At first I thought, wow, what did I do to deserve one of the top five? Turns out, nothing. When your buddy backed out, I thought for sure you would too, but here you are looking for playing time on a team that you don't want to be on."

I shake my head. "All you had to do was tell me you weren't interested instead of wasting my time."

"*I* wasted *your* time?" he says incredulously as if my time means nothing to me.

I nod. "You did, but I'm clear now. See ya around."

I turn and walk away with him calling my name. I run back to my dorm and pack my shit. I'm done with the Longhorns and Texas. I know what I want to do and I don't know if I'm going to succeed, but I'm going to die trying.

CHAPTER 25

AS soon as I leave campus the anxiety sets in. I was a macho piece of shit back there thinking my shit don't stink when I was talking to the coach, but now that I'm on the road, driving with no destination in mind, I don't know what the fuck I'm doing. I just left college without any hesitation or reason. I can stay and be a third string quarterback and get a free education. As long as I show up to each and every practice and do what's asked, they can't kick me off the team. So why leave?

I don't know.

I don't know anything right now. I don't know where I'm going. I don't know what I'm going to do. My parents are going to flip even though it's clear they don't give a shit about me, despite Sterling's attempt at making peace before I left. Going home isn't an option though. I don't care if I have to live out of my truck. I'll never live with my parents again.

I could enroll with Josie, but I don't want to play football and I know that would be expected of me and that's my fault or my parents with their stellar communication skills. I also don't want people asking me why I'm not playing. What do I say, I hate it? That all the pressure you had me under last year and the years prior finally took their toll? That I made the biggest mistake of my life when I chose the same school that Mason chose because I wanted to continue playing with my friend, but he bailed? I had the world at my feet and now I have nothing to show for it. Surprisingly, I'm okay with that.

Going to Los Angeles is an option. Betty gave me an open invitation. I'd like to introduce her to Josie. Maybe that will help her understand my parents better. I know talking with Betty gave me a different perspective. I'll never end up like my father and I'll never ask Josie to give up her dreams for me. I'm the one who doesn't know what the hell they want out of life, except for Josie. She's the only part of my life that I know is definite. I can see us lying in the sand with the waves crashing around us. I can find a job that'll keep me going until I know what I want to do, and she can go to college. We'll be together living the life that we want. My parents won't be there to interfere and remind me how much they don't like her. It will just be us, living in a fast paced city and enjoying life. The thought of her and I together in Los Angeles brings a smile to my face.

I'm going to whisk her away just like those many rom-com movies she's made me watch over the years. Chicks dig that, apparently. I'm going to make a grand show of it. I'll show up at her dorm with roses in my hands and tell her that we're destined for each other. Convincing her might be hard, but she'll come. We're in love and want to be together.

I speed down the highway toward Josie's school. While I hope she'll be excited with my decision, I know she's also going to be disappointed in me. There's no sugar coating why I'm showing up at her school like this, but she'll be happy. I know it. I'll make everything okay. We'll be okay. I'll find a way to make sure she can continue with school so she can get her education. For years she's been my cheerleader, it's time that I'm hers. I can do this for her. I know I can play, except…

The smile I was sporting is now gone with the sad realization that Josie doesn't support my music. It's not like I can blame her. I didn't give her time to really accept it. I played for her once, without warning, and never brought it up again. I blindsided her with something she had no clue about. She doesn't know how music makes sense in my jumbled up mind. Playing my guitar allows me to escape my life and I need that escape. I need to be able to shut my mind off and just play. I want to play for people. I'm not naïve in thinking I'm the next great singer, but if just one person likes what they hear from me, I'm complete. What if Josie doesn't understand that?

The hours pass and before I know it I'm pulling into the parking lot where her dorm is located. I shut off my truck and watch the other students as they walk by. I spot Josie, laughing as she walks into her dorm. It hits me straight on that she's happy here. She's happy and I'm not. Josie's living her dream, or at least she thinks she is. The thing is I can't continue to live like this. I can't. I can't pretend anymore, to her, to my friends, and to myself. I feel like my head is under a pillow and I'm unable to breathe. I'm suffocating and I don't know how to stop it.

I can't do this. Not to her. Not to me. I'm the biggest fucking joke of a boyfriend on the planet. We had this dream and when I was sixteen it sounded fucking fabulous but right now I want to throw a rock through the window and shatter that dream into a million tiny pieces. I don't want to play football anymore. It's not for me. Seeing her in this moment, laughing and joking with her new friends, I know that I can't do this to her. Taking her to LA with me, asking her to give up her dreams just so I can pursue something other than the plan we had, would make me just as bad as Sterling. I'd be pushing her to do something she doesn't want to do. Even if she doesn't know what's out there in California, it's not cheerleading and it's not football. It's not her idea of *us*.

She's going to hate me.

I get out of my truck slowly. My feet feel like concrete blocks are tying them down. Each step is heavier than the last. The common room of her dorm is bustling with students. Some are watching TV and others are playing pool. None of them look at me as I start to climb the stairs to her room. How I know where to find her is beyond me. I know nothing about this school, yet everything seems so familiar. Maybe it's because she's been so descriptive when we talk or maybe it's because I'll always know when she's near.

Her door is decorated with a white board and multiple paper flowers full of color. I raise my hand and knock twice. My heart starts racing, worse than when I first asked her to homecoming. Thinking back to that seems like so many years ago. Josie and I haven't had enough time together, not in this life. We're supposed to create greatness together and I don't think that's going to happen.

Standing before me is my girl. Her hair is down and she's wearing one of my t-shirts. When I look in her eyes I see happiness and confusion. She doesn't know why I'm here and now that I'm in front of her, neither do I.

"Liam, what are you doing here?" she asks the most obvious question. Yes, what am I doing here?

"I needed to see you," I tell her, unsure of my own words. Do I really need to see her, yes, but the calm I feel with her isn't there. And I can't figure out why.

"I'm glad you're here, you must be tired." Her hand finds mine, she tries to pull me into her dorm room but I'm not budging. My concrete feet won't move.

"You don't want to come in?" Her voice breaks. She knows something's wrong.

I do, but I can't. If I go in I'll never leave and nothing will change. My life will be the same pattern over and over again and if I don't change it I'm going to go nuts.

I shake my head just slightly but it's enough to peak her attention. "Something wrong Liam?"

My throat starts to close, my heart… it feels like it's about to burst out of my chest. I know I'm doing the right thing, but why does it feel so horrible. What if I'm wrong? What if she doesn't care about football and the life we thought we wanted years ago?

"I dropped out of school"

The first look of what is about to be a hissy fit spreads across her face. I have this face memorized from when we had our fight about Candy and me smoking. What she doesn't know is that I've been smoking more and more. It gives me something to occupy my time with instead of thinking about how much I hate my fucking life right now. She comprehends the words I just said to her. She's thinking about the plan. The plan I just deviated from. The all-American plan where I become an NFL football player and we live in a quiet neighborhood raising our two children, a boy and a girl, and she travels to my games and never misses one because she's my personal cheerleader.

"Okay, why?"

"I… um… I can't —"

"Can't what? You're scaring me, baby. Come in and we'll talk about it. We'll call your coach and fix this."

I feel a sense of relief wash over when she says we'll call my coach. That is exactly what I don't want and I know I've made the right decision. I don't want to play football anymore and she's tied to football.

"I can't be with you anymore, Josephine." I don't look at her when I say these words. I turn and walk away, ignoring her voice as she calls my name. I run down the hall, my feet suddenly free, zigzagging through the people that just witnessed my girl and I break up.

I stand by my truck waiting for her to come out. I keep telling myself that if she comes out, I'll throw her in the truck and take her with me. The sound of hurt and anguish comes from her building. I turn and stare up at her window, it's open and her curtains are blowing in the wind. She's crying. I can hear her crying and it's killing me. I try to go to her, but I can't. I'm frozen to the ground. If I could just move, I can go back in there and pull her to me and make everything okay. Or I can get in my truck, drive away and never look back. I love my girl. I love her so much. Hearing her cry is killing me, breaking me. When my eyes become unfocused and watery I realize I need her. I can't do this. I can't go to Los Angeles without her. I take a step toward her when I see Mason running toward her dorm. She called for Mason, not me. She didn't follow me out of her room when she could've. She could've come after me, chased me down the hall, but she chose not to. She could be standing in front of me, pounding on my chest and telling me how much she hates me, but she's not.

She chose not to follow me.

CHAPTER 26

BETTY meets me at a diner once I hit the city limits. I stumble into her arms the moment I step out of my truck. I know my eyes are bloodshot and for the first time in my life, I feel like a girl. I broke my own heart two-days ago and there's nothing I can do to fix it. I know Josie would take me back if I asked her to, but why should she? I wouldn't. I deserve to be alone and without love for the rest of my life. I've done the unthinkable.

I follow my grandma into the diner and we take a booth by the large window. I've never seen so much traffic and so many lights before. It's late, but the city isn't asleep.

"I'm so glad you're here, Liam, but you look so lost."

I bite my lip and tell myself I'm not going to shed another tear. For the past 48 hours I've thought about stopping and turning around, but couldn't do it. I did nothing but picture Josie curled up next to me, sharing Doritos and Coke for breakfast, while we navigated our way to California. I could see her, sitting by the passenger side with her hair blowing in the wind, looking at the map to keep me on the right path. Each vision would reduce me to a blubbering mess. It's not only women who end up with broken hearts. Mine is split with half of it dead and it's all my doing.

"I'm trying not to be lost, but …"

Betty reaches across the table and takes my hands in hers. "I can listen."

I shake my head and take a deep breath. "I left my girl. I wanted to bring her with me, but I don't think she'll understand why I need to be here."

"And why do you need to be here?"

I sit up straighter and reach for my glass of water. I take some ice in my mouth and chew before looking at my grandma. "Being on that stage at school gave me a purpose. People were there to listen to me because they wanted to be. They weren't there to watch me throw a touchdown so the team had a victory. They were there for me. I can't help but think I'm meant to do something else in life."

"And you want to try the music scene?"

I nod even though I don't have a clue what I'm doing. I have a guitar and two maybe three songs, which I've written, that probably make no sense to anyone but myself.

"I know it's going to be hard. I thought I could find a job during the day and play at some open mic nights. I don't think I'm anything special, but I want to play music. I don't have any expectations."

"That's good because the industry is cut-throat, Liam. They're vultures here looking for their next prey and I'd hate to see that be you. The first thing I'm going to tell you is trust no one who says they can help because they want something in return."

"Okay," I say.

"The next piece of advice is never change who you are on the inside. Be true to your craft. I've heard you play and can say your grandfather would be so proud of you. You're a natural. It won't take long for you to start turning heads and for people to start offering you the moon, but be smart about it. Don't sell yourself short. And finally, I have faith in you. You don't need a job. I'll take care of you."

"You don't have to do that."

"I have eighteen years of making up to do, of course I do. Now come on, let's go home. I'll let you go through your grandfather's stuff and see if there's anything in there that might help you. He started at an open mic night too."

That thought makes me smile.

STAND at the edge of my grandma's property and take in the view. She wasn't lying when she said her house overlooks Hollywood. The scenery is breathtaking and so lively. The lights alone make this place inviting. Her yard is manicured with lush green grass and flowers lining her brick walkway. Her house is white, with floor to ceiling windows looking out to Hollywood and nothing like the houses in Beaumont. Betty calls the style vintage Hollywood and laughed at me when I said everything looked so different here. The lights in her house cast a soft glow over me as I stand on the edge of her cliff. I'm trying not to think about the destruction I've caused, but it's heavy on my mind.

What's Josie doing now? Is she over me? How long until she'll move on? I can't help but think that Mason will have someone for her, seeing as she didn't hesitate to call him to comfort her after I broke her heart. Maybe he'll fix her up with someone who will help her live her all-American dream. As much as I want that person to be me, it can't be. Not right now.

I've been here for two hours and haven't moved. If I focus I can hear life moving around below me. It makes me wonder if other people are making life changing decisions and breaking hearts?

Every so often, a car's headlights shine off the cliff that my grandma's house is on. She says there are actors, actresses, musicians and every other Hollywood type in her neighborhood. She offered to introduce me, but I declined. I want to pave my own way and try to make a name for myself. After everything I've done, I need to earn my keep and deal with whatever comes next.

I don't even know what that is though. I can't imagine myself walking into a record company and saying, "hey I want to be a musician". I know it doesn't work like that. I wish it would. For the first time in years I don't have a plan. I'm still lost and confused. My emotions have gotten the best of me and I'm still not certain I've made the right decision.

I feel for the cell phone in my pocket. The display lights up with missed calls from Mason, and voicemails. I press the button and type in my code to hear my messages, except I don't want to hear what Mason has to say. I press the corresponding number to delete each message the moment his voice comes on. I know he wants answers, but I don't have any right now. I need to make a clean transition and talking to him and Josie will not help me do that. I look down at my phone and wonder how long it will be until this is turned off or he reports my truck as stolen. Those actions would be typical Sterling so I know it's just a matter of time. I pull out my phone and see no missed calls. I'm not gonna lie, it hurts to know she hasn't tried to call me. Maybe she needs time or is waiting for me to call. I want to. I want to hear her voice and tell her how sorry I am for leaving her and ask her to come here with me while I pass through this adventure, but I can't. I can't offer her the life that she wants or needs. Someone will be able to one day and when that day comes, it will kill me, destroy me.

"You look deep in thought." My grandmother's voice breaks my reverie. I wipe at my eyes, hoping that she doesn't see them longing for my girl.

"Just watching," I say without turning to face her. She steps next to me and sighs.

"Your mom was born here in this house. She grew up playing in this yard and swimming in the pool out back. I thought she wanted this life, but she surprised me when she just upped and left without any word. I tried to get her back but Sterling had given her other ideas. It broke my heart."

"That's what I did."

"What's that, Liam?"

I shake my head, pulling my lower lip into my mouth and biting. Right now thinking about Josie hurts too much. "I upped and left because I'm a coward."

Her hand touches my arm in a soothing, motherly way. It's something I've craved for so long.

"What's her name?"

"Josie Preston."

"How long have you been with her?"

I toe the grass in front of me and sigh, shaking off a shudder that is trying to work its way through my body. "I've known her for a long time, but we've been together since I was fifteen. We had this plan where I was going to go into the NFL and we were going to get married, but last year I started second-guessing everything and I tried to tell her, but either I wasn't saying the right things or she wasn't willing to accept that I was changing. Thing is, she had no idea about football being a career until I entered her life and I sold her on the idea and when I no longer wanted it, she did. I couldn't find a way to tell her what I want out of life without crushing her dreams. I love her more than anything and I just left her. I just walked out of her life and drove here. I did it because I didn't want her to get to the point where she resented me for this."

"That's how your grandfather left. I came home after being gone for a week and no sooner do I walk in, he's walking out. Said he was done. I said good riddance even though I loved him. I let him walk out because I thought he'd be back. I waited and waited and he never came home. About a month later I received divorce papers and cried my eyes out. I thought, "what the hell did I do?" but it wasn't me. It was him and his eye for anything blond."

"What about my mom?"

Betty waves her hand like getting divorce papers was no big deal. "Bianca and Charlie had the best relationship. He loved her so much. He never remarried after me and when he got sick, he moved back here and I took care of him. It's why I have all of his belongings. Well they're your mother's, really, but she doesn't talk to me so I guess you can have them."

I grow silent, just listening to the life that is happening below us. In Beaumont the moon can light your way, but here, it's the lights. The glitz and glam that is taking place just down winding road.

"Thank you," I blurt out, breaking the silence.

"For what?"

"For telling me to follow only my dreams. I had been following my dad's and a combination of Josie's and mine and was so afraid to veer off that path because I was going to lose her. I knew I had to leave or I was going to lose myself."

Betty steps closer and puts her arm around me. I lean into her, relishing in the attention. I hate that my parents took her away from me. I imagine someday, I'll ask my mother why, but I don't see myself doing that anytime soon.

"I want to try this music thing for a year. Give myself twelve months to see what I can do and if I fail, I'll go back to college."

Betty nods. "That sounds like a good plan. Now come on, let's go eat and you can unpack."

We walk back into her house, hand in hand. With how welcoming she's been and how loving, I don't think I'll ever want to leave her.

CHAPTER 27

I TIE the black tie my grandmother bought for me and let it hang against the freshly ironed white shirt. I have to wear a jacket tonight, but at this point in my life I'll do anything my grandma asks me to do.

Tonight, she's having a gathering as she calls it. What I found out from her housekeeper is that her gatherings include somewhere between fifty to one hundred people coming here to have cocktails and discuss Hollywood gossip. I've also learned, in the last two months, that my grandma can gossip with the best of them.

I've yet to perform since I've been here and even though that should bother me, it doesn't. It's giving me time to fine-tune my stage performance. I play in front of my grandma and the house staff all the time. They all say I'm good and can't wait to see me perform on stage. My grandma has offered to make some calls, but I told her that I need to do this on my own, no handouts. I know she wants to help, but I need to struggle. I need to feel like I'm accomplishing something for everything I've left behind.

I don't know what to expect from tonight. I do know a lot of industry people will be here and we'll be mingling. In all my years, I've never mingled. I'm not even sure I know how to mingle or be social. I am promised that no one will ask about where I came from or what I'm doing. Betty simply told them that her grandson has come to live with her.

Living here has been interesting. Navigating the streets is a nightmare and I know why my grandma has a driver, but I refuse to let Stan drive me anywhere. I have to learn my way around. I can't show up at a gig with a driver. That screams rich spoiled kid and that is something I'm not.

I slip my arms into my jacket and stand in front of the mirror. Everything about me is different. My hair is longer. The bags are gone from under my eyes. I feel like I stand taller even though I know it's not possible. I've taken full advantage of the swimming pool that's on the grounds and agreed when my grandma ordered a weight set for me to use. As much as I'm over football, I'm not over my physique and do want to keep that.

Days after I arrived, my grandma and I sat in her theater room and watched her old movies. We ate popcorn, laughed and she even cried a little. It's amazing to see her on screen and then sitting across from me at dinner in the same day. Each day that I'm getting with her is a blessing. She's truly an amazing woman and the fact that she's been kept from me for so long makes me more resentful toward my parents. They have no idea what they're missing.

When she pulled out my grandfather's old records and played them I did something I never thought I'd do – I asked her to dance. Seeing her face light up made me truly smile for the first time in months. Being here with her is worth the heartache I feel. I have no doubt in my mind this is where I belong.

I walk down the hallway and into the formal dining room where the party is already in full force. There are new staff members walking around with serving trays, all dressed in black pants and white shirts. One walks by, offering me a glass of champagne. I take the glass and quickly bring it to my lips, downing the contents. My grandma and I haven't talked about the vices I have, but I've seen her frowning when she catches me smoking. The habit should be easy to stop, but it occupies me and keeps me from thinking. It keeps me from wondering why I've been gone for two months and *she* hasn't called me yet. I thought she would've. I had hoped she'd call and demand I come back to her so we can fix us, but she hasn't.

The one request for tonight is that I mingle and introduce myself. It's an easy enough challenge. I was once the most charismatic guy in Beaumont, how hard can industry people be?

"Liam?"

I turn at the sound of my grandmother calling my name. She beams at me when I step toward her with an out stretched hand.

"I want to you meet a friend of mine," she says. "Liam this is Tess and her son Harrison James. Tess is the personal assistant to my casting agent." We spent a day going over all the jobs in the industry. There are so many that I got lost and like a true grandma, she made a list for me so I wouldn't forget. "Harrison plays the drums at a club called Metro. They have open mic nights if you're interested in talking to him about it," she whispers. I nod, acknowledging what she's telling me.

I step forward and shake both their hands. "It's nice to meet you both," I say.

"You too, Liam, your grandmother has told me so much about you. She's very happy you've decided to stay with her." I look at my grandma who is smiling from ear to ear.

She pats my arm. "Why don't you take Harrison out back and show him around?"

"Okay, grandma." I kiss her on the cheek and signal toward the patio door. Harrison follows, stepping out into the early evening sun. I walk until I'm at the back, where there is a table set up.

"Sorry about my grandmother in there. I think she's trying to make up for all the years we've missed." I sit down and lean my chair up against the tree.

"It's okay. I was pretty much forced to come here tonight." I inspect Harrison. He's a bit taller than I am and far skinnier. He has a few tattoos on his arms, making wonder if they're a necessity in the music industry. I quickly look down at my arms, curious as to what they'd look like with inked etched on them. One thing is for certain, my parents would flip and that thought alone makes me want one.

"Because of me?" I ask already knowing the answer but needing the confirmation.

He nods. "Yeah," he says without making eye contact. "My mom is close to your grandmother so they plotted and here I am."

"I'm sorry. If you want to leave, I can make up some excuse." I know what it feels like to be put in awkward situations. My dad has done it to me many times, which only spurred me to withdraw from him more and more.

Harrison shakes his head slightly. "I'm cool." He looks down at the ground or his feet. It's not like I want to stare, but I'm trying to figure him out. He runs his hand over his beanie, moving it back and forth before leaving it where it originally was.

"Do you mind if I smoke?" I ask.

He looks up quickly and offers the slightest of smiles. "Hell no, my mom said I couldn't, but if you are, I'm going to." We both light up and I don't know if this is some freaky guy bonding thing, but it definitely takes the edge off any awkwardness we have going on.

"Can I ask you about your gig?"

"I play the drums for the house band at the bar Metro."

"So you have, like, open mic nights?"

He nods as he takes a drag of his cigarette, exhaling into the night air. "Thursday through Saturday we do. We have some regulars and shit too. You sign up at four and wait your turn. The owner puts you on according to popularity. Usually by ten or eleven there are a few agents lurking around. We've had a couple of acts pick up agents and even sign deals from there."

"You're not working tonight?"

He looks at his watch and back to me before putting his cigarette out. "I'm doing the last few sets. My mom doesn't stay out late so I just asked for a few hours off."

"How do you know what to play? I mean, everyone comes with different music, right?"

"They do, but most of the time they're songs that we've all heard. Every now and again someone will come in with an original piece and once they start, I can usually figure out the beat."

"Just like that even without hearing it first?"

"Yeah, I have this weird music hearing thing. I don't know. I can't explain it," His brows furrow as he's telling me this. I wouldn't call it weird, I'd call it a talent. I had a similar knack with picking apart the defenses that I was facing. "My mom said something about you playing the guitar and wanting to sing?"

"I taught myself last summer and I've been playing a few songs. I'm on the list for the Roxy, but that list is freaking long."

"And they're hard to get into and you usually need a full band to play there. But that's how I learned to play the drums so it's cool that you taught yourself. You should come with me down to the club and check it out."

I think I like this guy and I want to scream hell yes, but I try to keep my cool. "Want to go now? I have a truck we can take."

"Sure why not? If we're supposed to hang so you're not alone, might as well hang where we can jam. Grab your guitar and we'll go."

Harrison doesn't have to tell me twice. I all but run back to the house and to my room to change out of my clothes and into black jeans and a t-shirt. I snag my guitar and find my grandma to tell her what we're doing. Her expression is a mixture of "I wish you wouldn't leave" and "go have fun". When I get outside, Harrison is standing by my truck, waiting.

"Stan said this one is yours."

"Sure is," I say as I hop in. I can still smell *her* perfume lingering in the upholstery. Half of me wishes it would dissipate, but the other half, the half that will love her forever, wants it to never leave. All of me wishes she was here, in the middle where she belongs, and going with me to jam because she makes everything better.

CHAPTER 28

FORGET when we're walking in the door that I'm a minor. If this were Beaumont, I'd be okay, but probably not here. I follow Harrison down a long dark hallway. The music being played is muffled and I can barely make out the beat, let alone the words. Harrison turns into a room that has a few people sitting around. One guy is sitting in the corner, strumming his guitar. Another sits on the couch, with a girl sitting on his lap. Neither of them makes eye contact with me.

"Thought you were going to be late, James?"

I turn at the sound of the female voice and step back. Standing there is a girl, no a woman, with raven black hair that looks blue under the florescent lights. Her lips are painted red and her eyes have barely any make-up on them. She's wearing leather pants with some incredibly spikey boots and a simple tank top. Thing is I don't think there's anything simple about this woman.

"Liam sprung me from party purgatory. I'm here and at your service, Trixie."

Trixie?

I avert my gaze once Harrison says her name. I look around the room taking in the walls that have band posters adorning them. The furniture is a bit rough, but looks comfortable and the guy in the corner seems oblivious to me just standing in the middle of the room completely out of place. This is where I want to be though. I *want* to be waiting for my name to be called up on stage. I *want* to feel the anxiety and pressure I've read so much about from other artists. I *want* to deal with stage fright and people hating my music. I just want to get up on stage so I can sing and play my guitar for people. I'm not looking for overnight success – I just want the satisfaction of playing for people. I want the sound of hands clapping because they want to, not because they're obligated too.

"Liam, huh? You're a virgin."

My mouth starts to drop open. I shut it quickly and clear my throat. "Excuse me?"

Trixie moves forward, almost pressing herself against me. She eyes me before continuing, "I'm not talking about your dick, but you've never been in a green room before. That makes you a virgin in my book."

I swallow hard, afraid of breaking eye contact with her. Trixie steps away, laughing. "What's your story, Liam the virgin?"

"Um... I'm just looking to play."

"Trixie is the owner, Liam. She's just giving you shit. But yes she can smell fresh meat a mile away. He wants to jam and I had a few hours to kill so I thought I'd bring him back here and hang out."

"Are you twenty-one?"

I nod and pray that she doesn't ask me for my driver's license. Her head moves up and down slowly before she purses her lips and gives me another once over and leaving the room.

"You can breathe now, dude," Harrison laughs as he pats me on the shoulder. "She's a firecracker, but she's trustworthy and faithful to her staff. I've worked for her since I was nineteen. She can be a little hard to take sometimes because this is her baby and all that shit."

"Got it."

"Right, so let me show you around. The band will be taking a break in a few so we can sit back here and jam a little before I have to go on stage. Do you want to watch the main act tonight? It's an all-girl band and they're pretty good."

"All-girl band?" I question. I sort of like the idea of watching girls play so I can get a feel for how they perform.

"Well aside from me and Burke who plays the piano for them tonight."

"Yeah man that sounds cool."As I follow Harrison around the club I can't help thinking about Mason and what he's doing. I'd give anything to be giving him a tour or standing out in this club with him by my side as Harrison fills me in. Harrison is very unassuming and keeps himself to himself. The drive here he just gave directions, nothing else. No conversation about the weather and he didn't ask about my life before Los Angeles and for that I'm very thankful. I don't know what, if anything, I'm going to tell people. The last thing I want is people to think I'm still that kid in Beaumont who's come to the big city to try to make it big. I don't want to be a statistic. If I don't make it, I'll go home and eat crow. Beg for forgiveness and find some way to pay my way through school.

Either way I need to do this as the new me, not the old one. Not the one that was so stressed out and anxiety riddled that I couldn't see straight. I need to try out the music scene, fail and try again in hope that I'll be something. If I can do that, I'll be something to me and that's enough.

"Hey you should put your name down for tomorrow." Harrison points to the sign-up sheet for open mic tomorrow night.

I grab the pen that's on the table and write *Liam* before pausing. If I'm doing this, I'm doing it with the new me. I close my eyes and picture myself up on that stage with a drummer and a keyboardist playing right along with me, enticing the crowd to sway their bodies or hold on to their dates. I see them to sing along or jump up and down to the beat of the music. This is what I want. I scribble *Liam Page*, the name that has echoed in my mind since the moment my grandma said it, and set the pen down. Tomorrow, I'm booked for my first open mic in Los Angeles, that's why I came here and now it's done.

"Trixie goes over the list at closing and calls people at nine a.m. sharp," Harrison tells me as he shrugs. "She's a sadist, but people love her and they keep coming back even after they're signed."

"That's good, right?"

He nods. "It is. Look outside." He points to the window where people are lined up. "She does two sets. The top talent gets the last set which is what you're going to watch, but she kicks everyone out after the first one so we can clean and get tuned up. Those people are lined up, trying to get front row."

I walk close to the window and look out, amazed by what I see. "They're here just to watch a band that hasn't been signed?"

"Yeah," he confirms, standing next to me. "These girls will get signed though, they're that good."

"And do you go with them?"

"What do you mean?"

I run my hand over my face, frustrated that I don't know what I'm talking about. "You play for them, right?" he nods. "So when they get signed with an agent or a record deal, do you continue to play with them or do they move on?"

Harrison fiddles with his lip ring and as much as I don't want to stare I am. You don't see those in Beaumont. Hell, you don't see people like Harrison there at all. That town is so pretentious and in need of a serious culture overall.

"I want to be in a band, but the right one hasn't come along. The people who perform here usually have their own ideas about music and are trying to make it as an artist. I'm an afterthought and just here to add the extra beat or rhythm to their set. The agents in here, they aren't looking at me, they're looking at the singers. Drummers are a dime a dozen around these parts. I'm going to go get ready. Take a seat up front and when we're done, just come back stage."

Harrison walks away before I can acknowledge him or ask him any more questions. I look back at the crowd forming outside, unsure how to respond. I could fail at this and have to go back home with my tail between my legs to face the music so to speak, but it's worth it to try. At least it is to me. I pull my phone out of my pocket and look at the dark, blank screen, which indicates that there are no missed calls or voicemails. *She* still hasn't called, nor have I called her. I don't know why, either. I should call her, but I don't know what to say. Telling her I'm sorry doesn't seem like it's the right thing to say and trying to explain myself will fall on deaf ears. I tried to show her this side of me and maybe I should've tried harder. Maybe I should've shaken her until she opened her eyes, but I couldn't. I shouldn't have to. She's supposed to love me, not the idea of me or what I can do to secure her future by my side.

I put my phone back and shake my head. With each day that goes by, the decision I made becomes easier and easier to deal with. As much as I want things to be different, as I look around this club, she doesn't fit in here. She would be uncomfortable and on edge and I need to focus on me and making this happen.

The doors open and people rush in, vying for seats up front. I'm taken back by the onslaught of people. Whoever this band is, they have a large following and I like it. I like knowing the potential is out there for me. I just have to work hard to achieve my goal and that's something I can easily do.

My goal – the words resonate in my head. I never thought I had a goal until now, but I do. I want this to be my crowd. Not tomorrow night and maybe not next month, but this will be my first milestone and I like that I have something to work toward, a milestone that I can take back to Beaumont and show *her* that I'm good at something other than football. I need to prove to her that

I left for the right reasons, whether she wants to believe me or not.

Harrison and Burke come out on stage, followed by two girls who I assume are in the band. The people move faster, racing for seats. The lead singer stands in front of the microphone with her legs standing shoulder width apart. Her hair is straight and long and a very vibrant red. Nothing about her seems real except for the way she's carrying herself. I sit down and watch as she gives orders to her female counterpart, and to Harrison and Burke as well. Everyone seems happy and poised for performance.

The lights dim and the crowd comes alive. The chanting of their name – it's what I want. My heart races for them. My palms sweat with excitement and I'm not even on stage, but they are and they're living a dream. I scan the patrons briefly; wondering if any are agents or scouts looking for new talent.

A guitar strums and I swivel back toward the stage. Sticks clank together four times before Harrison's arms move quickly and bang onto his drums. The crowd screams as the music starts and the lead singer takes hold of the microphone. The way she clutches it in her hand shows me that she's in charge. She owns the stage with her music and that is something I haven't grasped yet. She's putting on a show and I need to do that as well.

My eyes wander between her, Harrison, Burke and her guitar player. Each one of them commands a presence with their own craft. The lead singer moves across the stage, tempting her fans with the way her hips sway, the way her leg bounces as she belts out the lyrics to her song. They respond in kind by grappling for her, begging for her attention. She is what I need to be. I can't be this lump of body mass sitting on a stool singing about a love that I had and lost due to my own actions. I need to re-invent myself. I need to figure out how to command a crowd and bring them to their knees because that's what she's doing now. They're eating out of her palm and she loves every minute of it.

I'm going to love every minute of it.

CHAPTER 29

S this singer, whose name I need to learn, finishes her last song, the crowd is showering them with thundering applause and I can't help but join in. The band deserves it, each one of them, including Harrison and Burke. This is the first time I've analyzed a performance. Watching MTV does nothing for you when you can sit next to the stage and watch every single movement, hear the reactions from the audience and feel the vibration coming off the instruments. Each action is being cemented into my brain. This is what I needed to take my next step.

The lights dim, but the fans get louder. I can't help joining in with the celebration. I cup my hands over my mouth and scream loudly, begging them for an encore. The deafening cheers are enough to bring them back on stage. I look around and see just how infectious the singer is to her capture audience and that sentiment is returned when they look back at her. It's pure admiration.

They leave the stage after finishing three more songs and the lights come on. This must be Trixie's cue for people to start leaving. *Metro* is so different from *Ralph's*; it's like night and day. *Ralph's* is home drinking where people will spend hours just sitting at the bar telling Ralph, the owner, all of their troubles. *Metro* is art deco and Trixie doesn't care if you want to linger, you're in and out.

It's time to move on.

I walk backstage as Harrison suggested. As soon as I open the door I'm greeted with laughter. So much so, that I can't help smiling as soon as I walk into the room. The lead singer is shaking a bottle of champagne and lets its contents fly, dousing the room with sticky liquid. The excitement in the room is contagious and it leaves me wanting this for myself. I know I could've had it with football. Winning the big game for college or NFL – that's what it's like to be a part of a family, but it's not the family I want. I want this one or something similar. I want to be close to the fans and feel their elation permeate off them and onto me.

"What did you think?" I turn at the sound of a captivating voice beside me. The lead singer is standing next to me offering a beer to me. I take it with a smile and bring the cold, dark glass to my lips. The amber liquid is a welcome taste and one that I've missed sharing with my friends these past few months. I haven't dared drink in front of my grandmother for fear she'd disapprove and for some reason her approval is incredibly important to me.

"What's your name?" I ask, avoiding her question.

Since I've become acquainted with her on stage, it's only right that I know her name.

She smiles and turns away. Her grin is infectious and I find myself smiling against the lip of my bottle. There's something wild about her, you can see it in her eyes. They're honey colored and twinkling in the bright lights above our heads. She winks and that reminds me that I still don't know her name.

"A…" The words lodge causing me clear my throat. I look down at my shoe and shake my head. When I look up, I quickly realize that this girl could be trouble. Her lower lip is pulled into her mouth. Her eyes are bright, glossy. "Are you going to tell me your name?" I ask again, my voice barely above a whisper. I don't know what's come over me, but I need to snap out of it. This isn't me. I've never acted like this with a girl before. Not even *her* and honestly it feels wrong to be this way now. I take a step back to put some space between us, only she steps forward so we're almost body to body.

"My name's Layla," she reveals as she offers her hand and being the gentlemen that I am, I take it in mine and shake. When I let go she slowly traces her nails along my palm sending chills up my spine. "Did you enjoy the show?"

I nod, unable to find any words. I've heard stories about women who go after what they want, but have never seen any in action. I'm eighteen and fairly inexperienced and I have a distinct feeling the enigmatic being standing in front of me will eat me for a snack.

"I learnt a lot." I close my eyes in embarrassment. I bring my hand to my forehead to knock some sense into myself but realize that's probably pretty childish and right now I need to be a confident, self-assured man, so I run my hand through my hair casually. "Your show was jammin."

Layla laughs and shakes her head. "It's a set and no one says jammin', but I'll forgive you if you come out with us tonight."

"Us?"

She turns and waves her arm out over the room. I look around and my eyes find Harrison, who tips his beer at me. I return the sentiment, thankful that he's brought me here.

"All of us. We're going to a dance club down the street."

"Ah I don't really dance." It's a cop out. I can dance, I just don't want to.

Layla steps forward, eliminating the remaining space between us. "No one really dances. We stand there with our bodies pressed together and let the music move us."

My head dips, acknowledging her. "I'll come," I blurt out stupidly.

"Perfect," she says as she backs away. The smile that is plastered on her face never leaves. It hits me like a ton of bricks that she's just played me. For a brief moment I thought she was into me, but as I watch her work the room, it becomes apparent that she's just securing her entourage for the night. I'm nothing more than a pawn in her game and somehow I'm okay with that.

The room is brimming with people but I'm alone, sipping on an almost empty beer. Harrison is in the corner talking to the other member of the band and he looks like he's hitting on her so it's probably best that I stay where I am. I let my eyes wander around the room, acting as if everything is interesting. I have never felt so awkward, but I don't want to leave. I want to experience the nightlife. I want to see what I've been missing out on by living in Beaumont and never taking an adventure anywhere. We don't have nightclubs, we have the country club and the only time most of us hang out there is for Prom.

Layla breaks my musing when she announces we're leaving. I set my empty bottle down and walk toward her. To my surprise she links her arm with mine and sets our pace. The night air is still sweltering, another difference between here and Beaumont. It's not chilly and I have a perverse desire to strip down and go swimming. I'm guessing doing such a thing would probably be frowned upon.

It feels different to have someone else's arm inside of mine. Her other hand is clutching my bicep, a sure sign that she's marking some type of territory. From what, I don't know. Part of me wants to slide away from her, but the rest wants to stay and let her guide me. Just because she's holding onto me now doesn't mean she'll be with me in the club. Maybe this is nothing more than a friendly gesture so I don't get lost in the crowd en route to the club or maybe it's so I don't get lost when we get there. We squeeze through the door and the bass instantly vibrates through my body. A few of the others in our group raise their arms and head off toward the dance floor and we make our way to the bar. My stomach drops as I try to remember whether my fake ID is in my wallet or not. The last thing I want or need is to be thrown out of here because I'm underage. I've already lied once tonight, no need to push my luck any longer.

Much to my relief Layla orders and I'm not asked. She

hands me a beer, taps hers against mine and walks away. I don't know if I'm supposed to follow, but I'm thinking she meant to leave me here since I can barely make out her red hair among the masses.

I lean against a small open space on the bar and pretend to watch everyone. What I'm really doing is waiting for Harrison. I feel like such an outsider. I don't know what I'm doing. I know I should let loose and mingle, but I don't know how. I pull out my phone to occupy my time and see that I have a missed call. I flip it open and there's a voicemail and *her* number. It's too loud in here, but I'm afraid if I leave I won't get back in. Layla walked us right by the bouncer and he didn't even flinch. I'm no one though. I won't be so lucky.

I meander through the crowd and find the bathroom. Unfortunately it's the only way I'm going to be able to hear what she has to say. I lock myself in a stall and take a deep breath to try to calm my racing heart. I don't know what I want her to say. If she asks me to come get her, I will. I don't care if it's been two months and we haven't spoken. I'll leave tonight to go get her.

I dial the code for my voicemail and hold my phone to my ear. The seconds it takes to connect seem like a lifetime. Everything that I did to her comes rushing back. Leaving her in her dorm room, knowing I was making the right decision, but breaking my own heart weighs heavily. I wronged her. There's no sugarcoating what I did. Now that I'm here I know I should've pushed harder, but the times that I played my guitar for her and her felt her stiffen in my arms when she heard me on my stereo are at the forefront of my mind. She'll never understand why I need to do this for myself.

Her voice fills my ears and my eyes start to water. I close them, fighting back the tears.

I hate you. I hate you so much for what you've done to me. Are you listening to me? I hope you're happy and in a ditch somewhere. You've ruined my life.

I click save and replay it, again and again. Letting her words seep into my skin and burn into my mind.

She hates me.

She hates me.

She hates me.

I hate me.

I've ruined her life. She's eighteen and I've ruined her life. But I was ruining mine. Why couldn't she see that? I wasn't happy. I was suffocating and now I'm not. Now I'm breathing and am able to sleep at night. I can finally close my eyes and not see my life playing out in front of me like a bad dream. If I stayed, we wouldn't have made it. We'd be a statistic and that's the last thing I want.

I leave the stall and quickly wash my hands before heading back to the bar. I need to forget about what I left behind in Beaumont and the only way to do that is to numb my mind. She's right to hate me. I will never fault her for that. I want her to, if I'm being honest with myself. I don't want her pining away for me when I'm not coming back.

I'm pushed from behind and before I can turn around and punch someone, arms move around my waist. I turn slightly to see the red hair I was looking for earlier. I could fight her and ignore her attempt to get me on the dance floor, but I don't. I let her drive us into the barrage of sweating bodies.

She moves around me, her fingers dipping under my

shirt, dancing along my skin. I should tell her no, but I can't find the words. Layla dips down and slowly brings her body up against mine. Her hands move up my torso, over my neck and into my hair. My eyes close on their own free will. I hate that my body is reacting to her. It's not supposed to. I should be damned and sent to hell for causing my girl so much pain, but here I am enjoying the exhilaration coursing through my body because of the way Layla's touching me.

My eyes spring open when her fingers still. Her hand moves to her mouth and away. My eyes follow. Growing up in Beaumont I never realized now naïve I was until now. Sitting on her tongue is a white pill and she's offering it to me. My eyes move from her mouth to her hooded eyes and back again. People all around us are moving, gyrating to the music. Layla steps closer, allowing for no space between us. Her hand cups the back of my head while her other hand leaves a blazing trail down the side of my neck. My hearts is screaming no, reminding me of the damage I've caused. Telling me that I don't deserve happiness, but my mind is urging me forward.

I listen to my head this time and move toward Layla. She doesn't wait and touches her lips to mine, pushing her tongue into my mouth. Immediately, I'm filled with guilt and try to pull away, but I can't. My body won't move. I don't know what she's giving me, but I swallow it as her body melds to mine and my hands find her hips and then her sides. Before I know it, my hand is in her hair and I'm holding her to my mouth while we move to the beat of the music from the DJ.

My world is spinning on an axis that I'm not in control of. I'm flush, sweating. I can't get enough of Layla and it doesn't matter what I do, the thirst I'm feeling isn't being quenched. My hand slides under her shirt, my fingertips grazing her breast. She pulls me closer by my belt, rubbing herself against my erection.

Her mouth leaves mine, her teeth biting my ear lobe. "My place is down the street. Want to get out of here?" I don't know if I do, but I take her hand in mine and lead us to the door.

CHAPTER 30

WE hold hands and rush toward her place, having to dodge cars as we jaywalk across the street. Steps are taken two at a time and she fumbles with her key when I attack her neck. I nip at her skin as my hands move up her body, under her shirt and pushing her bra aside. My desire for her is building, pushing the boundaries that I've held together for so long.

The door finally opens and we stumble in. One of us pushes the door shut, but neither of us is really paying attention to whom. I pick her up, her legs wrap tightly around my waist as she grinds against my hard on. I moan, welcoming the pressure. I palm her ass in my hands as I walk blindly down the hall.

"Turn," she mewls and I do, crashing down on top of her as my knees hit her bed. She rolls, straddling me. I can barely make her out in the dark, but my hands feel her skin burn against the pads of my fingers. Her shirt is gone and mine is next. I should be doing something to help her undress, but her porcelain skin mesmerizes me.

I sit up and kiss the valley between her breasts, lowering her bra. She arches when I bring her pebbled nipple into my mouth, tugging gently. Her fingers grab a handful of hair as she pulls me back, pushing me onto her bed. Layla moves my arms to rest above my head. I keep them there as if I'm being tied down. The clank of my belt and the pulling of the buttons on my jeans is the only indication that she's still with me. My mind fogs over and the lights from the cars below create an array of colors and designs. My eyes follow the patterns on her ceiling as she pulls my jeans and boxers down.

I look at her briefly, the street light outside providing enough illumination for me to see that she's poised and hungry. Her eyes don't leave mine as her tongue snakes out and licks the tip of my cock. Steady and focused, she watches me as I watch her take me into her warm mouth. For a moment, my eyes roll back, lost in this euphoric state. I want to reach for her, but my arms are heavy, weighted down and unable to move. My hips buck as she sucks harder.

"She hates me," I blurt out, unable to control or even comprehend what I'm saying. Layla kisses a path up my torso, biting my nipple before kissing me deeply.

"I'll make it all better," she whispers against my lips as she sinks down on my erection. Her nails dig into my chest, inviting pain to surface. I scream out, encouraging her for more, begging her to put me out of my misery and she does. She takes everything that I can give her, pushing me to the brink.

"Fuck," I hiss as she rides me, our skin slapping against

each other. She throws her head back and screams my name.

My name on her lips in ecstasy spurs me on harder. I bring my hips up and push into her deeper, faster. She screams. Is it pain or pleasure? I don't know because I don't know her, not like I know... shit, this is wrong. Everything about her is wrong, but I can't stop. My body doesn't allow it. My dead carcass is the captain of my being and it's telling me what to do. I have no control. I am nothing, if not a pawn in its game to get over the hurt and pain I've caused.

I need this. I need to feel and be felt. I need to let go.

THE sound of horns honking and people yelling reverberate through my ears. I try to cover them, to block out the noise but to no avail. My head feels like there's a jackhammer in there creating a sinkhole only it's not for me to escape but to let more noise in.

I open my eyes slowly only to be blinded by direct sunlight. I turn my face into the mattress and smell perfume. Someone shifts next to me, causing me to stiffen. I peek out over my arm and see a mess of red hair and alabaster skin. I rise up on my arms as confusion sets in. Nothing about this room or the girl next to me seems familiar. I roll over and sit up, using the eggplant purple sheet to cover my waist. I scrub my hands over my face, but quickly stop because of the throbbing. I hold my head in my hands and try to remember the night before. It's all a haze. There was music, a few beers, dancing and Layla, the woman who captivated me on stage and offered to make the pain go away.

Layla stirs next to me, turning over to face me. The

energy and excitement she had last night lays dormant, waiting for her to come to life again. She looks at ease, peaceful, even as she lies next to me. There's no doubt she's beautiful, stunning even. It feels wrong and awkward to stare at her naked form, but I can't help it. I was with her last night and she'll never know the magnitude of what that means.

I never thought in a million years I'd be here like this. I honestly hadn't given much thought to how my life was going to be after I left Beaumont, but I never thought I'd end up in bed with another woman so soon, or even at all. I lie back down with hopes of alleviating the headache. I should get up and leave, commit the walk of shame that so many of my teammates have done in the past, but the effort on my part is lacking. I've never had such a bad hangover before and know it has something to do with that pill she gave me... no that I took from her without reservation.

First the smoking and now some form of recreational drug use. At least it wasn't snorting coke or sticking a needle in my arm. I'm not stupid enough to do that and I really hope I never get to that point in my life.

I roll onto my side and watch Layla sleep. What is it about her that would make me forget my worries; forget the pain I'm causing myself? From the moment I met her after her show, she had me captivated with the way she carried herself. I shouldn't feel like this, not after what I've done. I shouldn't want to reach out and let my fingers trail over her soft skin or push my hands into her hair, but I do and I am.

Her skin pebbles in the wake of my fingers touching her. I try not to laugh, but can't help it. Layla stirs, the sheet falling just below her breast, a breast that I became very acquainted with last night and have an urge to get to know again. I don't know the protocol here and I could be wrong for staying in bed like this, for wanting to touch her again.

"You're tickling me," she mumbles. I stop and rest my hand on my hip, realizing it's time for me to go. I don't know if I should kiss her on the cheek or just leave. What I do know is that I shouldn't be here, not anymore. This isn't right for me. I shouldn't want to touch another woman like this. I don't deserve to.

Before I can move, before I can get away with just the shame in my heart, Layla is staring at me with her honey colored eyes. Her make-up is heavy and still in place from last night, the complete opposite of what I'm used to.

"I'm going to go." I say this mostly for my own benefit and peace of mind. Does she really care if I stay, probably not?

Layla pulls the sheet down exposing me for all to see… or just her since we're behind a closed door. This is my cue and I'm taking it. I start to roll over, only to be stopped by her climbing on top of me and now I'm seeing all of her in the morning light with the sunlight kissing her skin.

"Do you really want to leave?" she asks as she kisses her way up my chest and to my neck, her body rocking against me creating friction. "I thought maybe we'd have breakfast."

She's thinking about food?

"Um… sure, breakfast sounds good." I swallow hard and close my eyes to try and calm down. I try to think about anything other than Layla being naked and sitting on top of me, but the ministrations she's providing is making it impossible. The last thing I want to do is walk out of here with a raging boner and run into her roommate, if she has one. I haven't a clue what to expect on the other side of that door, but I'd prefer to do it without a tent in my pants.

"Good, I really like breakfast in the morning," she whispers in my ear. The sound of foil ripping is enough to make my eyes spring open. I lift my head enough to follow her actions as she rolls a condom on my waiting erection. I hope, no I pray, that we used one last night. I hate that I don't remember and it pains me to think that we didn't because I was in too much of a haze to remember to put on a coat.

Layla slides down my cock, her head falls back and her mouth drops open. She uses my stomach as a tool to push herself up and down. Even though I've been here many times before, I'm at a loss as to where I should put my hands. All I know is I want them all over her. I need them to be on her to help me forget the pain that I'm living with. I want her to help me block it out. To shut out the voices that are constantly screaming inside of my head, telling me that I'm the worst of the worst.

She doesn't wait for me to stop fighting with myself. She reaches for my hands, placing them on her breasts as she rides me. I want to be in control. I don't remember much from last night, but apparently she does and it's about time that I do. I move my hands to her waist and flip her over. Everything about her is foreign, but what we're doing seems natural even if I feel like this is wrong, like I'm cheating.

I sit back on my knees and pull her hips to me, sliding

her up and down over my shaft. I can't read her, not like… I shake my head to clear the thought. I don't want to think about *her*, not right now, not like this. I lean forward and silence her moans with my mouth, morning breath be damned. We've already shared enough and we haven't even been on a date. That thought alone almost breaks me. I can't do a relationship. It's not in me to even try with someone else. I shouldn't even be here and if *she* hadn't called, I wouldn't. I wouldn't have needed someone or something to take the pain away.

Layla's frantic beneath me, her hands grab at any part of my body that she can get too. My head rears back when her nails sink into my back. Everything about this moment is intense and different from anything I've ever experienced before. I thrust into her harder as I feel her tightening around my cock. She bites my lower lip, I cry out, not only from the pain, but from my release as I fill the condom.

I collapse on top of her and carefully pull out making sure the condom stays in place. The last thing I need is an accident. I don't know her that well, but she's on her way to stardom and she doesn't need me complicating her life.

"Was that breakfast?" I ask, out of breath.

She laughs, her chest pushing against mine. I roll over and cover my eyes with my forearm. I'm exhausted and know for a fact that I didn't last that long. If I wasn't so tired and hung over, I'd care, but I don't. I can always show her again after a nice long shower and nap if that's what she wants. I'm thinking that's not what she wants though and I'd be okay with that.

"Yeah, was it good for you?" she snorts when she

finishes her question and I'm laughing right along the side of her. You always fear that stupid cheesy line, but when it actually happens you realize you can't help but laugh. "Oh God I just snorted."

"It was cute," I add to ease her embarrassment. "But yes it was good. I'm just sorry I didn't last longer."

"You were perfect and last night was amazing."

I wish I could agree with her, but I can't. Bits and pieces are coming back to me, but it's all in a fog. Something tells me though that she's one I won't forget even if I don't remember the specifics.

CHAPTER 31

WHEN I get home, I find my grandma sitting in her sunroom. The view is breathtaking, making it easy to understand why she prefers this room to the others. Her gardens are nicely landscaped with birds taking advantage of the late summer sun. I lean down and kiss her on the cheek, but she doesn't show any emotion. There's no reaction from her. For the first time since I've been here, my grandma isn't smiling at me. My chest tightens immediately with the knowledge that something is wrong.

"Sit down, Liam." Her voice is stern, commanding.

I do as she says, taking the seat next to her. My hands clutch the arm rests as I prepare for the worst. Whatever I've done, it's pissed her off and I know I'm going to end up paying for my actions. She's probably shipping me back to Beaumont, but I won't go. If I have to live out of my truck and bus tables, I'll do it.

"I'm not going to set rules for you, but I do have one request and if it can't be met, I can't have you living here. I'm far too old to be up worrying all night because you haven't come home. So I'm going to ask that you call me or let me know beforehand if you plan on staying out all night."

I hang my head in shame. I hadn't thought about what she might be thinking when I didn't come back last night. My parents – they didn't care – and I didn't give a shit if they did. I'd leave many times in the middle of the night and not give pause to what they'd think if they found that I wasn't in my room.

"The life here, it's different from what you're used to. The rules are different. The people – they don't care about you – all they care about is what they can do to make you be a pawn in their game. As much as you probably don't want to admit it, you're naïve. I don't want to know where you were or what you were doing, but I want you to be safe. I've been around long enough to know the cycle doesn't change with each generation. It just gets worse.

"I know you want to be famous, even if you can't admit that to yourself. Everyone at one time in their life thinks about being famous and you have the opportunity knocking on your door. I told you I can make some calls, but you asked me not to. And because of that you need to do it on your own. Your mom was the same way. I respect that about you, you're not looking for handouts, but you have to remember that each and every person you meet in the industry wants something from you in return. It's a never-ending cycle in Hollywood. Nothing is for free, despite what you're being told.

"Like I said, I don't want to know where you were last

night, but I want you to be careful. I want you to think with your head and not always your heart. The booze, drugs and women are on every corner and in every club, and if you're not cautious you'll end up in a hole that even I can't dig you out of. "

My grandma goes silent as I replay her words. I'm a total shit for not considering her feelings last night when I left and I'm sure at one point I had every intention on coming home, but Layla and her magic pill threw every inhibition I had out the window. Not that I mind except for the fact that my actions have hurt the one person who is supporting me not because of my dream, but because she's my grandma. She doesn't care if I'm a football player, a musician or a bum. She loves me for *me*.

My grandma eyes me as I scoot my chair next to hers. I have a feeling the chair wasn't supposed to move or hasn't moved in years. It's okay though, we're making all types of changes in our lives, her and I together.

I take her hand in mine and smile when she squeezes it. "I'm sorry, grandma. I truly am. The last thing I want to do is to disappoint or even upset you. I had every intention of coming back last night. I didn't mean to disrespect you and it won't happen again."

She squeezes my hand again and sighs. "Did you have fun last night?"

"Yes, I did. Harrison took me to the club he works at. There was a band playing and after we went to a dance club. I just lost track of time." I hate lying to her, but telling her that I ended up with the lead singer in some drug-induced haze probably isn't want she wants to hear. It was my first night out and while I had a great time, knowing that I've upset and disrespected my grandma doesn't sit well with me. I need to be more responsible and respectful of her feelings.

I also need to make sure that what happened last night never happens again. I'm not ready. As much as I want to be over her, I'm not. When I close my eyes, I dream of her. Some nights it's a nightmare and other nights, its memories of the times we've spent together. I replay in my mind the voicemail she left me last night. The anger in her voice and the knowledge that she finally hates me, is a relief in a way. I can't take the crying and the begging. She doesn't understand that I just need one weak moment and I'll be running back to her. If I do, nothing has changed. I'm still the Liam that she wants to love on the outside, but on the inside, I'm different and I don't know how to show her that. I'm weak and I don't deserve someone like Josephine Preston. I've had a taste of what I want and I need to try to accomplish that. I need to pay my dues and if I fail, I'll suffer the consequences. I'm prepared for that.

My decision to leave her the way I did still weighs heavily on my chest and in my heart. From the message I saved I know her heart is broken, but mine is too. The pain is evident with every breath I take. The cinderblock that is sitting on my chest isn't budging and after last night, it's only worse. I should've known better than to take what was offered on Layla's tongue, but my mind… it was replaying her voicemail over and over again and I needed to shut everything off. I wanted to mute the noise and just let my body feel nothing for a brief moment.

I sigh and relax in the chair. My grandma pats my arm, maybe understanding my pain more than she lets on. Someday I plan to ask her more about my grandfather and even my mother and how she met my father. I know it's not something she wants to talk about, but I have questions and I'm hoping that the day will come that we can sit down and she'll reveal everything with me.

"I'm sorry, grandma. I really am," I say without reservation. "I met some people and let the excitement of the night take over. It won't happen again."

"It will, Liam, and that's okay. I just ask that you call or tell me before you leave if you plan to stay out. When I go to sleep at night I want to sleep peacefully, but knowing you were out last night, you're first real night out in LA, I was worried. That's all."

I lean in and kiss her on her cheek again. This time she meets me half way and I know I'm forgiven. My cell phone rings and when I look at the number, it's one I don't recognize.

"Hello?"

"Liam? Trixie. Six-thirty." The phone goes dead before I have a chance to respond. I pull my phone away from ear and look at it as if it's offended me.

"Everything okay?"

I clear my throat. "Yeah. I think I get to play tonight at Metro."

"That's wonderful, Liam. Your first gig."

I shake my head and look at my grandma. I've already decided that my first gig will be when someone shows interest in me. Until then I'm just playing my guitar. "My first gig will be when someone wants me to perform so they can hear me. Right now and until then, I'm just playing to get to that point."

"You'll be there before you know it."

Her confidence in my ability overwhelms me.

"Hey do you think it's okay if I tag along or is that not *cool*?"

I chuckle. "If I didn't know any better I'd think you're asking me out on a date."

She fakes horror, but laughs. "It will definitely get me on the front page of Page Six if I show up with you on my arm. Oh imagine the tabloids."

I shake my head. "I'd be honored to take you as my date tonight."

Grandma claps her hands together. "I must go get ready." Before I can say anything or remind her that it's just after lunch, she's out of her chair and in the house leaving me here to contemplate everything that's happened in the last twenty-four hours. Two things are for certain. One, I'm hoping Harrison is there tonight and two, as much as I want to see Layla again, there cannot be a repeat of last night. I need more friends than lovers right now and I don't want to ruin what I'm hoping will be a good friendship.

CHAPTER 32

RAP my knuckles on the dark gray metal door and wait with my grandma by my side. Her hands are fiddling, making me wonder if she's nervous or maybe reminiscing about an occasion she did this with my grandfather. Each time I think about him, I want to sit her down and delve into her memory bank, but I know it's painful for her. She's lost both the love of her life and her daughter and it can't be healthy to bring up all those memories.

The door opens and I step back. We're greeted by Burke who nods at us before stepping aside to let us in. My hand guides my grandmother down the dark hallway. She's tense and probably wondering what the hell I've gotten myself into. I don't know if this is a trick that Trixie likes to do to people or what, but it wouldn't hurt to put some lights on back here. Then again, if you're in this part of the club you know where you're going, or at least you should.

The door to the green room is open and we step in. Harrison is sitting on the couch, spinning some drumsticks around his fingers causing me to stop and stare in amazement at how adept his fingers are at manipulating a simple piece of wood. I'm lucky to be able to play a chord without looking at my finger placement, but here is he as cool as a cucumber, acting as if twirling drumsticks is the easiest thing in the world to do. When Harrison spots me, he stands up and starts laughing.

"Man, what happened to you last night?" I smirk and give a sideways glance. Last night isn't something I want to talk about with my grandma within earshot.

"It's okay, Liam. I'll go and find Trixie."

My eyes bulge out and my mouth drops open. "W-what?"

Grandma pats my cheek and smiles coyly. "Metro has been around for a long time, Liam. Your grandfather used to play here when it was a jazz bar. Trixie's grandfather used to own it and he's passed it down. I know my way around here. I was a groupie once too, you know."

With that she effectively walks out of the room. I'm going to have to ask her what her nervousness was all about earlier because I'll be damned if I didn't think she was scared to be here. There's so much more to her than meets the eye. I can't help wondering if she played a part in getting me the call. If she did, I'm not sure how I'll react. I *need* to do this on my own. If I can't succeed in life without someone constantly helping me, what good am I?

"So last night?" Harrison asks. His eyebrow is raised and his arms are crossed. I run my hand through my hair, resting it on the back of my neck.

"It was great. I learnt a lot and now I know what I need to do to refine my performance." That's as close to the truth as I'm getting.

Harrison laughs. "If that's what you're telling yourself."

I nod, not knowing how to respond.

Harrison sets his hand on my shoulder and pushes me toward the corner of the room, away from Burke and the girls he's with.

"I wish someone had my back when I was starting out. I jumped into bed with the first girl who threw herself at me and regretted it the next day. I know Layla's hot, but she's trouble and you shouldn't stick your dick in crazy because it comes back to bite you in the ass."

"She's crazy?"

Harrison makes the crazy sign with his finger next to ear and I chuckle. "Loco, like off her rocker sometimes. She has a new boyfriend each and every week and the heartache is too much to bear, blah blah blah. We all hear about it until the next guy walks in. Don't get me wrong, she's a helluva performer, but love wise, she's a bit touched in the head."

I'm trying not to laugh at Harrison, he's so animated, but I get what he's saying. Last night with Layla shouldn't have happened, but it did and it's my fault. I let my emotions get the best of me when I knew my head wasn't straight.

"Did you at least wrap your junk?"

I bite the inside of my cheek and nod, looking away from him. I don't want to lie to his face, but the truth is, I don't know if I did. In six weeks she could come knocking and tell me she's pregnant and there wouldn't be shit I could do about it, except get a job busing tables. I know I screwed up last night and might end up paying a bigger price in the end. I try not to think about the one time I purposely didn't use a condom, but I had been with *her* since we were virgins and knew she was clean.

"All right man, I'm giving it to you straight. I get it. With all that free pussy, it's hard to say no, but you have to sometimes. I like to get to know them a little before I sleep with them, almost like that stupid three-date rule. I'm not a fan of one-night stands either, but I don't like relationships. I date them for a couple of weeks and move on. Usually it's mutually agreed upon because they become needy and clingy and I can't do that. I sleep late, stay up until the sun comes up and work in a bar. I'm not going to go for long walks on the beach or have a candlelit dinner waiting for them. I'm not open about my feelings either. I don't want to discuss that shit, but I'm at least honest with them. I don't give them false hope and I always wear a condom. No babies and no diseases.

"The more they see you, the sexier you become. You have to protect you and only you. Trust no one. Everyone here is out for themselves and will stab you in the back while you're staring at them," he pauses, allowing me to cut in.

"My gram says the same thing about trust."

"She's right, you know. I've known her since my mom started working for her casting agent and she's been real good to me and my sister, but I've seen people burn her just because of who she is. You should listen to her."

I nod and realize I have so much to learn not only about the industry but about people. In Beaumont, you can trust everyone.

"You're on in five, better get tuned up. It will just be me on stage so tell me what you're playing and I'll have your back." Harrison walks out of the room leaving me to contemplate everything he just said. I don't know if I should talk to Layla or leave it be. Either way, nothing can happen with her again.

TRIXIE goes over the rules before slapping me on the ass and yelling "good luck" as she walks away from me. I'm not sure how to take her. She's so different from everyone else I know yet, I find myself drawn to her. I don't know if it's because she holds my future in her hands or if it's because she knows what the hell she's doing. She can make or break me with the flick of her wrist if I'm not careful.

I step onto the stage and nod at Harrison. I hand him my two-song set list. That's all I get to make an impression, two songs. It's not much, but as I understand it, the time slots dictate how many songs I'll get. As with any artist the late slot is what we all want. I'm going to earn that spot sooner rather than later and if it means I have to sit on the street corner and play to get an audience, so be it. Either way, it will be mine.

I thought about playing the song I wrote for my girl, but I'm not ready for the questions that will come as a result. My grandma is in the crowd and while she knows, pouring my heart out to everyone else isn't something I'm comfortable with right now. Maybe next time I will be.

The wooden stool is hard, but familiar. The stiffness is a welcome feeling as I remember the many nights at the University that I sat and played. I rest my leg on the bottom peg and look out at the audience. I try not to let the size of the crowd deter me, but it does a little. There are maybe seven people out there and that's counting Trixie, my grandma and the bartender. Four people are here to listen to me sing.

"I can do this," I say as I strum the strings on my guitar. Harrison starts the beat for *Never Say Goodbye* by Bon Jovi. The lyrics come easy to me as I belt them out. My eyes close as the music takes over my body and my soul. I can see *her* standing on the dance floor waiting for me. She wants to dance, but Mason and Jerad are talking to me. I'm watching her sway her hips back and forth. Her finger beckons me and at this point who am I to deny her? I can't that's the problem. She couldn't accept this part of me so I had to leave her because had I stayed, I would've done anything she asked me to do and that would've destroyed us in the end. I put a stop to the dream so we can have a chance at a future… someday.

I open my eyes as I hit the last note. The audience has doubled and they're all clapping. I spot my grandma in the center. Her hands and covering her mouth, but I can see by her expression that she's happy for me. I reach down and pick up the bottle of water that is sitting on the floor and take a quick drink before setting it back on the ground.

"Thank you," I say as I adjust on the stool. "This is my first night at *Metro* and I'm very happy to be here. My name's Liam Page and this next song, everyone knows so please feel free to sing along. You'll make me sound better, I promise."

I can't contain the grin that spreads across my face. This has gone better than I thought. So what if I started with four people, they all clapped for me. I place my fingers on the proper strings and start the melody to *Don't Stop Believin'* and the few that are out there cheer loudly. Everyone can relate to this song and it's going to be my motto from here on out. If I believe that this can happen, it will. I just have to have a little faith.

A bigger crowd wouldn't be a bad thing either.

I leave the stage with a new surge of confidence. The size of the crowd doesn't matter; it's their reaction that solidifies that I'm on the right path. Harrison slaps me on the back and congratulates me before he returns to the stage for the next performance. My goal now is to sing three songs. I just have to figure out how to get Trixie to move me to the next slot. Baby steps, but I'll get there.

I stumble as I walk back to the green room as I catch the flying redhead in my arms, thankful that my guitar is still slung over my shoulder. Layla buries her head in my neck with her legs wrapped around my waist. I set my hand on her waist and push a little to get her to let go. She slides down slowly causing me to close my eyes and wish this wasn't happening right now.

"You were fantastic. I had no idea!"

I want to say of course you didn't because we don't know anything about each other except for what we learned in bed and that's not much to go by since I only remember a small portion of it.

"Thank you," I respond, hoping to end the conversation there. Layla has other ideas though and steps forward, placing her hand on my chest.

"Want to come over after my show?"

I look over the top of her head before looking back at her. "I can't, Layla —"

"Why not?" she asks before I can finish.

I step back. "I'm not in a place right now where I can do this." I motion between her and I. "I need friends right now. I need to focus on my music and not get wrapped up in something I can't control."

"I'm not looking for a boyfriend, Liam, just a good time."

"I get that, but I'm not even looking for a good time. I just got here, Layla. I need to establish who I am and figure out if I can even hack it in this industry. Can we be friends?"

"With benefits?" she asks with too much hope showing on her face.

I shake my head and step back, putting some space between us. "I can't do that, not now. All I can offer is a friendship and support."

"I get it. It's cool. We can hang and be friends."

"Thank you, Layla."

She steps closer and kisses me on the cheek. "Some girl is going to be lucky when they finally land you. I think I just went about it the wrong way."

I've already let her go, I want to say, but don't.

CHAPTER 33

LOS Angeles during the holiday season is drab. They try hard, but it's almost impossible to get into the spirit without cold weather and even a hint of snow. It doesn't snow much in Beaumont, but we'll at least get a few flurries and maybe a slushy road or two. But the fact that it's Christmas and I'm wearing shorts makes me feel more like a bah-humbug than a jolly ole Saint Nick.

My grandmother *loves* the holidays. I put major emphasis on love. It makes me wonder how much damage my father has done to my mother because she's not like this. The house is tastefully decorated, bringing enough festive cheer to make you forget that its eighty degrees outside. I never had this in Beaumont and I have a feeling my gram knows it. I have a distinct feeling that when she looks at me, she sees everything that I've missed out on and it must pain her to know that her daughter is not how she raised her. The most we've had is a tree, a fake one at that, which was large enough to take up the entire living room window.

Surprisingly, we never had a holiday party. You'd think with Sterling and his social agenda he'd be the first one to hold a gathering. Maybe he didn't want the outside world to see just how dysfunctional his house really was. What strikes me the most is that my father isn't riding my grandmother's coattails. From the months that I've been here, she's the epitome of social elegance and grace. I've escorted her to more high-priced dinners and red carpet events than I can count. I'm now the proud owner of an Armani tuxedo and a Rolex watch; all material items to me but important to her.

I help the staff hang the rest of the decorations. More are being added for tonight's party. I have to dress up and usually it doesn't bother me, but being home and dressed up seems like overkill. Grandma says that appearances matter and that I need to get used to that because when I'm signed, I'll want to carry myself with an aura of refinement. At that, I rolled my eyes and told her politely that I've been playing for months now and am nowhere near the pot of gold I need to make an impression on any agents or talent scouts. I still play for the happy hour crew who isn't really listening, but at least they're clapping.

I could put my name in at other bars, but I've grown fond of Trixie and Harrison has become a good friend. At least in my eyes he is. He still doesn't know how I ended up in L.A., he doesn't ask and I'm not one to offer up the details about my life before I arrived here. I wouldn't even know how to bring it up. It's not like it's an everyday topic and since I've changed my number, he doesn't look at me oddly anymore. I think he was probably wondering why

I was always silencing my phone.

Changing my number was hard, but I did it. I couldn't take the crying anymore. She wasn't even asking me to come back, just crying and telling me how much she hates me. I hate me, she doesn't need to remind me of it, but damn if I don't want her to ask me to come home or to call her. My heart breaks each and every time I re-listen to the message I saved. I know the damage I've done because I live with it every day. I wake up in a cold sweat wondering if I've made the right choice, but deep down I know that I have. I can't be what she needs, not right now. My only hope is that when I go back home in a year she can forgive me. I'm not counting on it. Hell, I wouldn't forgive me and I know I've got my work cut out to convince her to give me another chance. But on the off chance that she does, I know I'll never fuck shit up with her again. That's still my plan – to go back in a year – to fix things. I don't know if it will work, but I'm going to try. I have to. I have to show her that what I did, I did for us. That if we had continued down the path, I would've self-destructed and I couldn't take her with me.

I miss her. I miss her so much it hurts to breathe sometimes. I have a few pictures of us together that I keep in my bedside table, but I try not to look at them. I try not to put myself through the pain of seeing her smiling face stare back at me. I can hear her angry words, the sobs coming from her as she screamed into the phone. Each one twists like a knife in my heart making it shatter into a million pieces. Gram says I'll heal and that it takes time. For me, this feels infinite.

"Are you going to change?" I look down at my shorts and flip-flops and look at my grandma who is dressed in a gold shimmery dress. How I know what the word "shimmery" even is, is beyond me. It's amazing what you learn when you're the bag boy for a Rodeo drive shopping trip. I don't mind though.

"I do believe the clothes that are lying on my bed are for me to wear and not donate?" I ask, trying not to laugh. I finish hooking a string of lights around some garlands before giving her my full attention. "Yes, I'm going to change. I didn't want to get my suit dirty."

"Mhm," she says, giving me the stink eye. She loves me, but loves to act like I'm pissing her off. "The guests will be here any moment and I'd much prefer my grandson looking dapper and not like a homeless bum hanging on the Boardwalk."

"Hey now, I don't look like a bum."

She raises her eyebrow and I concede. I kiss her on the cheek and hustle off to my room. When you think about it, she's not much different from Sterling. Both have social agendas and high standards. My grandma just goes about things differently. Her thoughts on who or what someone should be isn't the "be all that ends all", not like Sterling. He has to be the only master in the house and you have to live by his rules. There's no live and learn where he's concerned.

WHEN I come out – dressed to impress per gram's wishes – there are already enough party-goers lingering that I have to side step to get around them. A man sits at the baby grand piano and plays Christmas carols while people gather around. The terrace doors are open allowing the overflow to filter out back. Chinese lanterns are floating in the pool, each one carrying a tea-light candle. And while we may be missing snow, the ambiance screams winter and Christmas.

I look around for Harrison, finally spotting him at the table that we often sit at. It's away from the crowd and noise and just about perfect for me. A few people stop me on my way to meet up with him and I have to make idle chitchat. Everyone here is an industry executive – that has been drilled into my head repeatedly – and while I haven't asked my grandma to call anyone on my behalf, I know the importance of who these people are. At any given time one of them could make or break me. I'd rather it be the former. I know they'll ask for a demo and I don't have one yet. I'm also trying to do this on my own. All I need is a little faith.

"Hey man," I greet him as I sit down. I pull out my pack of cigarettes and lay them on the table before taking one out and lighting it. I don't even know how this became a habit for me, but it is. I used to live by the adage that my body is a temple and all that shit. Not anymore. Aside from a daily run and lifting some weights, I'm not watching what I'm eating or putting into my system, nothing illegal aside from beer and a few different kinds of liquor.

"How's it going?" he nods his head.

I look around and laugh. "Another party," I shake my head. "I used to look forward to a good party, but nothing like this."

Harrison chuckles and kicks back in the chair. Once again he has a hat on and it makes me wonder how he gets away without dressing up for something like this. Everyone else is dressed to the nines and he's sitting here in slacks and a dress shirt. Makes me a bit jealous, if I'm being honest. I pull at my tie, loosening it a bit. I should be out there mingling and making connections. Grandma has expressed the importance of networking, yet here I sit far away from the party, watching from the outside.

"You know she's doing this for you, right?"

I look at Harrison questioningly.

"I'm just saying my mom is here maybe once or twice and then you show up and we're here every month it seems like, and suddenly I'm invited over."

"You hadn't come over before until I got here?"

He shakes his head, taking a long drag off his cigarette. "My sister, yeah, but not me. I tend to keep to myself and am usually at *Metro*."

"Why's she doing this?" I ask, curious as to what he thinks is going on with my grandmother.

He shrugs. "The only thing I can think is she's trying to get you noticed which is why she sent you with me that night. I know you don't know anyone, but if you look to your right, the man wearing fedora is Anthony Moreno. He's an entertainment guru, owns a few different companies. He's talking to Ness Cacco..." he trails off. He doesn't have to tell me who Ness Cacco is. Not only does he have mob ties, he's one of the best directors in cinematography. The girls have gone stupid crazy over his movies and now he's standing not twenty feet from me. The excited faces of the girls are flashing like a bright beacon in front of my eyes. They'd love this moment.

"Where'd ya go?"

I look down at the ground and shake my head slightly. "If she's doing this for me I should probably do something about it, right?"

"I would. I've been playing for various bands for a few months now and I think you have a lot of talent. Personally, I think Trixie is just messing with you. You're drawing a sizable crowd during Happy Hour and I think she doesn't want to lose it. If I were you, I'd be out there talking to these suits. Some might ask for a demo so make sure you have plenty on hand."

I look at him sharply, amazed that he can read my mind. "I don't have one."

"What?" he scoffs. "I thought you were a musician?"

"I am." I shrug. "I know I need one, I'm just not sure how to go about it."

Harrison laughs. "You ask someone for help. I'll help you make one. You're too good to be playing at *Metro*."

"So are you," I add.

He rolls his eyes. "Everyone says that, but no one is doing anything about it when they sign their deals. Besides, I like it there. It's stable and pays my bills."

I nod, pretending to understand. He's really good on the drums and better than some of the bands that come in. I've seen the way he looks at people when they're celebrating that they've just signed. I sit there and think about how he helped them. How he was an essential part in getting them the attention, yet they're not taking him with them. Maybe he's content being behind the scenes. That can't be me though. I came here to make it or at least try too lately I've been satisfied with sitting on the wooden stool with Harrison playing behind me while I entertain the working class. I see so many *suits* that I can easily say I have regulars. I don't care how much Trixie likes me playing that time slot, I need to move on or I'm going to be stuck in a rut with nowhere to go. I need to make a change.

And I need to make it now.

"Will you help me cut a demo?" I ask, unable to make eye contact.

"Yeah, I'd be —"

He's interrupted when someone screeches his name. My first thought is that my grandma has invited one of his groupies. But that thought changes when I see his face light up. The girl running toward him is excited to see him as well. He stands just as she jumps into his arms. I know I should look away, give these two love birds some privacy, but they're happiness is infectious. I had that once.

"I'm so proud of you," he says as he sets her back on the ground. "Let me introduce you to my friend."

When he says *friend* it hits me square in the chest. He's my first friend here and even though my grandma says trust no one, I want to trust him.

"Liam, this is my sister, Yvie."

My eyes bug out of my head. My initial thought of this girl being his girlfriend was so far off base, but the way they greeted each other was odd.

"It's nice to meet you," I say, standing and shaking her hand.

"Hi," she replies shyly, her voice soft and low. I nod at her and sit back, but not without noticing that she's biting her lower lip and her hands are fiddling with the hem of her sweater. She's dressed like someone from the fifties with her poufy dress and ballet flats.

"Yvie was just accepted into one of the best dance schools. The competition is tough, but she nailed her audition."

"Harrison, he doesn't want to hear about that. It's so stupid," she asserts in a hushed tone.

I disagree. "I think it's great. Congratulations."

She smiles brightly. "You do?"

"Of course."

"Thank you," she replies, her eyes in a dreamlike state. Her eyelashes are fluttering and her head is slightly bent. She glides slowly, as if she's dancing and sits down in the empty chair between Harrison and me. She rests on her hand and looks at me, making me feel somewhat awkward.

Harrison clears his throat. "So the demo?"

"Oh you're a musician?"

"Yvie, what are you doing?" Harrison asks, his voice quizzical.

She doesn't look at him when she answers. "Learning about Liam."

I smirk and fool around with my lighter. "Knock it off. It's creepy," Harrison adds. My lips go tight as I try not to laugh, but yeah I agree with him. "So about the demo, tomorrow?"

I nod. "Yeah that works."

"Great, now go network. Go meet people, Liam, that's why they're here."

I look around and notice the party has almost doubled in size, at least the people who are hanging out in the backyard has. I get up, take a deep breath and fix my tie. Here goes nothing.

CHAPTER 34

FINISH my four-song set and vacate the stage with Harrison quickly on my heels. It's been months since I started performing at *Metro* and I still haven't even come close to the coveted time-slot that I want. To say it's taking a toll would be an understatement. I don't know what else to do. I'm frustrated, tired and wondering if I'm ever going to get a look. If not, someone needs to tell me because my year is almost up and I'm either going back to Beaumont as a musician or a statistic. I prefer the former, but at this point I don't think it's going to happen.

Tonight, I don't feel like hanging out. I think Harrison knows this. He's quiet and sitting in his corner messing around with his drumsticks. He's more than likely feeling the same dejection I am. Since I've started playing here I've seen six artists get signed, including Layla. They all played the prized performance time and they all left Harrison behind. It has to get to him. Hell, I feel angry for him. I'm pissed for me. I know I'm drawing a crowd, but I'm not rewarded and I'm beginning to think it's time I start playing in other bars. I'm stupid to put all my eggs in one basket.

I zip up the canvas case that protects my guitar and sling it over my shoulder. Harrison looks dejected and I don't know if it's because I'm bailing or if he's genuinely hurt that he can't get a big time gig. He deserves it more than the people he's playing for.

"I'm going to head home," I tell him, stating the obvious. I have a lot of thinking to do and need to do it in the quiet of my bedroom. Since Christmas, I've sent out about one hundred demo tapes and have yet to receive a call. I knew it was a long shot, but thought with all the networking I've done at the parties my grandma had been having for me, I'd at least get a bite. This is probably a sign, a large neon blinking sign telling me that I'm grasping at straws.

"It's gonna happen, man. It just takes time." Harrison speaks not to me, but to the wall. He doesn't look at me, leading me to believe it's just words to keep me coming back.

"I should probably start playing in other bars. I have a feeling that Trixie either doesn't like me or doesn't think I can handle the after dinner crowd. I've watched acts move past me and get signed just like that. I gave myself a year to do this and that year is almost up."

"What happens after a year?"

I shrug even though he can't see me. "I go home."

"Which is where?"

I sigh heavily and realize I can probably tell him anything at this point. He's the only friend I have here so what's it going to hurt if he knows?

"Home is nowhere and everywhere I guess. I'm running from my previous life where I'm the town's prized possession and it didn't matter what I did, I could do no wrong.

"Anyway, I ditched, let people down and now I'm here. I told myself I'd do this for a year and then go home. I either go back a loser or I head home for a visit because I'm so busy I can't stay for too long."

Harrison rotates on his stool with his hands resting in his lap. "You shouldn't put a time limit on success."

I nod, agreeing with him, but this is different. "I know, but I have to make amends for my actions. I figured one year is enough time for people to take me seriously when I tell them that I needed a different life from the one they had planned for me. Thing is, if I go back a failure, my dad will never let me live it down."

"I get that. I feel like I'm always letting my mom down. Yvie…" he shakes his head. "She's going places with her dancing, but here I am playing drums in a house band. Like I said, I just want to play and it pays the bills, but I do wonder what's out there."

"We're not so different, you and I."

"No we're not," he agrees.

I dip my head in acknowledgment and head for the door. Something about this seems final, like I won't see him after tonight. I hope that's not the case, but when Trixie calls tomorrow to give me my time-slot I'm going to turn her down. I can't live as her puppet any longer.

"See ya around," I whisper when I get to the end of the dark hallway. I'm not good with goodbyes. This is how it has to be. When I step outside, under the cloud cover, I look back at the door. I feel a pang of regret, but I have to push it down. I need to expand, see what else is out there.

"Are you Liam Page?" My head turns sharply at the sound of my name. Walking toward me is a businesswoman. Her skirt stops above her knees and stockings cover her legs. Her heels are dangerous spikes that she can likely use as weapons if someone was to attack her. The closer she gets, the more features I can see. Her lips are painted red, her hair is long and very blond. She stops in front of me, sizing me up with her green eyes. She stands a few inches shorter than I do. I shift my weight uncomfortably. I don't think I'm a fan of being gawked at. "Are you Page?" she asks again.

"Ye…" I clear my throat and swallow hard. I don't know who this woman is, but she scares the shit out of me. "Yes," I say, my voice squeaking like a girl.

"Sam Moreno, *Moreno Entertainment*." We shake hands and I pull away before she can be disgusted with my sweaty palm.

"It's nice to meet you," I reply stupidly.

"I'm not a fan of back alley business, but since you left stage so abruptly here I am. My father sent me to listen to you play. He said he met you at a party and you later sent him a demo. We don't care about demos. We like to hear… to feel… the artist. Anyone can fake it on a tape." She looks around and I can tell this is not her normal job.

"Thanks for coming."

"Right, anyway. My father wants to meet you in his office. I like you and he listens to what I say."

"Um… okay," I stammer. "When?"

"Eager, that's good. Eager talent means you're willing to work your ass off to make a name for yourself. That's perfect really."

I nod eagerly. I don't know what I'm supposed to say or do right now.

"Do you want to know about *Moreno Entertainment*?" she asks.

"Oh… um… yes. Can you tell me?"

"For someone who wants to succeed you should know the players. *Moreno Entertainment* is one of the best agencies out there. We handle everything you can think of and have our own in-house distribution. If you want a traditional record deal with *Capitol Records* or with us, it's done. We don't dick around with our clients; each one is a top priority. Our talent managers keep their client list to a minimum to afford each of the best service. We have some of the most sought after talent signed with us and we're interested in you."

Hearing her say that they're interested in me sends my mind reeling. This is what I've been waiting for and I was about to give up. My nerves are on edge, I feel like I'm going to burst. My hands shake and as I fight to control them I try to come up with the appropriate response. Somehow "where do I sign" doesn't seem like the right one even though that's what I'm screaming on the inside.

I bite down on the side of my cheek, hard and likely drawing blood, but it brings me back to the now. "I'm definitely interested," I say as calmly as possible.

"I figured. Here's my card. I'll see you tomorrow at nine a.m." I take the card from her hand and examine it. Samantha Moreno, Talent Manager. I look up as she starts to walk way.

"Excuse me, Ms. Moreno. Are you only interested in me or my band?"

She stops suddenly and by her stance, I know she means business. Her long legs are barely a shoulder width apart, one foot is jutted out and her hands on her hips. "I wasn't aware you had a band?"

I nod quickly. "A drummer," I say, hoping that Harrison will come with me. If not, I'll just look like a fool when I show up tomorrow.

"Bring whoever you want, Mr. Page, just show up tomorrow. I don't have time to mess around."

"Yes ma'am," I mutter as she stalks away, disappearing in the blink of an eye. I look back at the business card I'm holding and finally allow myself to smile. I pump my arm in the air a few times and yell as loudly as I can. The busy street traffic blocks out my bellow so I don't have to worry about anyone coming to see if I'm okay.

I rush back into the club and pray that Harrison isn't on stage. Someone's playing, but it sounds like an acoustic set so my chances are good that he'll still be in the green room. When I walk in, I find him in the same place I left him, except this time his face looks like someone just kicked his dog.

"What are you doing tomorrow morning at nine?"

He looks up, startled. He doesn't show any emotion when he answers. "Nothing," he huffs.

"Great because we have a meeting with *Moreno Entertainment*, they want to sign us."

Harrison shakes his head. "They want to sign you."

I step forward and hand him the card. "Not this time, Harrison. You're coming with me."

CHAPTER 35

MORENO *Entertainment* isn't anything like I thought it would be. Honestly, I was expecting some corporate America building like you see on television, where you walk in and have to stand awkwardly and wait for the receptionist to stop yapping on the phone so she can tell you where you need to go. Instead, we walk into this old warehouse that has character and charm. The ceiling is exposed with its heating ducts and beams adding to the ambiance. It's very industrial and not stuffy at all. I thought I'd feel intimidated but I don't. I feel very at ease sitting here waiting for Ms. Moreno to greet us.

Magazines litter the table in front of us and along the wall there's award after award, evidence that *Moreno Entertainment's* talent is top notch. This is what I've wanted. I may not have earned it the way I thought I would, but I'm here and I'm ready.

My leg bounces from nerves and my hand pulls at

my tie. Harrison sits across from me and for the first time he's not in a hat. His dark hair is slicked back and if my grandma had seen him, she'd be telling him to get a haircut. He's dressed in a suit as well; neither of us are taking any risks that may indicate that we're not serious about being here.

"Are you scared?" I ask Harrison. He shrugs and shuffles a few of the magazines around on the table.

"If you are never scared, embarrassed or hurt, it means you never take chances."

"Who said that?" I ask.

Harrison chuckles. "I read it in a fortune cookie. It sounded good so I memorized it. I never thought I'd have a chance to use it though."

The sound of heels clackity-clacking on the floor comes from behind us. I stiffen from nerves. My palms sweat and my heart races. I've never been this on edge before. Everything that I've worked for is either going to be made or destroyed today. She could change her mind. She could decide that we're not what she's looking for or tell me that Harrison's not needed. Thing is, if she says that, I'm out. I want to do this with him.

We both stand when she comes into view. I pull at my suit jacket, straightening it out. I assume Harrison does the same. I'm too scared to look away from Ms. Moreno to check and see if he's as on edge as I am.

"Liam, happy you could make it."

As if I'd pass this up.

"I'm Sam," she tells Harrison as they shake hands.

"Harrison James."

"Follow me." She turns and walks away and we follow. It's then that I realize I'd follow this woman anywhere because I have no doubt she's the key to getting what I want. She leads us into a large office and sits in a chair similar to Sterling's.

"We'll cut right to the chase," she says as she pushes a stack of papers toward us. "We want to represent you and cut your first record. I have no doubt that you want a bigger label, but that's not always best. You'll be a little fish in a big pond and here you'll have my full focus and access to the best of everything."

We leaf through the papers. There are words that seem foreign, like royalties, percentages and rights. Each time I read a new sentence my head spins a little bit more.

"I think we should have a lawyer look at this," Harrison says and I agree. All of this seems to be too much.

"Understandable and expected," she says, leaning forward. "Forgive me for being forward here. You're young, Liam. I'm guessing about twenty."

I stiffen and adjust in my seat. I can feel Harrison's gaze upon me and I'm afraid to look at him. I didn't lie to him about my age. I just never corrected anyone when they assumed I was older. There's a difference.

"Nineteen," I correct, clearing my throat.

"And naïve. You should hire counsel, either together or separately. Take them the contract and have them call me with any questions. It's standard, straight across the board. Same you'll find with any other agent."

I nod, holding the papers in my hand.

"Take a couple of days, read it over, talk to your lawyer. When you're ready to sign, I'll be here."

I read through the papers one more time questioning whether I really need a lawyer. A hundred thoughts race through my mind. What if he tells me to ask for more or seek out another agency? I don't want that. I want to perform. I want to be somebody. I wanted this before I knew I did and now it's in my hands. I can find a lawyer and he could tell me one of two things: sign it or walk away. And I'll be damned if I'm going to walk away.

"Can you give us a minute, Ms. Moreno? I'd like to talk to Harrison in private."

"Yes, of course." She leaves her office, shutting the door behind her.

"What are you thinking?" Harrison blurts out his question before I have a chance to even formulate a thought.

"I'm the first to admit I don't know jack shit about contracts other than what I've learned from my grandma. I've seen a few of hers and I know they're not the same. But do you really want to take a few days to find a lawyer or do you want to sign?"

"You're only nineteen?"

I nod, feeling a bit ashamed for not coming clean. "I dropped out of college to move here. I was on a scholarship to play football at the University of Texas and I walked away from everything to start over."

"Holy shit."

"This is what I want," I continue. "This is why I'm here. If you're not feeling it, you can walk away with no questions asked, no hurt feelings. I want to sign. I don't want some overpriced lawyer trying to dick around the contract to make it more lucrative for them."

Harrison runs his hand through his hair, undoing the work he's put into it to keep it from falling into his eyes. "When we arrived I asked if you were scared and you said yes. I said if you were never scared you'd never take a chance. I think we should be scared and take a chance here. The contract is for three years which, when you think about it, isn't a long time. We're going to make a record and they're guaranteeing airplay. Those are two things that we don't have now. It doesn't say I have to quit *Metro* and you live with your grandma so it's not like we're hurting for money right now."

Every point Harrison makes is valid. "Do you think we should sign?"

"Yeah, I do. We have nothing to lose. I have one concern though?"

"What's that," I ask.

"She's young. She just graduated from college." He points to her diploma on the wall. "Do you think she can do for us what we need her to?"

I shrug. "You saw those awards on the wall. We'll be part of the company and her father owns the business. It's a family here." Family is what I really don't have aside from my grandma.

And he's right. I have nothing to lose. Everything I had, I walked away from months ago. In my heart, I know I can only gain from being here. I stand and walk to the door, opening it slightly to let her know we're done talking. When Ms. Moreno returns, she sets down two cups of coffee. Harrison and I both reach for our respective cups. The hot liquid feels good even if I can't stand the taste. Somehow I think living off coffee is going to be a requirement of this business.

"Are there any questions I can answer for you?"

We both shake our heads. "Can we use your pen?" I ask. Her eyebrow rises in question as she hands her pen over.

"We discussed everything and we've decided to sign," Harrison says as I scribble my name on the line. I hand him the contract and he does the same before he pushes it back to Ms. Moreno.

"Now what?" I'm eager to start whatever it is I need to do to get my career off the ground.

"Now we get into the studio. We'll start with a small EP and set you up as an opening act with an established artist. Everything's going to be moving really fast from here on out so be prepared for long hours and missed days at home. Is there anything I should know about? Any skeletons in your closet?"

Both of us shake our heads. I could tell her everything, but why? It's not like any of my family members have come looking for me. My parents even know where I am, but they've yet to call or even show up demanding that I return home. It's like I don't exist to them and honestly, that's fine. I'm happy here with my gram.

"I just want to thank you for this opportunity, Ms. Moreno," Harrison says the words that have been sitting on the tip of my tongue since I met her in the alley.

"You're welcome, but please call me Sam. The 'miss' part makes me feel old."

Harrison gives me a sideways glance, mocking me. Yes, she's young and very attractive, but I have no doubt she'll do a good job for us.

"Do you have a band name?"

I glimpse at Harrison before turning my gaze back on Sam. "No, we don't, but we can come up with one."

"Perfect. Now come with me, I'll introduce you to the team, show you where you'll have studio time and we'll grab lunch."

I peek at my watch and see that we've been here for an hour and half already. It's funny how fast time moved when I thought it was slowing down and torturing me. As Sam shows us around the building and introduces us to the people we'll be working with, everything comes down on me tenfold. Just over a year ago I played a song for my girl only to have her look at me like I had two heads. Without words she made me feel like I was doing something taboo. She made me feel like I wasn't good enough. In hindsight, I should've helped her see what I was trying to do instead of surprising her. I want her by my side. I want her holding my hand today, but that's not possible. She couldn't bring herself to understand that I was suffocating in the life I had. Since I've been in Los Angeles, despite the smog and pollution, I can breathe easily. The freedom I'm afforded to be myself allows me to be a new me.

Sam knocks and opens a door, ushering us in. Anthony Moreno stands and greets us. I met him at my grandma's during her holiday party, but this meeting is different.

"Come in and sit down." He motions to the open seats in front of his desk. "So I hear a welcome is in order?"

The man I remember at my grandma's party stands in front of us. He looks different today, more businesslike and not like he's schmoozing at a party.

"Yes, thank you for the opportunity," I reply, grateful that I'm here today.

He leans back in his chair and makes a teepee with his fingers. He's appraising us, watching for a sign that we're about to crack. I'm stoic. Reserved. I refuse to crack again. I did that once, but it's turned out for the best.

"Sam will treat you fellas right. She's young, but hungry and wants to climb the corporate ladder. Isn't that right, sweetie?"

"Yes, daddy. I already have big plans."

"Excellent that's what I like to hear. Welcome aboard boys, you now belong to *Moreno Entertainment*." He stands and shakes our hands, effectively excusing us from his office. His last words resonate. I don't want to belong to anyone but myself and now doubt runs through my mind. Did we make a mistake?

CHAPTER 36

"OKAY here's the deal." Sam throws open the studio door and tosses a stack of papers down on the table. Her cell phone is attached to her ear and she's clutching a *Starbucks* cup in her hand like it's a lifeline. In the months that we've been working with her we've learned a few things: Don't mess with her talent; she loves her *Starbucks*; and she's always in heels. We've also learned that each and every one of us gets her undivided attention and she's a spitfire. Everything that she said she was going to do for us, she's done. We've been in the studio since we signed and our first EP is coming out in the next few weeks.

Tomorrow we're having our first performance or as Sam's calling it, our first gig. Harrison balked, but she reminded him that we aren't being paid, we're trying to gain a fan base. I don't care either way. I just want to play and we'll be playing in front of thousands of people at a huge music festival. It will be our first time performing at something of such a grand scale, and to say I'm scared shitless is an understatement. I don't think I've slept in days and the closer the day of the performance gets here, the more my anxiety builds.

Sam continues to yammer in her phone. Her coffee cup is now on the table, which is good since her hand is flying around wildly. I strum my guitar quietly. She interrupted our practice session when she busted in here.

I look at Way Johnson, the ole timer who Sam picked up to round out our band. He's been around for a long time and says he knew my grandfather, but never had the opportunity to play with him. Says it would've been a great honor and is more than humbled to be playing with his grandson. It's times like that when I wish I had known him, even if it was only in memories. Way plays every instrument you can think of; the piano, bass, cymbals and he can play multiples at the same time. He performs in a suit or African grab and a hat. He also moves like he's blind, even though he isn't.

Way brushes his finger across the cymbals and gets Sam's attention. She looks at him, rolling her eyes. He laughs, but I know it pisses him off when she does this. We only have tonight left to practice and she's wasting valuable time. There's no reason she can't be behind the glass having her conversation.

She finally closes her phone and sighs. "Sorry to interrupt. I thought he'd shut up as soon as I told him I was walking into the studio."

I pull a stool out and sit down, waiting for her to finish.

"Anyway, tomorrow you've been moved to the main

stage. The time slot is 5 p.m., but it's an all-day show so the crowd will be exceptional. The organizers want a band name and frankly I don't know why I didn't of this sooner. Here are my suggestions: The Liam Page Band or Page."

I look from Harrison to Way and back at her before looking at the laces on my *Doc Martens,* my first purchase when we signed our deal. It's the first time I've used any of my savings. I thought after I dropped out of school my dad would cut me off, but he hasn't. My inheritance from his parents is still being deposited monthly. I'm trying not to spend it, at least not too much at once. The last thing I want to do is raise any red flags with him.

I don't like any of the band names. If this was just me and I hadn't brought Harrison, maybe I'd go with The Liam Page band, but he and I are together. Way, is employed by *Moreno Entertainment* and floats from group to group. He'll be performing with someone next week or whoever needs an all-round musician and percussionist on tour. But Harrison and I are in this together.

"I hadn't thought of a band name, have you?" I ask him. He shakes his head, his lips in a thin line. "Do you have an idea?"

"Nah, not really."

"What's wrong with the names I gave you?"

I shrug and feel this could've been handled a month or so ago when we were told we'd be performing. "It's not just my band; I think a name should encompass both of us."

Sam throws her hands up in the air before picking up her cup of coffee. "Pick something. I don't care, but just make it good," she says before raising the paper cup to her red painted lips. There's never a chance of mistaking what cups are hers around here, anything that has lip paint on them, regardless of the color, belong to her. My grandma says she must go through a tube of lipstick a week.

"What about 4225 West?" I blurt out.

"I like it," Harrison says as he hits his drums.

"What does it even mean?"

"Um…" I run my hand through my hair. "The date and time we're playing?"

"Are you asking me, Liam?" Sam says, incredulously.

"N-no," I stammer. "I think that should be our name."

"What's the West part?"

My last name so *she* can find me, I want to say, but don't. I have no idea if she's looking for me or if she even cares since so much time has passed. "Harrison and I met on the west coast."

Sam looks at Harrison who nods. She huffs. "Whatever you want." Sam waves her hand as she walks away from us and into the other room, signaling for us to continue practicing.

Harrison starts laughing as he bangs on his drums and Way hits a few keys on the piano. I strum my guitar and stand in front of the microphone. I hum to get my vocal cords warmed up. Tomorrow at this time, I'll be in front of thousands of people and they'll all be staring at us, waiting for me to mess up. They'll either love me or hate me.

THE sun is beating down and right in my line of sight. Sweat is dripping into my eyes and nothing I can do makes it stop. Sam had me dressed me in all black. Big mistake. I'm sweaty and miserable.

Harrison is the smart one and why he wasn't given a dress code is beyond me. He's wearing khaki shorts and a tank top. He has a few new tattoos showing and I keep thinking that I want one, but I don't know what I'd get. The typical rocker tattoo of a heart and the word "mom" on my arm definitely doesn't appeal to me.

"How can you wear that hat?" I ask. I'm sitting here sweating my balls off and Harrison has a damn beanie on his head. It's scorching out there and his head is dressed for winter.

"I'm used to it I guess."

"Used to what, the hat?"

He shakes his head as he puts a cigarette in his mouth. "The heat. I'm used to it. I've lived here my whole life and you're a newbie. You'll get used to it."

I roll my eyes. "I doubt it. And why are you wearing shorts?"

He looks down at his clothes and shrugs. "Why aren't you?"

I throw my hands up. "Sam told me to wear this."

Harrison takes a drag and blows the smoke in the air. "Sam doesn't care what I wear. You're the talent, the sex God that's going to sell records. I'm just the guy behind the drums."

I choke on my tongue. "Sex God?"

"Yeah that's what I heard her call you the other day. I'm cool with it. It means I won't have any extra duties and I won't be called to do any press conferences." He puts his hand on my shoulder. "Believe me when I say I'm so very okay with this role. I just want to play music and I am because of you."

I scoff. "I'm no sex God."

Harrison leans back on the wooden divider that's blocking us from the stage and points out into the crowd. "All those women are going to go nuts for you. Just remember to keep your clothes on."

"No problem there," I say, never intending to strip for the audience. "Hey" I say, changing the subject, "I was thinking of getting a tattoo."

"Yeah? That's almost like a rite of passage for rockers. We'll go after the show. I need a new one anyway."

Before I can respond, our name is called and Harrison walks away. There's a roar from the crowd that reverberates through me. This is what I've been waiting for, dreaming of. This is why I left my life and my girl behind. I wanted to feel this moment. I want to see if I can entertain people like they're entertaining me now.

I step out onto the stage accompanied by Harrison's drumbeats. Way follows stealthily behind me and hits his notes on the piano. My guitar hangs at my side. I stop in front of the microphone stand, my hand holding onto the top of it as I turn and look at the crowd.

"I'm Liam and we're *4 2 2 5 West*," I yell into the microphone.

"I love you, Liam," someone yells back and as much as I want to tell them that I love them too, I won't. I'll never utter those words to another person as long as I live. I can't see myself loving anyone but *her* and unless she's out there yelling at me, I'm not saying it back.

"Thank you," I say, instead. "We want to play a few songs for you and we hope you like them. If you do, our CD is for sale and if you don't like it… well you can buy it and give it your enemy or something as a nice gesture."

Harrison plays *ba-dum-tsh* on the drums and

everyone laughs. Perfect, they think I'm a comedian. I glance over at Sam who is shaking her head and moving her hand in a circle, telling me to get things going. I nod and look over my shoulder as Harrison begins the beat to the song I wrote for my girl. I didn't want to record it, but he encouraged me to. I changed some of the lyrics, but it's still her song.

"Here's our first single," I say into the microphone to the excitement of the crowd. We've had some airplay on the major station in Los Angeles to get us ready for today's show. Not gonna lie, as soon as I heard my voice on the radio I had to pull over, roll up my windows and turn it up. Chills enveloped my body as I sang the words that have haunted me for almost a year. *Her* face flashed before my eyes, her sitting on my bed with her arms crossed over her chest, watching me, wondering what the fuck I was doing.

As the lyrics take shape in my mind I look out at the crowd and look for her. Is she here and if so, will she try to talk to me? Will she make her presence known? Most importantly will she tell me that it doesn't matter what I am or what I do for a career, she'll love me for me?

I can only hope.

I strum my guitar, my hand and fingers moving fluidly. That is one thing I'm very appreciative of Sam for because she had me take lessons. I can play comfortably now and have been learning to play the piano as well. I used to think music calmed me, but now I feel like I'm in a trance-like state. I love the way each note, whether from the guitar or piano, makes me feel, the way the sound works its way into my body, into my soul.

Before I open my mouth to sing, I spot my grandma

off to the side of the stage sporting a *4225 West* t-shirt. I have to laugh at the pure sight of her not dressed to impress, but dressed like a groupie. It dawns on me that I have a groupie and regardless of who she is or how old she is, she's mine.

I belt out the lyrics that mean so much to me. Hell, each song I've written is about her. I have a feeling Harrison thinks I'm a sap, but oh well. When your heart beats for one and that one isn't with you, nor do you know how to stop her from consuming you day in day out; what else can you do? Nothing, that's what. Your life takes on a different meaning when you break your own heart.

The last verse bellows from my mouth and I'm surprised and humbled to see fans singing along. Is that a sign? If so, I'm taking it and running with it. If I can create something that others can relate to maybe this is my destiny.

The first thing you're gonna see with the sunrise
Is my arms wrapped around your body so tight
As we reflect on the love we shared
We'll realize it's not a one night love affair.

Girl I never wanna leave your side
Don't want to be strangers in the night

I let my last word trail off and the roar of the crowd is deafening. I can't help smiling My grin is spreading across my face like wildfire as I look back at the crowd. They're clapping, some are jumping up and down and there are even a few who are locked in embraces with their significant others.

I own this moment.

"THAT was amazing." My grandma greets me first with her hands on my cheeks before pulling me into a hug. "Oh my word, Liam, I'm so proud of you."

I return her hug and pick her up off the ground, twirling her around like the many times I've seen in her movies.

"Thank you for coming. I know it's hot out and you'd rather be inside with air conditioning," I tell her as I put her down.

She slaps me playfully on the chest. "Do you really think I'd miss this because of some heat? You're my grandson and you just had your first official gig. This is exactly where I want to be."

Sam comes up to us as poised as ever with her clipboard in her hand. She clutches it to her chest and stands in front of me. "Not bad, Page."

"Not bad?" grandma scoffs. "I know you better than that Sam Moreno. I saw you shaking your little tush."

Sam tries not to smile, but I see it. She's slowly cracking her tough as nails façade.

"Be honest, how was it?"

"You're leaving on tour in three days!" she announces excitedly, jumping up and down. Harrison and Way are hooting and hollering and my grandma is clapping. I'm standing here, with my mouth wide open, catching flies.

"W-what?"

"*Blaze* an all-female group and one of the headliners here start their tour in three days and they've asked that you join them. You'll have your own tour bus, you'll earn money and you'll be able to record while on the road. This is what you're looking for."

"Where do we sign?" I blurt out excitedly.

"Here," she says as she drops her clipboard and hands me a pen. I pause and look at Harrison and Way, who are both nodding. I sign my name and hand the pen to Harrison who eagerly jots down his signature.

He looks at me and smiles. "Come on, it's time for that tattoo."

"HARRISON," a very large man greets Harrison when we walk into the parlor. "To what do I owe the pleasure?"

"Things are looking up Zeke. I'm going on tour with my buddy here and he's an ink virgin, let's change that."

Zeke sizes me up and I feel about two feet tall. In fact, I feel like the incredible shrinking woman, only in male form.

"Come on back, we'll get started."

Harrison pushes me forward to get my feet moving. Suddenly, I'm a ball of nerves. I just performed in front of thousands of people and didn't have an issue, but now that someone is going to going draw on me permanently, I'm freaking out.

"Have a seat," Zeke says as he sits on his stool. "What do you want?"

"I…" I shake my head. "I don't know. I want one, but not sure how to decide."

Zeke snaps the plastic glove onto his hand, making me jump. He laughs. It's clear that he's enjoying my agitated and nervous state.

"What's close to your heart?"

"My girl," I admit without much thought. I glance at Harrison who looks at me questioningly. I'll have to tell him about her now and he'll probably wonder what other secrets I've been holding on to.

"What's her name?" Zeke asks, without looking at me. I break eye contact with Harrison to look at Zeke who is hunched over a table with a pencil in his hand.

"Her name is Jojo."

He nods and starts writing or scribbling. I can't tell. I'm glued to the chair I'm in, afraid to move. I look around at all the artwork on the walls and wonder if Zeke drew these or if they're tattoos that people came in for.

"Who's Jojo?" Harrison asks, breaking my avoidance tactic.

"My girl back home. Or she was my girl. I left her to come out here."

"Is she why you want to go home after a year?"

I nod and look away. I don't think I'm going to cry, but when it comes to her, you never know.

"It's good to have someone waiting," is all he says. He's wrong though. She's not waiting. When I say I left her, I left her. She's not sitting in her room writing me love letters or waiting for me to call her at the end of the night. She's moving on, or at least I hope she is. In my mind she's planning a future without me. She's finding a new love, one that will treat her right and not disappear on her. She doesn't need me to fill her thoughts or dreams any longer.

Zeke shows me the drawing and my heart breaks all over again. The words I uttered to her replay in my mind. I sit up and pull my t-shirt off and show him where I want the tattoo. He smiles like he gets it and places the transfer paper onto my skin.

"Harrison's told me about you and I have a feeling you're as private as he is. If I was you, I'd never take my shirt off after this or your girl will become famous."

His words strike a chord with me and I make a mental note to always stay dressed when I'm on stage. I know other artists like to walk around with their chest showing, but I don't need to do that. Not now that *her* name is a part of me forever.

CHAPTER 37

SHE *crawls over my body with her mouth teasing me. Her long dark hair creates a veil, shielding her face from me. My hand brushes her hair aside, cupping the back of her head. My fingers guide her up my torso as her lips blaze a path on my skin. Her blue eyes shimmer in the morning sun. I beg her with my eyes to please put me out of my misery.*

"Josie," I whisper as our lips meet. "God, I've missed you," I tell her as I bring my hips up to meet hers. She peppers my face with feather light kisses, pulling me to the edge. I can't hold her in my hands long enough to quench the thirst I feel for her.

"Liam, don't leave me," she purrs in my ears. Her words break me, shatter my heart. Why does she think I'd ever leave her? Doesn't she know she owns me? "I love this," she says against my skin, her tongue reaching out to trace her name. The name I had inked so I'd never forget her. "Do

you love me Liam?"

"More than my own life," I reply as I place my hands on her leg, pulling them away so she's straddling me. I need her. I need to feel her wrapped around me. "Marry me," I murmur against her mouth. This is not the type of proposal I wanted for us, but the words are out of my mouth before I know it.

"Yes," she replies as I plunge into her and she bites down on my lip. Her back arches as I move my hips. I hold her to me, afraid that if I let go, she'll disappear. I just got her back. I can't let her leave me.

"Oh Liam," she moans as her hands push against my chest. I try to hold her, but she's moving away.

"Stay. I want you to stay."

"I can't."

A loud crash startles me. I sit up and rub the sleep from my eyes. They're damp as if I've been crying. I know I have, but I can't admit that, at least not out loud. This dream or nightmare was disturbingly vivid. I can still feel her lips on my tattoo. I touch my scarred skin and wonder why my mind works the way it does.

I throw back the cover and groan at the sight of my erection, a wet dream nightmare – wonderful – sign me up for the next case study in Dream Studies 101 I'm surely a top candidate. I throw on some sweats even and pad my way into the kitchen. Grandma should be awake by now.

"Gram?" I call out, but receive no response. The coffee pot is on so I know she's awake. I walk into the living room and stop dead in my tracks.

"Grandma?" I say my voice barely above a whisper. She's lying on the ground with her coffee cup shattered next to her. She's the loud crash that woke me from my dream.

"Grandma!" I yell this time as I kneel next to her. I shake her slightly at first then more firmly, but she doesn't come around. "Holy fuck, Grandma, wake up, you're scaring me." I shake her some more, but there's nothing. I feel for a pulse, trying to recall what I learned in health class, but can find nothing. I put my head on her chest and wait for the rise and fall of her breathing. Nothing.

I reach for the phone and dial 9-1-1.

"9-1-1, what's your emergency?"

"My grandma fell, I think, and I can't find a pulse and I don't know if she's breathing."

"Okay, what's your address?"

I recite the address and listen to the lady on the other end guide me through CPR. Why didn't I pay attention in class when this was taught? I breathe into her mouth and start chest compressions, counting out the required times that is needed before breathing for her again, losing track of time as I repeat the process.

"Grandma, come on. You can't leave me," I cry out. In the background I hear sirens, but I don't stop. I can't. I need her. "Grandma," I yell as I push on her chest, one-one thousand, two-one thousand. I'm lifted off the ground and away from her only to be replaced by someone in blue.

"What's her name?"

I stare at him while his lips move, but I can't hear him.

"What's her name, son?"

"B-b-betty." I clear my throat. "Betty Addison."

Realization stretches across his face. He knows who she is and I don't know if that makes him move faster or what, but he's yelling out instructions and people are moving around her at lightning speed.

He rips the top of her nightgown open, exposing her breasts and I have to turn away. I don't need to see my grandma like this. It's taking every ounce of self-control that I have to not pummel him to pieces, but I know he's trying to help her. I hear "clear" and turn my head in time to see him place paddles on her chest. Her bodies convulses before slamming back down onto the floor. I look at the monitor that the paddles are hooked up to and see a flat line. I'm not a doctor, but even I know that a flat line isn't good.

"Clear," he says again and it's the same. He does it again and again, nothing changes.

"Call it," I hear someone in the background say. What does that mean?

"Time of death, 10:31 a.m."

"Wh-what? I stammer.

"I'm sorry, son." The man in blue says as he stands. Someone walks behind him and places a sheet over my grandma, blocking her from my sight.

My eyes begin to water as this man steps in front of me. His hand rests on my shoulder, but I'm looking past him. I'm afraid to take my eyes off of her. They roll her onto a board and place her onto a stretcher.

"What are you doing?" I ask.

"We need to take her to the morgue."

I shake my head. "I don't —"

"Is there someone you need to call?"

I look at him as if he's an alien. Who would I call and why? I grab my hair and step away from him. I'm gasping for air. Something is pressing down on my chest making it impossible for me to breathe.

"I have no one," I repeat, over and over again. The man in blue puts his arm around me and directs me out of the room. He takes me outside and sits down with me on the bench.

"I'm sorry for your loss, son."

I hate that he keeps calling me his son.

"You'll need to come down to the morgue and fill out some paperwork so they can release her body to you for burial. Here's the address."

He sets a card in my hand and leaves. The blue and red lights are spinning, but no siren. I suppose that's not needed any longer since the emergency is over.

"Hi, I'm here on behalf of Betty Addison." Sam's voice carries down the empty corridor. I don't remember how I got here, or even calling her, but here she is. And here I am sitting in a hard plastic chair with the smell of formaldehyde invading my airways.

"Your name?" the lady behind the desk has an annoying, nasally voice that makes me what to gouge my eyes out.

"Sam Moreno. I'm Mr. Page's manager. His grandmother was brought in and I'm here to make arrangements for her body."

The clerk presses keys on the keyboard, each one more jarring than the next.

"Her name?"

"Betty Addison," Sam repeats while handing the clerk a piece of paper. "Please sign this."

"What's this?"

"Your standard non-disclosure agreement, which I'm sure you've signed in the past. Mr. Page would like to keep his grandmother's passing out of the press until such time he's ready to make a statement."

"But she's famous."

"Of course she is, this is Hollywood, isn't it? Please sign it."

"You know I don't have to," the clerk responds with a snotty tone. I watch as Sam nods and pulls out her phone. "Barry, how are you? Great, listen I'm at the morgue and need a lawsuit drawn up against the Los Angeles Country Morgue. Oh you know, the norm, leaking the deceased names before we can get a press release out —"

"I'll sign it," the lady huffs and Sam closes her phone.

Sam takes the paper from her and stuffs it into a folder. "Please be so kind to remind the pathologist that he has a standing order with the county and that Mr. Page isn't afraid to sue."

The clerk nods and hands a file to Sam. She walks over to me. She sits down and places her hand on my leg. The gesture, I find, is calming.

"I'm sorry, Liam. I know how much she means to you." It doesn't escape my notice that she talks about my grandma in the present tense, as if she hasn't left me yet.

"I don't know what happened. I heard something and it woke me up and I found her on the floor. I tried to bring her back but I couldn't." My voice breaks and I collapse into Sam's arms. She holds me while I sob, soaking her jacket with my tears. She rubs my back, but not the same way my grandma would. Sam is almost detached and I forget that she works for me. She's not here to comfort me, only here to make sure shit doesn't go wrong. I pull away and shield my eyes from her. I can't afford to be weak in front of her ever again.

Sam pulls a file out of her briefcase and flips through it. "It says cause of death is a brain aneurysm, Liam. There wasn't anything you could've done to save her. The crash you heard was likely her falling which is in line with the bruising she sustained."

"She didn't tell me she was sick."

"She wasn't, these things just happen."

Death just happens. Just like that, she's gone and I'm alone again. I have nothing with her gone.

"I'll take care of everything. I know you don't want to think about the future, but it's like a flashing beacon in your face. You leave for your tour tomorrow, but need to get her affairs in order. I've already contacted her lawyer, she left everything to you. You just have to decide what you want to do with it all, but you can wait until you come back."

I shake my head. This is too much to handle. "I can't go back there."

"That's fine. I'll send someone over to pack your clothes and you can stay at Harrison's tonight."

I shake my head. I can't do this without her support. She's the reason I'm where I'm at today.

"I can't go on tour."

Sam sighs next to me. "Listen, Liam, I spent all of yesterday with your grandmother. She's so proud of you. She wanted to be in the front row while you performed instead of being back stage – that tells me something about a person. She's a remarkable woman and she'd want you to go out on tour and live your dream. I'm not going to sit here and pretend I understand what you're going through because I've never lost someone close to me before. I understand the importance of family and that's what I'm here for. I can't take the place of your grandma, but I can help you live out her memory and I can be your friend.

"She wouldn't want you passing up your dreams like this. You can hold her in your heart when you can't hold her in your hands, Liam. I'm not trying to pressure you, but I've seen this before with my father's clients. Everyone has their own way of working out how they cope with grief. I'm just asking you not to let down Harrison and Way with your decision."

I think more about Harrison than I do Way. He's been around the block before and he's just along for the ride, but Harrison's a different story. For years he's been nothing but the house band drummer that helps people develop their sound. I helped make this happen for him. Once again, I'm letting someone down with my decision. Seems like no matter what I do, that's always how things are going to be. If I bail this time, I'm letting myself down too.

"I'll go, but I can't go back to the house, not now, not ever. Sell it or donate it, I don't care."

"And what about her belongings?"

"Put it in a storage unit, I guess, until I can find a place to live."

Sam nods and has her phone out before she's out of her seat. She's all business and for that I'm thankful.

CHAPTER 38

THERE isn't a playbook or a call sheet that prepares for what life is like on a tour bus. There's no one on the sidelines yelling calls out to you and there's no one to pick you up if you fall down. When you see reports of an artist entering rehab and the cause is exhaustion – they're not lying. Rehab is the only place where people can't bug you twenty-four seven and you can sleep. Believe me, I've thought about it.

I haven't fallen, but I feel like it sometimes.

Sam is a Godsend. If it wasn't for her we wouldn't have clean clothes, food on the bus or even know which way we're heading. Disorientation is my sixth sense. I'm always disoriented. Is it night or day? Am I north or south? It doesn't matter because Sam is there to make sure I'm where I need to be, when I need to be.

Life on a tour bus, not gonna lie, it sucks. Yes we have all modern day amenities, but the constant movement is jarring. The first three days, I was sicker than a dog and thankful we were only performing five songs because anything more and I would've hurled onto the fans. '*There, take that for standing in the front row with your barely there tank top on*'.

Sam, Harrison and Way have been like a family to me. We've been on the road for a month now and despite the fact that I had reservations, I'm happy I didn't give up on this and that they didn't give up on me. I could've turned into a *has been* before I was even a *been*. What a joke that would've made me.

I miss my grandmother though and I don't think that feeling is going to go away, not as long as I'm Liam Page. She's so much a part of me, a part of who I am and who I'm becoming, that I can't let go. The sleepless nights and writer's block, I blame on her. I try to channel her thoughts into my lyrics and just when I think I have her lifeless body flashes before my eyes and I'm back to square one again.

I finish the last verse and hold the note longer than usual. The crowd erupts and as much as I want, an encore isn't happening. It's not allowed. There's another act after us and the stage has to be set up for them. We rush off and the roadies start to break down our set. Sam meets us in our dressing room with bottles of water and fresh fruit. She's not very strict about any underage drinking on my part, she reminds me daily that she's not my mother. But she does protect me and for that I'm grateful. She's kept me away from a few sticky situations and her intuition is usually spot on.

"There's an after party tonight that we need to attend."

Harrison and Way both roll their eyes. Way is likely

not to attend, but Harrison and I will because we want to stay in the good graces of *Blaze*.

"I thought we could go to dinner first," Sam says, as she hands us clean clothes. She starts to leave but turns back. "We're almost done guys and let me just say, it's been worth it. I think you'll like the new contract that *Moreno* has drawn up and if you don't, we can market elsewhere." She shuts the door, leaving us to change.

"Did she say new contract?" Harrison asks, as he slips a new shirt on.

"Yeah, could it be we're already done with our first one already?" I shrug because I can't remember what we signed. I know Sam is our manager for at least three years. "I'll ask her at dinner."

DINNER is a quiet affair in a small Italian restaurant. Sam has made sure all our meals are balanced, no fast food and nothing that is going to weigh us down or make us sick. One stipulation that Harrison asked for is that he be able to run each day and she's made that happen. She says it won't always be easy so we should enjoy it while he can. She's right about the easy part. About a week ago I ventured out with one of the guitarist from *Blaze* to the mall for clothes shopping. She was spotted immediately and all hell broke loose. Needless to say, our adventure was cut short.

"Sam, can I ask what you meant earlier about a new contract?"

She sets down her fork and raises her napkin to her mouth wiping away nothing. She's the most impeccable eater I've ever seen, nothing like Harrison and I who shovel things in our mouths constantly.

"If you remember correctly, *Moreno Entertainment* agreed to cut one EP, which we've done. Now I've told you before, we can look for a record deal with another company or you can stay with *ME*. It's your choice."

I nod, remembering the conversation.

"We'll want to look at the new contract before we make a decision," Harrison adds.

"Of course, Harrison, I'm not saying you have to sign it and we can shop around and see what offers I can pull in. Either way, we'll be cutting a new record when we get back to Los Angeles. Hopefully that has you excited."

"I'm excited," I tell her. My fear was that this tour wouldn't go so well, but it's exceeding my expectations. I think that's easy when you don't know what to expect, but every time I think something is going to fail or completely fall apart, it doesn't. The road crew that is on the tour with us is fast and efficient. They take care of our equipment as if it's their own. Each stop has been a thrill ride and *Blaze* and *The Saplings* (yes, they named themselves after baby trees) who come on after us, have been amazing to work with. On our nights off we get together and jam in the parking lots where we stay.

The tour bus isn't that bad either. At first I hated it, but we have our own space, a kitchen to cook in, a table to sit at and a television to watch. There's a small seating area that we can gather in for a pre-show game plan, but Sam usually holds those meetings in our dressing room. She likes to walk around and wave her hands wildly when she speaks.

We finish dinner and Sam pays our bill. We're not naive in thinking she's covering the tab; we know we are footing the bill for everything she does. Way says we'll be lucky to break even. I'm not in this to make money, just music and right now she's helping me do that.

Our walk to the nightclub where the party is being held takes us all of five minutes. Sam informs the bouncer who we are and we're let in right away. This is something else to get used to, the VIP treatment. I've yet to be accosted by a fan and I won't lie, I'm sort of waiting for that moment just so I can say it's happened to me.

I'm eating the words as soon as I think them when I'm almost bowled over with arms and legs wrapped around me. The intense shrill of screaming in my ear immediately makes me go stiff. I gently put my hands on my assaulter's hips and push her off of me. But one look at the red hair and I know.

"Layla!"

I pick her back up and twirl her around. When I set her back down her lips are on me in an instant and as much as I don't want to, I give in. I admit it, I'm lonely. I never thought I'd feel it until now.

"What are you doing here?" she asks.

I run my hand through my hair and look for Harrison who is at the bar chatting up a blond. I look around for Way and Sam, but they're nowhere to be found.

"Harrison and I are on tour with *Blaze*, we just performed. This is their after party."

"Holy shit, Liam, I knew you'd make it." She steps back and shakes her head. "Wow, look at you. Maybe I should be pissed that you dumped me. I should've tried harder."

Her words make me blush, but I know deep in my heart things would've never worked for us.

"You're looking good, Layla. Come on, let's find a

table."

I take her hand in mine and lead her through the crowd until I find an empty table with the words *Reserved* and Sam's name on it. I let her slide into the booth before me. I place my arm on the back of the pleather seat and lean in so I can hear her.

"So what's new?"

"Not much," she starts. "My manager is a douche and I need to hire a lawyer to get out of my contract. He's a total creep and only wanted to get in my pants."

I want to ask her if she let him, but that's none of my business. Sam appears at the table with drinks in her hand.

"Is this your girlfriend? She's beautiful, Liam." I make eye contact with Sam when Layla asks me that and notice that Sam's blushing. She looks down at the drinks and back at Layla, avoiding eye contact with me.

"This is Sam, my manager." Not correcting Layla about Sam not being my girlfriend seems like the proper thing to do. There was something in the way Sam looked that told me I'd hurt her feelings if I explained any further.

"It's nice to meet you. I'm Layla."

"Nice to meet you as well, Layla. How do you know Liam?"

"We met at *Metro*, hooked up and the next day he ditched me. You know classic groupie addiction."

Sam looks at me suspiciously. I shake my head, telling her that it's not true. She once asked me for skeletons in my closet and I told her no. I honestly thought I'd never see Layla again.

I glance back at Layla who is staring at Sam. For some reason there's tension between them and I don't understand why. I pick up my drink, a rum and coke courtesy of my manager, and chug it down. I think I'm going to need a lot of liquid courage to get through tonight. I have a feeling Layla wants to hook up and Sam isn't going to leave my side.

The night moves on fluidly. I have blinders on I admit it. Each time my drink is empty, Sam refills it, but before long Layla pulls me out on to the dance floor for some tension release. This time when she shows me her little white pill I pull it out of her mouth and toss it on the ground. If I'm going to be with her and that's a big if, I want to remember the whole night.

I let her kiss me because it feels good and my body craves the attention. The feeling of her pressed against me gives my body the attention it needs and I didn't realize it was missing. She's pointing out the obvious. I'm lonely. She feels amazing pressed against my body and it seems my body agrees. My senses are heightened with her in my arms and I love it and hate it all at once. I don't want to feel this way with anyone else, but I can't help it. I lead her back to the table where Sam is sitting. Harrison is long gone and Way retired hours earlier. Sitting there waiting for me is another rum and coke, which I knock back, not bothering to nurse it or even slow down. I'm sweating enough on the dance floor to keep my wits about me.

"Layla!" she turns and drops her hand from mine. "What the fuck?" the guy behind me roars.

I turn in time to have his fist connect with my lip. I stumble back into the table and hear Layla yelling beside. Sam is by my side immediately with a napkin wiping the blood that is gushing from my lip.

"What the fuck?" I exclaim, taken off guard at the

sudden contact. Sam's eyes are wild and I feel sorry for whoever is on the receiving end of the verbal barrage she's about to let loose.

"I can explain," Layla says as she looks at me sheepishly. Her hand is pushing on the man's chest, keeping him away from me.

"Let's hear it."

"Remember when I said earlier about my manager?"

I nod, not willing to add to the conversation.

"I married him."

"Oh you've got to be fucking kidding me. Are you shitting me, Layla?"

She hangs her shaking head.

I pick up whatever Sam was drinking and down hers, along with Layla's and walk away. I know Sam is hot on my tail, but I don't care. I need to get away. I can't believe I got into this mess with her. She was trouble the first time I was with her when she gave me her little magic drug, I should've known better. Harrison warned me that she was loco, but I had no idea until now just how crazy she really is.

"Fuck," I yell when I'm outside the club. Just when I think I'm on the path to something good, it gets all fucked up. I lean against the brick wall and hold my head in my hands. Sam's next to me, her hand rubbing my shoulder.

"You didn't know?"

I shake my head. "I'm not about to mess up someone's marriage whether they're happy or not. I'm fucking nineteen for God's sake, I don't need the drama."

"I know you don't, come on. Let's go back to the bus. Way and Harrison are both off with whoever they picked up you'll have it to yourself tonight."

As soon as the cold air seeps through my body, my drunken state rears its ugly head. The moment we step onto the bus, I realize just how alone I am. Everyone that I love is gone and it's too late for me to go home and fix everything.

I walk straight to the kitchen and pull out the bottle of whiskey. I twist the cap and drink it neat.

"I don't think you need that tonight," Sam says, her hand calmly taking the bottle from me. I want to yell and scream at her, remind her that she's my manager and nothing else, but I can't. Her green eyes are boring into mine, they're dangerous and heated. Her hand brushes against mine as she takes the bottle away from me.

"I'm lonely." The words have more meaning than I'm willing to admit. She nods, understanding what I mean. She slides her jacket off, dropping it to the floor. Her fingers start at the top of her blouse as they nimbly work each button open. Her white lace bra is visible, exposing her voluptuous breast.

My hand shakily reaches out, my fingers touching her skin just above the lace. Her eyes close briefly before she looks at me again. I swallow hard, unsure if I'm supposed to be doing this or not.

Her hands go behind her back, the sound of her zipper the only thing competing with my labored breathing. I watch as her skirt pools at the bottom of her feet. I suck in a gulp of air at the sight of her black garter belt.

"Holy shit," I breathe stupidly. She stands here in front of me, baring herself and that's all I can say. "You're fucking hot, Sam."

She bites her lower lip, stepping out of her skirt. She walks toward my room as I watch her ass sashay in her thong. My erection is straining against my jeans, begging for attention. I bend down and pick up her clothes. The last thing I want is for the guys to come back and figure out what's about to happen because for all I know this is against the contract and I'm probably getting us fired in the morning.

I shut my door behind me. There's not a lot of room to maneuver. She stands before me, her bra straps sliding down her arms, leaving her breasts in full view.

"Holy, fuck me."

"I plan on it, Liam."

I fumble for the hem of my shirt, ripping it over my head. I move toward her quickly and capture my lips with hers not mindful of my busted lip. I hiss, but relish in the pain. I deserve it. She pulls at my belt and yanks the fly of my jeans open as my hands palm her ass. My fingers inch toward her pussy, feeling how wet she is. She wants me. She's just not giving herself to me. Her hand rubs down my shaft giving me the friction that I need.

I spin her around and set us down on the bed. I sit up and shimmy out of my jeans, unlacing my boots as quickly as possible. Her legs are spread for me, inviting me.

"Are you sure?" I ask, as I reach for my wallet to pull out a condom.

"Yes," she answers as she unhooks her garter belt and slides her thong down her legs. "I want this with you." She kisses me hard, pulling me forward. I rest on top of her, letting her feel my weight before sitting back on my knees. I rip open the foil wrapper and sheath my erection.

"Who's Jojo?" she asks, her fingers tracing the name inked on my skin.

"No one you'll ever be," I reply, capturing her lips. It's only when she stiffens do I realize my mistake, but it's too late. She's already encased me and unless she tells me to stop, I'm not going to. I need this. I need this to feel whole again and not so broken.

CHAPTER 39

PULL at my bow-tie as the limousine drives at a snail's pace down Hollywood Blvd. I've been nervous a lot in the past year, but this time my nerves are frayed. I down a shot of whiskey from the bar and settle in my seat. My date, Valerie Penn, sits beside me looking out the window at the fans waving.

Tonight is a new adventure for us. About six months ago, one of our songs was chosen to be on a movie soundtrack. We didn't think anything of it, thought it was cool and we went on about our business until Sam told us we were invited to the red carpet event. I wanted to blow it off, but she said it was important for our image and that we should want to walk the red carpet and greet the reporters and fans. If there's anything I've learned over the past year or so, it's to listen to what Sam says. Well mostly. I don't listen to her when it comes to my love life because she's not happy with my decisions, and that's only because my decision doesn't involve her. We slept together once, and it was a mistake. I was lonely and we were on the road. I just had my lip busted by an angry husband. Needless to say, it's a night I planned to forget. Sam, sadly, had other ideas. At first, I didn't think anything of it. She'd bring me breakfast in the morning and sit with me while I ate. She started taking me shopping and calling all the time to see how I was doing. She became more touchy-feely with her hand always on my arm or brushing my leg. I finally put a stop to it when she came over one night to drop off some paperwork and acted like she was too tired to go home. It hit me like a ton of bricks what she had been doing – trying to get back in my bed – and I wasn't having any of it.

So I started casually dating. I'm not looking for anything too serious and it's only with women who have some type of celebrity status so both of us can benefit. The women know this going in and more often than not, our publicists set us up. We both gain from our mutual interest in each other and there are no hard feelings when one of us wants to go in a separate direction. That's usually me. I'm becoming bored very easily. A few have become clingers, but I've become too much of an ass to really care.

My car door opens and I reach for Valerie's hand, pulling her behind me. We step out to massive screams. The sounds are deafening, but very welcomed. Sam assures me this will catapult us into super-stardom. She's hoping that we'll be headlining our own tour after tonight.

This is an A-list event and my relationship status will be confirmed in the press by this time tomorrow. Valerie has been my rumored girlfriend for a few weeks thanks to her publicist making sure we're in the same place at the same time. Like I said, I don't mind playing along. It's fun for a while. Valerie's beautiful and will make an amazing wife for someone, but not me. She agrees. We're strictly friends when we're off the camera. We have zero romantic chemistry at all.

I wave to the crowd and wait for Harrison to get out of his car so we can walk the red carpet together. His door opens and the decibel of the cheering moves up a notch to bordering at hysteria. Since we've done a few videos, Harrison has gained some fans. I think it's great. It takes some of the spotlight off me.

He joins Valerie and me with his sister as his date. When Yvie reaches me, she goes up on her tiptoes and gives me a kiss on the cheek, much to the chagrin of the crowd. Yvie loves it. She's had a crush on me since we met, according to Harrison, but I see her as a sister. It would probably make sense for us to date since we're close in age, but the things I've seen and done in the past year ages me far beyond her reach. I may be only twenty, but I feel thirty.

Sam meets us and guides us to the crowd. Right now we're only signing autographs. When we actually step onto the red carpet, the interviews and photos will start. Fans ask us for photos and Sam obliges, taking photo after photo until she tells us it's time to hit the carpet.

Valerie and I step onto the carpet first, followed by Harrison and Yvie. Sam is in front of us with her clipboard out and an earpiece in. She's talking to our publicist who is securing interviews along the carpet for us.

Photographers and journalists yell our names

at the same time. I'm thankful for Sam and her list because without her, I wouldn't know who to talk to. She knows where we're supposed to go. She directs us to *Entertainment Weekly*. Harrison and I step up to the makeshift barricade, ready and willing to answer anything. Well almost anything. There are some questions that I refuse to answer and a simple shake of the head tells Sam that I'm ready to move on. Harrison does the same thing. We're adamant that we won't answer any questions about our family, especially my grandma.

"Well hello Liam Page and Harrison James," the reporter coos our names as she bats her eyelashes, turning on the full charm. "Tell me boys, how are you enjoying your first premiere?"

I look around with a smile on face. "I'm loving it," I respond. "Look at all the beautiful women." I wink and cock my head sideways causing her to sigh. She blushes, score one for Page.

"You know I've heard about the Page Pantydropper and I do believe I just experienced it."

I lean over the barricade slightly. "Well maybe I'm losing my touch because I definitely don't see your panties down around your ankles."

"O-wh-," she steps away and fans herself. I wink at her one last time since Sam is pulling on my arm.

"Why do you do that, Liam?"

"What's that Sam?" I look down on her. Tonight she's not rocking her usual stilettos, which honestly is a bummer for me. I may have made the mistake of sleeping with her last year, but I can't discount that she's smoking hot and her heels turn me on.

"You flirt like they have a chance with you."

I lean in, my lips grazing her ear. "Maybe they do. You know Valerie and I aren't sleeping together and I get lonely." I let my hand brush against her ass. I know what I'm doing and I'll likely pay for it later with some epic off the wall rant, or she'll turn totally emotional and cry in my ear for an hour.

I like Sam, I do. At times I wish she weren't my manager because I'd probably date her. She's confident, feisty and sexy as hell. But she's a valuable asset and she's helping me make a name for *4225 West* and that's far more important.

THE *Vogue* after party is in full effect when we arrive. How Sam scored us tickets to this event is beyond me, but I love it. Keeping with the façade, Valerie and I hit the dance floor. There's an elite league of photographers allowed in so we are afforded some privacy at least.

I spin Valerie around and hold onto her hips while she grinds against me. It's either flashbulbs or the strobe lights, either way I'm sure our pictures are being taken. This will appease everyone for a while until it's time for both of us to move on.

I catch sight of Sam sitting at the bar. She's not working the room trying to score us another deal or tour, she's staring at me. It was probably a mistake, me flirting with her earlier, but she makes it so easy. She's like putty in my hands.

Valerie turns in my arms. "I need a drink."

I nod and place my hand on her waist as I guide her to the bar. She's of age, I'm not, but I don't get carded. Hell, I haven't been carded since I arrived in Los Angeles. This place is a haven for turning a blind eye on underage drinking. I order her a martini and some whiskey for me. It blows my mind how I went from beer to hard liquor so quickly. The hard stuff numbs the pain and takes longer to wear off.

I hand Valerie her drink and notice a photographer getting close so I lean in and act like I'm telling her a secret. The flash goes off and now he's moving on to his next pay dirt photograph.

Valerie leans into me and almost spills her drink. I rub my hand up and down her back. "Are you okay?"

Her head rests on my chest and barely moves. "I'm not feeling so great, Liam."

I down the rest of my drink, placing it on the bar. Once I set her glass down I take her hand in mine and walk toward the exit. I'm hoping some fresh air will do her some good.

When we're outside, I lean her up against the wall, but her head falls forward. "What the hell, Val?"

"I don't know, but I'm sick, Liam."

"Do you think someone spiked your drink?" I try to think of who would've had access, but the truth is, anyone. The bartender, the guy next to us where we were standing, hell even the waitress brushed up against us. The possibilities are endless.

She barely nods and it makes me want to go in there and punch the shit out of him. I know I have to take her home, but can't just leave the party.

"I need to go tell Sam we're leaving, but I'm not leaving you outside by yourself, can you walk back in with me?" Valerie stumbles two steps before falling into my arms. I'm more carrying her than she is walking at this point. As soon as we step inside, Harrison is at the bar, his lips attached to some blond.

"Hey man," I say loudly enough to get his attention.

He turns and wipes his mouth with the back of his hand. I have no idea who the chick is, but he's digging her, so good for him.

"Val's sick. I think that douche spiked her drink. I'm taking her home. Can you tell Sam what's going on?"

"Yeah, no problem." He slurs his words and turns his attention back to the blond. I eye her up and down and can't really blame him.

I all but carry Valerie to a waiting limo. The driver hurries to the let us in. "Where to?" he asks. I give him directions to my place. There's no way I'm letting her go home alone.

We arrive at the hotel where my penthouse is located. Sam found this place for me after my grandma died. It's perfect for me. I don't have to cook or do my own laundry and I have all the privacy I need. The security is also top notch.

I slide my keycard in and carry Valerie into the elevator. "I'm going to make you throw up when we get to my apartment. You need to get this shit out of your system." She just nods. Her arms are limp around my neck. As soon as the door slides open I'm opening my door and rushing her to the bathroom. I set her down, helping her bend over.

"You have to stick your finger down your throat, Val."

"I know, but leave please."

"What?" I question.

"Leave me. I don't want you to see me puke."

It takes a moment for me to realize what she's talking about, but when I do, I bolt out of the bathroom and turn on the stereo so I don't have to hear her either. I don't count the minutes while she's in there, I just pace. Who the fuck spikes people's drinks? Hollywood is a mecca for sex. Hell all you have to do is ask.

The bathroom door opens and I can already tell she's better. There's color in her cheeks and her eyes seem more focused.

"Better?"

"So much. Thank you for bringing me here."

"I care about you, Valerie. You may be my pretend girlfriend, but that doesn't mean I don't care."

Valerie walks toward me and places her hands on the lapels of my tuxedo. She rises up on her toes and her lips brush lightly across mine. I wish I felt a jolt or a yearning, but I don't.

"You're going to make a damn good husband someday, Liam Page." With that she walks away and out my door. I don't know how long I stand there, staring at the spot where she was, but it must be long enough for my legs to stiffen. Her words reverberate through me and thoughts of home filter through my mind.

I'm going home in a… I head for my wet bar and grab the bottle of Jack, forgoing a glass. I kick my chair over to the floor to ceiling window and sit my ass down. The liquid burns as it coats my throat, but I welcome it. I finish the half empty bottle and throw it against the wall. The sound of it shattering against my wall does nothing to curb the foul mood I'm now in.

I told myself I'd have a year in California and then I'd go home. I would get *her* back or I'd make her tell me how much she hates me. I dig around for my phone, pulling it out of my inside pocket. I scroll through my saved voicemails and press play. The screaming and crying, the hurtful words, the hate and venom from her telling me how much she hates me cut like a knife. If I go back now, it will be worse.

"Liam," the voice is soft, soothing. I lean my head back over my chair to find Sam standing behind me. I sit back up and look at the lights of Hollywood twirling through the night sky. "You okay?" she asks as she surveys the broken glass on the floor.

"Fine."

"Where's Valerie?"

"Home, I guess. Someone drugged her, I think. Who does something like that?"

"Desperate people do desperate things sometimes." She kneels before me, her hands spread out on my thighs.

"What're you doing, Sam?" my voice breaks.

"I just want a chance, Liam. I know I'm your manager and if you want I can hand some of my duties over to my dad, but we deserve a chance to see where this can go. I know you feel it."

"I'm fucking twenty and you want me to commit?"

She shakes her head as her fingers deftly undo my belt and slide down my zipper. I close my eyes when her hand reaches into my boxers. I should tell her no, but I can't. I won't. "I just want to try."

"Fine," I say gruffly. I'm giving in and I know it, but the resistance isn't worth it. I'm attracted to her and I have been for a year now. There's that word again. Year. I stand abruptly, pulling her up by her arms.

"Turn around, lift your dress and bend over. I want all of Hollywood to watch us." She does as I say, painstakingly slowly. She turns her head, eying me over her shoulder.

Her plump ass is bared for my taking. I slap her once and slide her thong over. She's glistening, ready.

I thrust into her with wild abandon. She screams out, but doesn't stop watching me. I pull out and plunge deeper into the darkness that is threatening to swallow me. I rip her dress away from her body and lean forward, pinching her nipple. Her cries encourage me. Spur me to take complete control of her body.

I fall back into the chair, still buried deep in her. Sam knows what to do as she rides me into oblivion. I close my eyes and imagine she's someone else. Sam has become *her* behind my closed lids and for the first time in years I'm letting myself go.

CHAPTER 40

THE sunlight filters through my window, waking me slowly. I roll over onto my side and immediately regret moving so suddenly. Last night's activities play like a black and white movie in slow motion. I'm the star, of course, but so is a blond haired, brown eyed woman that I don't want starring in my life.

I scrub my hands over my face and groan. I don't need to see her to know she's in the other room watching TV. I can picture her clearly. She'll be in my t-shirt, her feet tucked underneath her legs. There will be a bowl of fresh fruit on the table, but she's only picking at it. Her hair is piled on top of her head in a messy bun and she's wearing her librarian glasses. Papers are spread out all over the table and a pen dangles dangerously close to her mouth.

I've seen this image so many times before when we were on tour. She doesn't feel the need to hide herself and I can't really blame her, she's beautiful. Harrison and

Way didn't seem to care, but I did for a time and it looks like last night I started caring again. I think I have two options: I can get up, head right to the shower then rush out the door to the studio or to Harrison's or I can get up and walk out there like nothing has changed, except everything has. I can tell my heart over and over again not to feel anything, but the sad fact is, it does. Sam gets me. She understands the industry. She knows about this life. As much as I've been resisting her, my body responds to her with admiration. I'll just never accept that I love her, I can't.

I sit up and swing my legs over the edge of my bed. My sheet barely keeps me covered. I look on the floor for something to wear, knowing I left sweats there last night before I left for the red carpet and find nothing. Of course when I need Linda, my housekeeper, to not be so efficient she is.

The closet it is, which ends up being option three. I find a clean pair of sweats and put them on, leaving them loose at my waist. I give my body a once over, barely looking at the tattoo on my chest. That one pains me the most. Each day that I live, I feel the needle tearing my skin so I can bleed ink.

I close my eyes and take a deep breath before I pad out to the living room. Sam is exactly as I thought she'd be. It's Sunday and she's working, trying to make her clients the most money. For all of Sam's faults, and believe me there are many, she's an excellent manager.

I don't know what protocol here is. I could lean over the couch and surprise her from behind by kissing her on the cheek or I can go about my morning as if she's not here. I know if I kissed her – if I made the first move

– she'd be happy. A happy Sam, means a less stressed out Liam. But it also means I'm doing something I'm not sure I'm ready for. I don't want a girlfriend. Valerie reminded me of that last night when she said I'd make a good husband someday. I won't because I'll never ask anyone to marry me. I don't even want kids. At one point in my life I did. I could see myself standing in my front yard with a white picket fence, a wife and child. But not anymore, I destroyed that part of my life and I'm in no way eager to even start reconstructing it.

I'm too young to be tied down. I want to have fun. I want to live and wake up one morning and decide to take a drive and not have to report to anyone. I don't want to worry about what's for dinner or if I'm going to be home by a certain time. Relationships do that to people and that's why I've taken the route I have this past year. No strings, no feelings. Two adults enjoying each other's company without the touchy-feely shit getting in the way.

I don't know what to do, so I sit down next to her. I see her smile even though she's trying to hide it. I know she wants a relationship with me, but I'm not so sure I can do this with her. I pick up the remote and turn the volume up on the television, waiting for the commercials to stop so I can see what she's been listening to.

My stomach turns when I see the name of the college that killed my dreams. I'm not talking my football dreams, but the one that took my family away from me.

"What're we watching?"

"Football," she says without looking up. Sometimes I wonder if she knows about my past, but I think if she did, she'd say something. I'm shocked that it hasn't come up in an interview or someone has tried to claim to know me.

It's not like I changed my looks, just my name. Maybe I'm such a disgrace that no one cares.

The announcer says Mason's name and I lean forward, resting my elbows on my knees. They show his player profile and his stats. I scan them quickly and match them to what he had in high school. Why I remember those numbers is beyond me. He's doing okay in college. Not great, but he's making a name for himself. I block out other noise and focus on what the announcer is saying. He's married!

"I'll be damned," I mutter.

"What's wrong?"

I shake my head. "Nothing."

I turn the volume up a bit more to see if they're going to say anything else about him, but they move on to their next profile. It must've been halftime because they cut to the field and there's Mason sliding his helmet on and taking the field. A pang of jealousy works its way through my body, stopping at my throat. I know if I start to speak now, nothing will come out.

Mason lines up on his quarterback's right. The defense is going to blitz, I can see it, but the quarterback doesn't. He's not changing the play. The ball is snapped and before he can finish his third step, he's down. The play is over.

The next play is a hand-off on the left and the quarterback doesn't see that Mason probably has fifty pounds on the outside linebacker and he could take him. They gain five yards and now it's third down.

I will the quarterback to give the ball to Mason. I want to see him run again. I want to see him break tackles like he used to in high school.

The quarterback takes center and is shouting

something. I wish he were mic'd so I could hear him. Watching this game takes me back and for a moment, I miss it. I miss the excitement and the rush of the crowd. The crowd I have now is nothing like the ones from our games. The camera pans over the fans and I jolt forward to look for *her* face. The camera moves too fast and I silently pray that they go back over again to show Mason's wife because surely they're still best friends.

The focus is back on the field. The ball is hiked and passed off to Mason. He has the pigskin in the crook of his arm and runs like his ass is on fire for a forty-yard gain. Everyone goes wild and I'm looking for that one face again. I just need to see it, even if it's only for a moment in time. That one moment will tell me everything I need to know.

The announcers come back on to tell us they're switching games to one that is tied with only seconds left. I want to scream and tell them not to change the channel, but I can't. I can't let Sam know that I have a past.

"Are you okay?"

I look at her, her face full of concern. I adjust myself on the couch when I notice that I'm on the edge and barely hanging on. I sit back and relax my posture.

"I'm fine."

"I didn't realize you like football. I can get you some tickets to the USC if you want."

I shake my head adamantly. "No, I don't like it."

"Okay, Liam," she says to appease me. I know she can see through whatever wall I'm putting up. I just hope she doesn't pressure me into sharing my feelings and shit. That is something I can't do, not anymore. As far as I'm concerned those are buried deep in my soul and it will be a cold day in hell before I bring them out again.

CHAPTER 41

I'S amazing how quickly one can fall into a routine. When I first started playing at *Metro,* I'd stay 'til the early hours of the morning and party it up with Harrison. I'd sleep late the next day, waking in time either to have lunch with my grandma or barely before it was time to return to *Metro.* On the days I wasn't performing, I'd be up making breakfast with my grandma. That routine changed when I went on tour. Late nights and sleeping all day became my habit. I've kept that pattern for the better part of a year, except for now. Now, I'm up at the ass crack of dawn on a Saturday to go shopping at the Farmer's Market.

This is Sam's idea of being domesticated. I hate it. I live in a penthouse above a hotel so I don't have to do my own laundry or make my dinner if I don't want to. The last thing I want to do on a Saturday is don a baseball cap, sunglasses and pretend I'm having a blast picking out fruits and vegetables. But I'm here, trying. I told her I would and that's what I'm doing.

We hold hands as we stroll through the different vendors. Aside from the norm, there's pottery, flowers, homemade soap and clothes and that's just to mention a few of the staples you can buy here. I'm not interested in any of it. I want to be home sleeping or lock myself away in my studio writing.

We're due to cut another album for *Moreno Entertainment* but I'm having reservations. I feel like I've spent most of my life second-guessing everything and my gut is telling me I'm right about this one. This would be our second full-length album and aside from having one song in a major motion picture, we haven't done shit. Our sales are lackluster and we still aren't headlining our own tour.

Something has to change and I think it's the label, but I don't know how to approach the subject without coming off like a total diva. Harrison agrees with me though. We need something different and if it's not the label, it's our sound that has to change. Our first record was gritty, heavy. That's not Harrison and me. We're mellow. We prefer to sit on the couch and jam. The screaming shit isn't for me. I knew the record felt wrong, but Mr. Moreno assured us that was what we needed.

Now I want to change and I'm not sure how to go about doing that. Right now I'm not a fan of talking business with Sam and she must know something's up since I haven't been in the studio for weeks, but she's not asking nor demanding new material. I wouldn't be able to give her anything. My mind is blank. I get a headache just thinking about writing lyrics down.

I carry Sam's purchases in my free hand since she

refuses to let go of my other one. She wants press pictures. She wants the paparazzi to know that she's with me. It's a status thing for her. She made sure the press had a field day with Valerie and my 'break-up'. Sam didn't even wait twenty-four hours before her and I made a public appearance and the cameraman caught us with her tongue down my throat. I'm convinced it's all for show. I know she doesn't like my publicist and this was her way of showing her who's boss.

Sam hands me another bag full of God knows what. Her fingers linger on my arm, brushing back and forth. There's a want in her eyes that's indescribable. She loves me and that is my fear. I don't want her to. I don't want to hear those words from her or have her expect me to say them back, because I won't. I can't. I'm not capable of loving another human being. Shit, half the time I don't even love myself. I move my arm so she can't touch me. Her face falls and that's not the reaction I want from her either. Truth is, I don't even know what I want right now. I put my arm around her and pull her into me. She puts one arm around my back and the other is clutching the front of my t-shirt. I don't want clingy either, but it's better than seeing her face fall.

I don't know what I'm going to do about her. I feel the *talk* coming and I'm not prepared to let her down. This is exactly why I didn't want a relationship. This is why casual dating works so well. No attachments. If you're friends with benefits, you hook up and scratch the itch. If you're just friends, you do the occasional meet for dinner, drinks, take her out and show her a good time then retire to your separate apartments or spend the night on each other's couches. This domestic shit kills me because she's not who I thought I'd be doing this with.

I direct us back toward my apartment. I'd rather be alone with her behind the privacy of my own walls than out in public. There are too many prying eyes and loose lips around here. The gossip-mongers are relentless and the last thing I want to do is hurt Sam. Most know she's my manager, but for those who don't, I don't want those assholes blurting out my indiscretions in front of her. She'd have to do damage control because she wants to be with me.

"Want to stop for coffee?"

"Not really, Sam." I strong arm her back into the hotel and let go of her as soon as we're a safe distance from the door. She slumps against the elevator wall, avoiding eye contact with me. "I just don't want coffee right now."

"I know. I was just trying to stay out longer. The sun felt good."

I step closer and kiss her lightly on the lips. "We can go to the pool? Sit up on the roof?" I don't know what spurs me to kiss her or ask her, but it feels good. She smiles and nods as the doors slide open. "Let's go change."

WATCH Sam in my small kitchen. She's cooking and to me that's such a novel idea. I haven't had a home cooked meal since I was living with my grandma. Maybe Sam remembers this, I don't know. She was my rock when my grandma died. She took care of everything. I would've been lost without Sam in that moment. I don't even know if I thanked her for everything that she did.

She's wearing a white, see-through cover-up over her red bikini. A swimsuit that I happen to like and am thinking she needs to take the cover-up off. We spent two hours laying in the sun and lounging in the pool. I should spend more time up here, but never think about coming up here by myself. I feel energized and relaxed. I need to get back into running. It's been so long since I ran. I miss the feel of the wind against my skin. Running on a treadmill won't cut it. I need to run near my grandma's old house on the trail system. Be one with nature.

Sam turns and smiles. "What are you staring at?"

"You. Is that okay?"

She rolls her eyes and turns back to whatever it is she's doing. "Go sit down, Liam."

I do as she says, relaxing into the couch. She appears in front of me with a plate of food and a glass of milk.

"Milk?" I deadpan.

"It's good for you."

"I haven't had milk since I was eighteen."

She shakes her head slightly while placing a napkin in her lap. "That was two years ago, surely you know how to drink milk."

Ouch on the age comment. She doesn't need to rub in the fact that she's older than me. "Fine. I get why I'm drinking milk, but why are you?"

Her hands still in her lap and she clears her throat. She shifts slightly and faces me. Her smile is forced. I sit back and wait for her to deliver whatever it is that's sure to ruin our day. She reaches for my hand and I let her hold it. I don't have a clue what's going on and how just a few minutes ago everything was fine but now there's definitely something wrong.

"I'm pregnant."

My heart stops.

I forget how to breathe.

Everything about this moment is wrong.

She's supposed to be brunette, not blond.

She has brown eyes, not blue.

"Say something."

I shake my head. I have nothing to say. I've only wanted to hear those words from one person and she's not her. I don't care how long I live for, I don't want children with anyone but *her* and that's never going to happen.

"Liam?"

"Don't," I say through clenched teeth. "Don't say my fucking name."

"Okay," she replies nervously.

I stand, kicking the coffee table over. Food and milk crash to the floor, ceramic and glass breaking. Sam jumps, but right now I don't care. "What the fuck?" I scream while holding my head.

"I thought you'd be happy," she says weakly.

I drop my hands and glare at her. I see nothing but red when I look at her. "What gave you that fucking idea? I'm twenty years old and am barely making it in life. My band isn't going anywhere and our last record fucking flopped. What part of that screams I'm ready to fucking settle down?"

"Nothing, but we can get a nanny and I have money. You have the money from your grandma. We can get a bigger place."

I stand there, staring at her like she has three heads. "You've got to be kidding me! You're what, a minute pregnant and you're already talking about a fucking nanny? You want some stranger raising your kid?"

"Our child."

"This is not fucking happening."

"Well it is, Liam." She stands and walks over to me. As soon as she touches me, I shy away. I can't do this with her, not right now. I sidestep her and rush out of my apartment. As soon as I'm in the hallway, I'm out of the emergency exit and literally flying down the stairs.

I'm standing outside without a hat and sunglasses. Not that I'm expecting people to come up to me, but I like the security having those items provides. I hail a taxi and give the driver Harrison's address. I lean back in the seat and close my eyes. I don't know what I'm going to say to him, but this can't go on. We're better than this and something has to change.

I pay my fair and climb the steps to Harrison apartment. He wants to move, but we're still not making any money. At this point we're better off having a minimum wage job and playing out of a garage. At least what we make would be our own. Right now everyone is dipping their hands into our cookie jar and when all is said and done, we're lucky if there's a crumb we can share.

I rap my knuckles on his door. He answers straight away and lets me in. I've interrupted his time with his game console and wish I could sit down next to him and play like I used to with Mason. Maybe that's what I need, a trip back to Beaumont. That would put my life in perspective. I can take Sam home and introduce her to my dad. She's exactly the trophy wife mold that he wanted for me. I could go to junior college, play football and still attend the NFL combine.

My destiny is in my hands except I can't grasp it. Every time I try, it slips through like sand.

"What's up?" he asks as he turns off the television. "Want a beer?"

"Yeah or ten."

He laughs and returns with two, one for him and one for me. I pop the top and guzzle as much as I can without choking. This is better than milk any day.

"What's on your mind?"

I run my hand through my hair and down the rest of the bottle. "I need a hiatus or a break to figure shit out. We're better than that record we put out."

Harrison sighs. "I've been thinking the same thing. I've picked up some nights at *Metro* because I have bills to pay."

"I can give you the money."

He shakes his head. "It's not that. I'm not feeling the sound. It's different."

"I agree. I want to ask Sam to shop us around. I don't want to do another album with *ME*, their direction isn't where I want to go."

"Me either."

At least we agree on something. He may not agree with the next thing I'm going to tell him, but I need to give myself some space to think logically and I can't do that here.

"Listen, I'm going to take off for a bit and get my head straight. I don't like myself much right now and I'm afraid that I could damage what we're trying to do. I want to go someplace where I can get my shit in order, stop smoking and maybe not drink so much. I want to write and not worry about people taking my picture or who my girlfriend is."

"Yeah, I hear you, that's cool. Where are you thinking?"

"I don't know. I figured I'd pack a bag, hit LAX and see what's on the board. I'll have my phone with me though, so you call if anything comes up or you need me, right?"

"Yeah, man. Have fun."

I stand and feel like I need to hug it out with him, but don't. I don't want this to be goodbye, but something tells me that he's not going to call and I may not come back.

And if I do, I won't be the same Liam Page I am now.

CHAPTER 42

THE ocean waves crash around my feet. My toes burrow deeper into the sand with each wave. I have to leave my paradise tomorrow and return to my life. For the past seven months I've been living in Australia, on the beach, and wearing mostly board shorts. Of course when I arrived, I landed my sorry ass here in the heart of summer. Now that their winter weather is moving in, I'm freezing my ass off.

Flying here wasn't planned, but after leaving Harrison's that day, I knew I was going to do something drastic. I just didn't know what. After returning to my apartment to find Sam with a list of nanny's and a baby catalog already out, I knew I had to get out of there. When she mentioned the word marriage I packed a bag, grabbed my passport and fled before she could ask me the question I knew I'd say no to.

Sam and I are okay now. We're not great and we're

not going to be parents, ever. She miscarried at her two-month mark. I wasn't there to hold her hand or comfort her, and I had to convince her that it was for the best. I wasn't going to make a good dad. I didn't want to marry her and she really didn't want to be a mother if she was already thinking about nannies.

She asked me to come home and I told her I would, once my head was clear. I'm not sure if it is or not, but Harrison needs me. He called this morning, frantic, asking me to come back. For him, I will. For Harrison I'll leave my little slice of paradise and return to the concrete jungle known as Los Angeles.

I'm not the same Liam I was when I left. I've spent hours learning how to surf, running on the beach and lifting weights. In the time I've been here, I've cut down on my drinking severely and stopped smoking. I feel good and there's only a slight fog in my mind. I have a feeling that it's always going to be like that. I'm empty and I know that's from missing my grandma and *her*. It's been over three years and I still can't say her name.

I look down at my chest. My reminder of the pain I've caused her has been freshly retouched. The black ink is no longer faded. On my shoulder I now sport a barrage of art. There's a skull, a flower and an eagle that took two days to do making my arm almost a full sleeve. I never thought I'd get another tattoo after the one I had put on my chest, but the pain helped me feel again and feeling was the key to get me to write. I have a pile of songs that I'm eager to put music to.

Harrison and I are ready to get back into the studio and I've told Sam that we need to revisit what *4225 West* is about. We want a new record and she told us to lay down the tracks and she'll send them out. I thought she was going to fire us as her clients after the stunt I pulled, but she didn't. In fact, she forgave me, not that I was looking for her forgiveness. I know she loves me, but I've told her I'm not worthy of anyone feeling that kind of emotion for me.

Harrison and I also talked about adding a third member. It's time, but we want to hold auditions. As much as we like Way, he's a floater and doesn't care where he plays as long as he does. We need someone who is going to be devoted to the band and willing to contribute with their own piece of artistic flair to get us to the top.

I take one last look at the ocean and bid it adieu. It's time to go home and face the music, so to speak.

DESPITE the jet lag that is kicking my ass, I head straight to Harrison's. I'm hoping, for the sake of my sanity, that Sam is not in my apartment. I never asked her to leave after she moved herself in, but I would like to think she knows we're over. I've been happy and drama free for months and the last thing I want is to start in with her about why I've been gone so long and why, when Harrison said jump, I asked how high. It's hard to make a woman understand that you don't want them without destroying their self-esteem. I've said this from day one, she's a good-looking woman and I care about her, but I don't love her and it's best that we keep everything professional. Whether she'll be able to do that or not will be the test. The last thing I want do is fire her, but I will if I have to.

I knock on Harrison's door and a pang of regret surges through me. He still shouldn't be living in this dump and had I stayed around or figured my shit out quicker, we could be on the road to success. We're not and that's my fault.

The door swings open and his mom greets me, enveloping me in one of the biggest and best hugs I've had in a long time. It's funny that you don't think about the people in your life when you're gone, until you realize how much you've missed them. I've missed Mrs. James and everything she represents in my life. She's the one person that I know who knew my grandma the way I did.

I pick her up off the ground and twirl her around.

"Put me down before you break your back." She playfully slaps me on my shoulder and I do as she says. I give her another hug before letting go. Maybe she is what I need – a mother figure to fix me. I wouldn't dream of doing that to my own mother, but hugging her like that felt good. "I've missed you, young Liam."

"Sorry I was gone for so long."

She places her hands on my cheeks and her eyes start to water. "You look healthy. Your grandma would be so proud of you."

I shake my head and my lips go into a thin line. I'd hate for my grandma to see me like this or like I was. "I don't know about that. I lost myself for a bit. I'm hoping to change that real soon though."

"I have faith," she says, taking a deep breath. "Might as well go in and see what's been happening in our family." She nods toward the inside of the house.

I look around the door jamb for anything out of place or for something that might jump out of at me before looking back at her.

"Everything okay?"

"Everything is perfect." Her smile is infectious and lights up her face. She pats me on the back, pushing me into the apartment. When I enter the living, I stop dead in my tracks. The thoughts that run through my head are enough to make my stomach turn because sitting on the floor is Harrison and between his spread out legs is a baby. Now, I'm not doctor, but the baby looks brand new.

"Is that… did she…"

"This is my son, at least I think he's my son."

I sort of stumble onto the couch, in a less than graceful manner, unable to take my eyes off the baby. I glance at Harrison. I look at the baby. Back and forth my head goes.

"What?"

Harrison plays with a lip ring; he does this when he's deep in thought. It looks like both of us made some changes in our life. His is probably outweighing any of the drama I had going on.

"I don't know much. A couple of days ago this girl shows up and she's carrying this car seat. She sets it down in the middle of the floor and says *it's* mine and walks out."

"What the fuck?"

"Language, Liam." I shrink back when I'm scolded.

"Sorry," I apologize to Mrs. James. "So is it yours?"

"He," Harrison corrects me and it takes me a minute to realize that the baby is a boy.

"He." I nod. I can do this with Harrison. I can play along. "Is he yours?"

Harrison reaches out and touches the baby's foot, wiggling it back and forth. I lean forward, wanting to see his reaction. There's a light in his eyes that I've never seen before. Harrison admires the baby in front of him and the reaction he gets. The baby squeaks causing Harrison to smile. I've never even held a baby, let alone looked at one up close. He's tiny and all arms and legs. He doesn't have much hair and his head is cone shaped. It sort of reminds me of that *Conehead* movie that Dan Akroyd made back in the 80's. I just want him to say the baby is his so my heart can stop pounding. If he tells me this is Sam's baby I think I might jump off a cliff. I'm not ready to be a father.

"Mom says he looks like me, but I don't know. I don't remember the girl or the night."

"So she just showed up?"

He nods and the baby starts to fuss. I sit back, waiting for Mrs. James to come running, but she doesn't. Harrison picks up the baby and holds him to his chest. My mouth drops open in amazement as his little baby turns his head into Harrison neck. I feel like I'm invading his privacy by watching, but I can't help it. I wanted this at one time, with my girl. It's hard to admit that now, that I knowingly had sex with her without using a condom, but I did. I was desperate to stay. I wanted her to tell me to stay and if she had, I would've. I turn away when Harrison leans down and kisses this little boy... his son on the head. It's too personal and I don't deserve to be a part of it.

"I answered the door and thought, wow what a hot little surprise for me. She had a sweet ass body, but she was carrying the car seat I was confused from the get-go, but I let her in. She told me that we met at a show and she was backstage. She said we went to the bar and she bought me a drink. Thing is, now that I've been thinking about it, I vaguely remember someone spending the night, but I couldn't tell you who and she's someone I would've remembered. And now this little guy is here. It's been three days and she hasn't come back yet."

"I can't even think of a show we did nine months ago."

"Alicia – that's her name – she said it was ten months ago, but I don't know. I'll have to get a blood test and all that shit."

I think back to ten-months ago and come up blank. That time in my life is buried deep because I want to forget everything.

"So what are you going to do?"

Harrison bends his knees and places the baby on his lap. He touches every part of him that's not covered with clothes. Part of me wants to hold him, but he's so tiny and fragile, I'm afraid I'd break him. Besides, I wouldn't know what to do, but Harrison does. He seems like a natural. His mom must be a miracle worker if he's already that comfortable.

"I'm going to keep him until I know for sure. Mom says he's mine. She can feel it. I need to be straight with you. If you're not into this whole band thing anymore, I get it, but I have to be serious, especially if this little guy is mine. I watched my mom struggle with raising Yvie and me and I won't do that if I can help it. My apartment is a shit-hole, I have a crack dealer living next door to me and my car is a piece of shit. I need to provide better for my son. So you and I are going to either get our asses into the studio now and make something of ourselves, or I need to find another gig."

I'm a bit taken aback by his words, but he's right and I couldn't agree more. I came to L.A. to make something of myself and as of now I haven't done jack shit. It's time to piss or get off the pot. "Does he have a name?"

"I'm calling him Quinn."

I nod. "I like that, Quinn James, rocker in the making."

Harrison laughs, shaking his head. "I don't care what he does as long as he's happy." And yours I want to add.

Mrs. James appears with a bottle in her hand and it's like Quinn already knows. He fusses a little bit, but Harrison is on it. I marvel at how attentive he is, especially with not knowing if the baby is his or not. Harrison holds him up and kisses him on the nose before handing him to his mom. The look on her face, when she holds him, is priceless. I take my phone out and snap a picture. It's a memory that I want to keep and maybe someday look back at it and think of what my grandma would've looked like if she had held me in her arms.

"You boys go on, little Quinn and I are going to have some lunch and take a nap before Auntie Yvie comes over to play." Mrs. James sits down, holding Quinn in her arms. There's an ache in my heart knowing that my grandmother and even my mother will never have a moment like this.

"Mrs. James, can I hold him before you stick that thing in his mouth?"

She looks up with nothing but pure elation on her face, nodding. I sit down next to her and wait.

"Hold your arms like this." Harrison demonstrates the proper way to hold a baby.

"Dude," I say, laughing. He shrugs, clearly loving what's happened to him in these past few days.

Quinn is placed in my arms and the first thing I notice is how light he is. He's also warm and squirmy. He makes these little sounds each time he moves and I'm assuming that's okay otherwise either his dad or grandma would take him from me.

"Hi, Quinn," I say softly, wondering if he can hear me. I reach out and touch his little hand, only to have him grab a hold of my finger.

"Such a sweet boy," Mrs. James coos as she rubs his head.

I've been in love before, but what I'm feeling now is completely different. Quinn is bringing something out in me that I didn't know existed. I know he's not mine, but I don't want to let him down.

"I think Harrison and I need to get to work, Mrs. James." I reluctantly let him go. As soon as he's out of my arms I realize that I'll be a staple in this household because this little boy just gave me something to work for.

CHAPTER 43

Three Years Since Beaumont

"ARE you ready?"

I look up from my notepad to find Sam standing in front of me. Her toe is tapping impatiently on the floor and her hands are perched on her hips. It's seven a.m. and I'm still in the studio from last night or maybe it's the night before. I've lost track. It's been a year since I asked Sam to find us a new label. She promised me it would happen, but yet here we are with a full album and no producer. We have enough new songs to make another one, but no one wants us.

We almost cut Sam loose but in the end decided to sign with her again. If all else fails, we can make the record with *Moreno Entertainment*, but it's not what we want to do. If someone told me that it'd take this long to get a decent label, I would've laughed. I had such high expectations when I first signed and now I'm just spending night and day in the studio, writing.

I look at Sam questioningly. This is her new game: Cat and mouse, the Sam version. She asks a question and waits painstakingly long to continue, or until I cave and speak to her. I've learned that speaking to her too much gets me in trouble, so I try to keep my mouth shut as much as possible. If I phrase something wrong, or if there's a slight hint that I might want to see her later, she's like a cougar ready to pounce.

I can't go there again. I care for her, I do, but I care for my sanity more. I had to leave town to escape her and get healthy, and my fear is that she'll drag me back down again. She the puppet-master to my vices and knows how to pull my strings to get me to cave. I haven't had a cigarette in years, but she makes me want to inhale an entire pack just to calm my nerves. I prefer the mellowness of my apartment and my cat. How I ever ended up with him, I'll never know. He was sitting in a box, shivering. It was raining and I was running down the street. Why I stopped to look still baffles me, but I did and I brought him home. He doesn't have a name though. I thought long and hard but couldn't come with anything that I thought fit him so I stuck with Cat. I thought he'd be a good companion, but he hisses anytime I go near him. He's a good cat though. He loves Quinn and lets him pull on his tail and ears and never scratches him. It's just me that he hates.

"How long have you been here?"

I glance at the clock on the wall and shrug. I don't even pretend to know what day it is. She steps forward and that's when I get a strong whiff of what she's wearing. My leg starts to jerk and I'm biting the inside of my cheek hard enough to draw blood. I've never smelled this perfume on her before and it can't be that popular, so why is she wearing it? Why does she smell like *her* all of a sudden? Never have I had reason to compare them. That's why Sam is so easy for me to be with and dismiss. She's the opposite of everything I want, everything that I had with my girl. I don't care how many years it's been; to me it feels like yesterday. To this day I still have her hate filled voicemail that I listen to when I need to remind myself why I'm here. I can still see her eyes when I'm telling her that I can't be with her. I was a coward that night. I still am a coward. So many times I could've gone back and told her everything. I could've answered any one of her calls, but the thought of letting her down, the thought of her being so disappointed in me, broke me.

I know what I did was wrong and someday I'll make it up to her. I don't know how or when that will be, but it will happen. I'm still a nobody. I'm still the young kid that sat on a stool hoping that a bar owner would like him enough for that coveted nighttime spot. I wasn't even good enough for that, yet here I am pouring my heart out on a piece of paper because it doesn't talk back. It can't look at me with disgust and I can't hear the disdain in its voice telling me how much of a loser I am. The paper doesn't mock me, it absorbs what I'm telling it, what I'm feeding it.

Sam stands in front me, her expression one of contempt. Does she know what she's doing to me? She can't know. I've kept everything a secret and never gave any hint or inclination as to what awaits me in another town. I stand and move the other side of the room. My breathing is sporadic, coming in short spurts. This whole time I've done everything I could to protect my girl and now, somehow after years, Sam's wearing *CKOne*.

Everything about this moment feels wrong and I hate it.

"What do you want, Sam?"

She stalks toward me. I have a feeling she knows and she's doing this on purpose. The question is how does she know about *her* and what am I going to do about it? Do I pretend she's not invading my senses to the point where I want to grab her… and kiss her, or does she think I'm acting like the typical dick that I am? I hope it's the latter. If she's having those thoughts, my life is easier.

"I don't get you, Liam. Sometimes you want to be near me and other times you act like I'm carrying a disease."

You are, I want to blurt out. The 'let's try to kill Liam slowly' disease.

"What do you want, Sam?" I ask again. Her eyes brighten and I realize my mistake. I should know, no open ended questions.

"Well since you're asking. We're good together. I don't know why you insist on fighting it."

My head shakes slowly. I pinch the bridge of my nose and wish she would disappear. I sense her closeness before she touches my arm.

"But we can discuss that later. Right now, I want you to get the guys together and meet me at Capitol, they're making an offer."

I drop my hand and gaze at her. My eyes bore into hers. She's telling the truth. I can see it in her features.

"What time?"

"Half past ten. Don't be late." She turns and purposely sways her hips, showing off her ass because she knows I'm an ass man. "Liam, you can thank me later."

As soon as the door closes I want to scream out in joy, but instead I bang my head against the wall. If this deal hinges on me being with her, I'll take one for the team. I'll hate it, but they guys deserve it more than anything.

HARRISON, JD and I sit in the reception area of Capitol Records. When we arrived, I stood outside and stared up at the iconic building. The very same building that I could see from my grandma's yard and now here I am. I'm about to sell my songs to them and in return they're going to put their label next to my name.

Harrison and I are nervous, but not JD. He's used to this. JD, or Jimmy as he's named, came to us after answering an ad. We started jamming as a three-piece and he never left. He started as the bassist, but is a man of many talents, much like Way. One of the first songs we recorded with him was the song I wrote for my girl back in high school. It was one of the EP's Harrison and I released early on, but adding JD's piano mix to it gave it a whole new sound. I don't know if a producer will want to run with it again, but if they don't we have plenty of others to offer.

"If you're ready, I'll take you through now." I gawk at the very tall female standing in front of us. Of course, her heels make her six inches taller than she truly is. Her hair is the Hollywood blond, platinum and styled perfectly, but her face is fair with little make-up. I eye her up and down, causing her blush and believe me I'm enjoying the reaction I'm getting. She turns on her heel and I'm the first one to step in behind her. Her ass is the perfect shape and her skirt is tight enough to show just how round and firm it is.

She stops and holds a door open for us. My arm purposely brushes against her tits. She coyly bites her lip probably hoping I won't notice, but I do. It's been a while since I've been with someone, but after this morning with Sam and her perfume, I need to find a release and this one just might be it.

We sit down at the long conference table. Anthony and Sam sit across from us and at the end are the Capitol executives. These men are going to either make or break us. I'm praying that I walk out of here a happy man. If not, I need to seriously consider going back to Beaumont, but I don't know what I'd do there. I have nothing to offer anyone.

"Good afternoon, gentlemen. We've just spent the last hour going over everything with your agent and manager and we're happy to make an offer."

Papers are slid toward us, each of us grabbing our own set. The words blur on the page after I read "five record deal". Nothing else is making sense. *This* is what I've been working for. *This* is why I came here.

"Holy shit," Harrison exclaims quietly as he turns the page. I follow suit and agree. We have creative freedom. Sam stays as manager, Anthony as our lead agent. And the money, it's there. Harrison will be able to move out of his apartment and get Quinn a nice place. He'll be able to help pay for Yvie's ballet school and JD will be able to marry his girl, Chelsea. But most importantly someone likes my lyrics enough to want to buy them, and that right there is enough for me.

"Where do we sign?"

A collective sigh emanates throughout the room. Anthony claps and Sam pats him on the back. He can't take all the credit though; Sam does a lot of the legwork. She may only be a manager, but she also doubles as our agent more often than not.

Pens are passed around and the final contract is placed in front of me. I sign my name willingly. Harrison is next and JD goes last. When JD came to us, he just wanted a place to play, didn't care about anything else. His father is James Davis, a musician who's been around for a while and his grandfather tells me that he played with mine. I took the old man for his word, not really interested in going through my grandma's stuff to find out.

I never did get to sit down with her and talk about my mom and grandpa. I never found the time and always said I'd do it tomorrow. Thing is, tomorrow never came. I'm not sad about not knowing about him. I can't go through my life regretting my decisions. Had I stayed in Beaumont, I would've known my grandma and she would've died alone in that big ole house on the hill. If I stayed, I'd be a mill-worker or a mailman and we'd probably have three kids and be heading for a divorce. I wouldn't have been happy.

All the work, the blood, sweat and tears, the late nights and epic frustrations has all come down to this. The contract is sent back down to the other end of the table where it's signed. The sexy little thing that helped us out earlier comes in and I get an eyeful of what she's offering.

"Tonight, we celebrate," Anthony says as he stands, placing his fedora on his head. For a man who has as much money as he does, you'd think he would take better care of himself, but no. He's pudgy and is often caught rubbing his rounded belly.

Yes, I will be celebrating and I think it's going to be with the hottie out in the hall.

"**D**O you want to know my name?" she asks as my lips attack her neck. I push her up against the stall in the bathroom, ripping her nylons away from her body.

"No," I breathe out. The last thing I want is her name. I don't care. I just need her to scratch the itch and move on. No phone numbers will be exchanged and no, we won't be going back to my place to cuddle. I need a quick and dirty fuck – that's what this is.

I release my cock from the confines of my slacks, not even bothering to undo my belt or the button, zipper only. I fumble with the condom while trying to hold her. For as hot as she is, she's a fish and just waiting for me to do everything. I move her panties slightly and plunge into her. I swallow her scream with my mouth, keeping my lips pressed to hers while pound into her. Her nails dig into the back of my neck. The pain is a welcome feeling. I want it. Crave it.

As I work her into a frenzy, her head falling back. She looks at me, her eyes hooded. She runs her fingers through my hair and I want to tell her to knock that shit off – it's too personal – but I'm too focused on getting her off so I can come.

Her head falls forward again and her breathing picks up. Her body starts to react. I reach through our tangled bodies and find her swollen clit waiting to be stroked. I apply enough pressure to cause her to get a little wild. As much as any man enjoys sex, they're usually hoping their partner is into it and she's not.

Her walls start to squeeze me and I thrust harder, deeper until I'm spent. I pull her off of me and dispose of the condom. This was a mistake, yet another one to add to my long list of dumb things I've done. Once I'm tucked back in I open the stall door and head right to the sink to wash up. I have lipstick on my neck that needs to come off. I wash up, making sure there's nothing on the front of my pants.

I stiffen when she saddles up behind me, placing her arms around my waist. I don't want a clinger, but yet I have one. The bathroom door opens and for a minute I think we're busted. I look at the mirror to find Sam standing behind us. Her eyes are pooling with tears.

"Fucking great," I mutter.

"How could you?" she cries out.

I sigh. "Sam, we're not together. I've told you this repeatedly."

I turn and look at the girl who is shaking her head. "Why?" Sam asks, her lip quivering. I hate it when she cries and I feel the need to comfort her, but she has to know her boundaries.

"Are you really asking me why?"

She shakes her head. "You're my best friend. We share an apartment. You know how I feel about him."

I look from Sam to the girl and back again. This is not good.

"I'm sorry," she says, grabbing a hold of my arm. I shake her free and step away.

"Look, I'm going to go." I don't wait to see how that mess in there is going to turn out. I bail, leaving everyone behind at the club.

Stepping out into the night air makes me realize that Harrison has it made. He gets to go home to someone who loves him unconditionally. Someone who lights up at the sound of his voice and makes him feel whole. I need that, and then maybe I won't be such a shit all the time.

Maybe I should get a dog.

CHAPTER 44

Five Years Since Beaumont

"**W**HY the hell aren't you on the plane?"

I hear her before I see her. The studio door swings open, crashing against the wall. It's a damn good thing the walls are padded or there'd be a dent in there now. Sam stands there with her hand on the end of the door, her breathing is labored as if she's just ran a marathon in her heels. Her face is red and blotchy, but there's something different about her. I cock my head to the side in wonder before I realize what she's done. My eyes have to be deceiving me. I stand slowly, dropping my headphones onto the ground. She's gone too far this time. It's one thing to start wearing *her* perfume, but to go and dye her hair the same exact color is something else.

I look into the other room and see that it's empty. Both the sound techs and the producer have vanished leaving me alone to deal with a very pissed off Sam, which is fine. This is how I like it. I can take her on without any witnesses because she'll just drag them into our twisted trap when she's done. I've learned over the years that the one lonely night on the road has been the catalyst for a slowly self-destructing Sam. Apparently it's my fault and the brief period when we dated, was the happiest she had ever been up until I subsequently left her. There's no excuse for my behavior or none that I'm willing to make. Shit happened, I was young and that's it.

Sam stalks forward with her finger pointing at me. When she stops in front of me, she stabs me. I try not flinch but her fake nail hurts. I breathe deeply through my nostrils. Today... no, this week is not the week to be messing with me. My chest puffs out in anger, but she doesn't step back.

"I'm so sick and tired of your bullshit, Liam Page." Her words are venomous with a hint of pain. If I play my cards right, I can get out of this without making her cry. That's a win for me.

"What in the fuck are you talking about? I could ask you the same thing." I bite back, the anger boiling in the pit of my stomach. What gives her the right to barge in here and assault me like this? Doesn't she know what tomorrow is?

"I'm talking about how you're not on the plane flying to New York City to do the interview with the *Today* show." She rights herself and steps back from me. I don't know if she's trying to calm down or what. She clears her throat. "You have a contract obligation. There's a red-eye flight tonight, you'll be on it."

"The hell I will," I fire back.

"Excuse me?" her eyes are like daggers, piercing and cold. Her steely stare sends a cold chill down my back.

I've never seen her like this. Her eyes are void of any emotion and her normal hue of brown is so dark I'd dare say they've turned black.

"I think you heard me and since I know you're listening. Why the fuck did you change your hair color?"

"Don't you like brunettes?" It's a valid question, but one that isn't getting an answer from me.

"Have you ever seen me with a brunette?"

She steps forward, her head shaking slightly. "No, Liam, I've seen you with blonds, red heads and a few with jet black hair, but never have I walked in on you getting your dick sucked by a brunette."

"Maybe you should knock first."

Over the years I've made major mistakes with Sam. It's hard to say I regret them, but some I do. I should've never slept with her, period. We crossed the line and turned what was potentially a decent working relationship into hell. After my grandma died and she took care of everything, I didn't question her. I should've. She's listed as an emergency contact on my penthouse, so she always has access. I can't change it and she uses it to her advantage. Thing is, I'm such a dick to her that I've made sure she's caught me in the act, because it's the only way to get through to her sometimes. She needs to see me with other women to know we're never going to be an item.

"Well, if I knocked, I would have missed seeing your glorious body in the flesh." Just like that her tone has changed. Her finger trails down the front of my shirt. I grab her hand and push her away.

"No more, Sam. You need to get that through your head and if you can't, we're done."

"Is that so?"

"Yeah, it is." I bend and pick up my headphones and set them on my stool. "What do you want?"

"I want you to show me the respect I've earned!" she screams. I turn in time to duck from her briefcase flying toward my head.

"What the fuck?"

"Get your ass on that God damn plane, Liam. I'm done with your diva attitude."

"I'm not going anywhere, Sam. What part of that isn't clear? You know better than to schedule anything this week. Harrison and JD can do the interview, they don't need me."

Sam begins to pace. I'm afraid to move for fear I won't be able to dodge anything that she throws at me. I look out into the other room quickly to see if anyone's back yet. I'd like to know what she told them to get them to leave. I could really use some interference right now.

"For years..." she sighs. Her back is to me and right now I think that's more dangerous than her looking at me. I can't see or read her expression from here. "I made you, Liam Page. You weren't anything but a lowly teenage boy thinking he was going to make it big in the city. My dad," she shakes her head. "He didn't care. He respected your grandmother, but wasn't going to give you a chance, until I saw you play." She turns and faces me. She looks defeated and I'm trying not to care.

"I took one look at you and I saw something I could mold into a superstar, but you held back. You played like you were missing something. It didn't take me too long to figure it out, but short of bringing her here..." she shakes her head, biting her lip as looks down at the ground. I

334

process her words, wondering what the fuck she's talking about. I have a feeling, but I don't want to ask in case I'm wrong.

"I tried to be what you needed. I'm so much more than you ever gave me credit for. I know I'll never be ..."

"Be what, Sam?" I swallow hard, remembering the words I said to her the first night we were together, "someone you'll never be". The pit of my stomach is telling me that my worse fear is about to come true. She knows about my life back in Beaumont. The one I've tried to protect by forgetting. I don't care if she knows about Texas and football, but Beaumont is off limits.

"Sam?" I say, pleading with her.

Her head snaps up, her eyes on fire. "I know I'll never be like your precious Josephine. Is that what you want to hear Liam Westbury?"

I lurch and fight back the nausea. She knows, but how?

"How?"

She laughs and waves her hands in the air. "I'm rich, Liam. So fucking rich, yet I can't have the one thing I want out of life and that's love. I'm in love with you and at one time you were in love with me, but then you stopped. I can't even buy your love because you're so fucking hung up on someone who doesn't want you. I'M RIGHT HERE IN FRONT OF YOU. And you ignore me. I made you." She stalks toward me and pushes me with both her hands. "I made you, Liam, not her. All of this is because of me and you can't do something as simple as love me back, yet you pine away for that brunette like she's your dying breath. If it wasn't for me, you wouldn't be here right now."

I want to tell her she's wrong, but she's not. She discovered me and maybe if I had waited to see if anyone else wanted me things might be different, but they're not. I chose Sam and everything that came with her and now I'm paying the price now. I've been gone far too long to pick up the telephone now and call. I don't know if Sam's been to Beaumont or not and frankly I'm too afraid to know.

"How?" I ask again.

"Private investigator. After that night on the bus when you told me she's someone I'd never be, I had to find out who my competition was. It wasn't hard once I went through your grandmother's stuff and found out who your mom was."

"You bitch." There's no force behind my words. I'm stunned, hurt and breaking piece by piece on the inside. She invaded my life – the one I needed to leave behind to do this.

Sam smirks and laughs. "Yeah I'm the bitch. I fucked you and pushed you aside. I told you I would try at a relationship and bailed at the first sign of trouble."

"So what?" I yell. "So fucking what? That gives you the right to invade my life? There's a reason why I didn't want you to know about who I was before I moved here. That life doesn't define me."

"But it does."

I shake my head. "That's where you're wrong Sam. I left everything behind to be here. I ruined everything because I had this dream and someone in my family was willing to stand by me while I pursued it. My life there is none of your Goddamn business."

"I'm your manager - *everything's* my business,

including the barflies you bring home nightly. Your past indiscretions? I'm the one who cleans up after them. I pay Jorge to make sure they get home safely. You dismiss them like trash." She's pointing at herself. There's a light sheen of sweat on her forehead. This is the first time we've fought like this and it's scaring the shit out of me. This is why we aren't good for each other.

"They're one night stands, Sam. You drove me to them." I scream out, holding my head, bent at my waist. It all makes sense now.

The perfume.

Dying her hair.

She's trying to be Josie to get my attention.

"Get on the plane, Liam. I'm not telling you again."

I shake my head. "It's not happening."

"If you don't, it's a violation of your contract. I'll terminate you for insubordination." Right now I think it'd be worth it.

I nod and look her square in the eyes. "Fine, but I'll be meeting with your father in the morning and telling him everything. I'll tell him about all the late night phone calls. About all the times you've crawled into my bed when I've told you over and over again that I don't want to be with you. I'll tell him how you supplied all my alcohol when I was underage. How you took advantage of me on the bus that night. Two can play this game, Sam, and you may be his daughter, but right now he's sitting pretty with the royalties that this band is bringing in. The wall of fame is looking pretty fresh with the Grammy's we've won. You didn't win those. You didn't write those songs. I did. So while you think you've done so much for me, take a long hard look at what we've done for *Moreno*

Entertainment.

"I'm on vacation, Sam. This is the week that I've taken every year since my grandma died. You know that, so why you decided to schedule an interview during this week is beyond me, but I won't be going. You can either let the show know that you've made a mistake or tell them I'm ill, but I'm not leaving."

"You'd leave if *she* called you," her voice is quiet, broken. I try not to show that her statement gets to me, but I can see it in her face. She knows.

"That would never happen."

I leave her in the studio to figure her shit out. I don't know if we'll have a manager tomorrow or not, but I'm not going to let her strong arm me into something I'm not comfortable doing.

As soon as my feet hit the sidewalk I'm taking ten steps and walking into the bar that's adjacent to the studio.

"What can I get ya?" the bartender places a bowl of nuts in front of me after he wipes down the bar.

"Whiskey, straight."

"Tough day?"

I nod as I grab a handful of nuts and toss them into my mouth. He sets the whiskey down in front of me. The dark amber liquid mocks me. It's been years since I've tasted the burn. I move the glass back and forth, watching the booze slosh around.

I wish I could close my eyes and go back to the night that I stood at *her* dorm room door. I wish I'd let her pull me in so I could feel her in my arms one more time. Things would be different, but I'd be with her or we'd be in the same town. I could be admiring her from afar or even hold her at night. But I'm here in Los Angeles like

I wanted to be, living a life that I thought I wanted. If eighteen year old me could ask twenty-three year old me what his life would be like, I'd tell him to stay in college.

Life is not what I thought it would be. I'm cynical. I prefer to be alone most of the time until someone steps in front me and I think they can numb my pain long enough that I can function properly. The dullness only lasts until sunrise and then I have to start all over again. The same routine day in and day out. Nothing changes until I'm on tour and that routine is just as bad.

I suppose I'm living any man's dream. Women throw themselves at me. I smile and they're putty in my hands. Why? Is it because I'm in a band, because I sing? I don't see it. I don't feel the attraction. Each one is just a painkiller.

"I can make you forget her."

I shift my gaze to the woman that's just sat down beside me. I eye her bare legs and dress that is riding up her thigh. I pick up my glass and down my Jack, never taking my eyes off her.

CHAPTER 45

Ten Years Since Beaumont

WHISKEY at ten a.m. is not usually my thing, but then again reading about a man I once called my best friend wasn't my plan either. I fold the article that I printed early from The Beaumont Daily and place it in my back pocket. The internet, while I've used it plenty to keep tabs on people, is the bane of my existence right now. The day I stood on my grandma's cliff and told her I would try this for a year haunts my memory. Twelve months and I would go back to Beaumont and make amends, except I didn't because one year turned into two, which turned in five and now ten and now it's too late for me to go home and fix what I had done.

Right now, I'd give it all up. I'd give up the personal appearances, the late nights, the all access parties with the hottest celebrities, just for one moment where I can apologize for being an epic douche. I don't know if he'd understand, but I'd try my hardest to make him. I always thought I'd have a chance to let him into my life, this life that I've built for myself, so he could see how much better off I am... or used to be.

This business – it's deadly. I used to love it. I used to thrive to be on stage in front of thousands of people. To hear them chant my name over and over again. To sign autographs and take pictures. That soon faded. It became a hassle, a chore. Now it's become my reality and nightmare because I can't escape the life I've built. Not that I want to, but I would like something different. I don't deserve it though. I made the decision ten years ago to change my life and with what I'm staring at, I don't have the right to feel the loss that I'm feeling.

I press her number on my phone and wait for her to answer. She's not going to understand this, but I need to do this for me.

"Hello?"

"I need you to book me a hotel."

"Why?"

"Because there's something I have to do."

Sam sighs, but I can hear her moving around to get a pen. About five years ago Sam and I had a huge fight. We both said things we didn't mean and I walked away. I threatened to quit and her father was livid. Sam took a year off from the band to get her head straight and came back full-force. She booked us on a yearlong US and international tour that was a huge success. We also had a few more songs appear in movies and added two more Grammy's to our list. Since then, everything has been on an even keel. There are no more romantic feelings and she's been very professional.

"What hotel?"

"Um…" I try to remember the name, but I'm not sure if it's even there anymore. "There's a Holiday Inn on Route 15 —"

"Liam, why are you going to Beaumont?"

I close my eyes and pinch the bridge of my nose. I forgot that she knows every possible thing about Beaumont, thanks to her trusty private investigator.

"There's been a death. I need to go and pay my respects."

"Why?"

"It's just something I have to do, Sam. I can't explain it. I'll be gone three days. In and out and I probably won't talk to anyone. I'll stand in the back of the church and no one will recognize me."

"Mhm… I don't like this. I'll go with you."

My head is screaming no. "I'll be fine. I'm going to take my bike. You can have a suit sent to the hotel. Besides, someone needs to feed the cat."

"Linda can."

"I'm going by myself, Sam." I take a drink of the whiskey sitting in front of me.

"Are you drinking?"

"No," I lie. Right now I don't need a lecture from her.

"Liam, this hotel is a three-star. You've got to be kidding me. I'll find you another one."

"No, Sam, that one is fine. It's on the highway; no one will look for me there."

Sam huffs. "Fine. Anything else?"

"Just the hotel." I hang up and pay my tab. After one sip of the whiskey, my stomach is turning. The early morning sun is blinding when I step out of the bar. I slip my helmet on and straddle my bike. I need to get away before my mind explodes. I kick start my bike and let the engine roar before taking off toward Harrison's. His apartment is the most peaceful place I know.

I don't knock when I get there. The sliding glass doors are open and the wind is blowing through the curtains wildly. This place was made for a woman and whomever he settles down with will be in love with this condo. I walk through his place and step outside and into the sand. Harrison and Quinn are surfing and are the only ones on the beach. Solitude, that's what he has out here. Solitude and happiness. He's a changed man since Quinn came into his life.

As soon as I'm a close enough, Quinn ditches his surfboard and runs to me, wrapping his wet arms around my waist. "Uncle Liam, did you come to surf?"

"Nah, buddy," I say, ruffling his hair. "Just came to see what my favorite boy is doing."

"Just hanging with my dad."

Harrison has done an amazing job raising Quinn on his own. I know his mom and sister helped, but he's done most of it. Quinn tours with us and for a kid who doesn't have a set routine, he's pretty damn smart and well grounded.

"What's up?"

I shake my head. "I gotta leave town for a few days, but I'll be back by Monday."

"Everything cool?"

I nod. "Yeah." That's all I can say. I don't know if it is. I don't know what it will be like when I get to Beaumont. In and out, just long enough to pay my respects. Me being there won't do anyone any good and I'll just be a disruption. As far as I know he wouldn't want me there anyway and I don't want to ruin the day for him.

"When are you leaving?"

"Tomorrow."

Harrison nods and picks up his and Quinn's board and we walk back to his place. I sit down in the sand and watch the tide roll. It's a great day for surfing, but most people are at work. Quinn sits down next to me and buries his toes in the sand.

"You look sad."

I hang my head. "Maybe I am. I don't know, Quinn."

"Do you know what grandma does when I'm sad?"

"What does she do?" I ask, knowing he's about to tickle me.

He jumps and starts moving his little fingers all around my body. I laugh and pull him into my arms and hold him. I remember the first time I held him. He was just days old and Mrs. James put him in my arms because I asked her to. I loved every minute of it. He gave me a new perspective on life. I thought I was going to break him, but in hindsight he's really the glue that has kept us together. I never wanted Harrison to fail so I worked my ass off to make sure we were the best. Unlike me, he had someone in his life that needed him and I wasn't going to let this little boy down.

TOLD Harrison I was going home, but I made it as far as the bar. I need something to shut my brain off. I need a numbing agent to keep me from picturing what my life could've been like had I stayed. Sitting at the bar, I can't help but wonder if I would've eventually made it to the NFL. What if I had taken my dad up on his offer to help me switch schools and gone to play for someone who wanted me? Would I be married with kids and a house with a white picket fence? That's the one thing I'll never know, because at the time I couldn't handle what life was giving me. I needed something different.

I down the whiskey and signal for another one. There are women on both sides of me and it's just a matter of time before one of them makes their move. This is my hangout, everyone knows it and I've taken plenty of women home from here. I'd like to think tonight will be different since I'm leaving in the morning, but I doubt it. They want the same thing I want, but for different reasons.

The woman to my right has a large ass rock on her ring finger. She's out of the running. Having some other man's property, possession, wife, is not my style. She needs counseling if she's here trying to hook up with me. Or it's a trap. Get yourself knocked up by a celebrity so you can collect child-support for the next eighteen years. No thanks, go find some other unsuspecting bastard. That's not me. I'm never having kids. If I'm feeling the urge to be a father figure, I'll borrow Quinn.

Each sip I take brings back another memory from Beaumont. I'm here to cloud my memory, yet everything is vivid – like I'm watching a real life movie. Now that I've committed to going back, even to say goodbye, the floodgates are open. I've done everything I can to forget where I came from, not because I'm ashamed, because it was easier to block out what I was missing. I never thought I'd be here, like this, away from the ones I loved. My family.

I know everything is my fault. I could've picked up the phone when she called. I could've called her back. But

I didn't. I had something to prove and by the time I had the success I was looking for, it was too late.

I swallow my final drink. It's late. I need some sleep. The woman on my right left long ago, but the one on my left has been biding her time. So why not? Why not live up to my reputation one more time?

"Want to get out of here?" I ask, not really waiting for her answer. I grab her hand and pull her behind me. The night air is muggy as we walk to my penthouse. She's trying to keep up in her heels as I drag her. I could stop, but that would ruin my mood.

I'm on her once we're in the elevator. She's eager and willing.

"Don't you want to know my name?" she says, out of breath.

"Nope." I push her down the hall once the elevator opens. I slide my keycard in and push my door open. I strip myself, not willing to wait for her to get around to it. This is sex and nothing else.

We fall onto my bed and I make the mistake of looking at her. She thinks she's got me where she wants me. "You're afraid," she whispers against my lips. In this moment I should get up and escort her back downstairs, but that's not my frame of mind. She's right, I *am* afraid. I'm afraid of dying alone and tomorrow I'm going home to stand in the shadows while my once best friend is buried. He'll have people there to mourn him. People are going to grieve for him. No one would care if I died.

I'm going home tomorrow – to the unknown – and I'm scared shitless. For all I know, my life is going to change and I'm going to be worse off than I am now.

Sneak peak of the Beaumont series
series
Book 1

Liam Returns To Beaumont...

CHAPTER 1

A LIGHT snore reminds me that I'm not alone. The heaviness of a body sprawled out, sets me off immediately. The stale smell of day old perfume lingers in the air and on my sheets.

The curtains are pulled back, the sun shining through the large window which affords me the best view and privacy.

Rolling over, there's a face I don't remember. A face that holds no name in my recollection or any vivid memory of how she ended up in my hotel room let alone my bed.

The bed part I can probably figure out.

The blonde hair tells me that I didn't bother to get her name or ask her what her favorite drink was. Guaranteed our conversation was eyes, hands and lips only. There is one hair color that can make my heart beat and blonde isn't it.

Neither is red.

Eyes too.

Never blue.

They have to be brown or green, never blue.

This isn't a downward spiral or some drug induced moment. I don't do drugs, never have, but I may drink excessively on occasions like last night. This is me coping with my mistakes and failures. I may be successful when I'm on stage, but at night I'm alone.

And so freaking scared of dying alone.

I reach for my phone to check the time. Instead I pull up the gallery that holds her image, my thumb hovering over her face. I'll see her when I go home and I don't know what I'll say.

I know she hates me.

I hate me.

I ruined her life. That is what her voice message said. The one I've saved for the past ten years. The one I've transferred from phone to phone just so I could hear her voice when I'm at my lowest. I can recite every hateful word she said to me when I was too busy to answer and never found the time to call her back.

Never found one second to call and explain to her what I had done to us. She was my best friend and I let her slip through my fingers just to save myself from the heartache of hearing she didn't want me anymore.

I had dreams too.

And my dreams included her, but she would never have gone for it. I'm not living her American Dream. I'm living my own.

My decision destroyed everything.

My nameless bed cohabitant reaches out and strokes my arm. I move away quickly. Now that I'm sober, I have no desire to be anything to this person.

"Liam," she says through her seductive tone that sounds like a baby. It makes my skin crawl when women talk like this. Don't they see that it makes them sound ridiculous? No man worth his nuts likes this sort of thing. It's not sexy.

Wrapping the sheet around my waist I sit up and swing my legs over the edge, away from her and her wandering hand. My back tenses when I feel the bed shift. Standing, I pull the sheet tighter to keep myself somewhat covered. I shouldn't care, but I do. She's seen me in the dark, but I'm not affording her or her camera another look.

"I'm busy." My voice is strict, a well-practiced monotone. "Jorge, the concierge, will make sure you get a cab home."

I sleep purposefully facing the bathroom so I never have to look at them when I tell them to leave. It's easier that way, no emotions. I don't have to look at their faces and see the hope fade. Each one hopes they will be the one to tame me, to make me commit.

I haven't had a steady girlfriend since I entered the industry and a one night stand isn't about to change that. These girls don't mean anything and never will. I could change. I could settle down and marry.

Have a kid or two.

But why?

My manager, Sam, would love it, especially if it was her. She's my only repeat lay. The first time was an error in judgment, a lonely night on the road mistake. Now she wants more. I don't.

When she told me she was pregnant I wanted to jump off a cliff. I didn't want kids, at least not with her. When I think about having a wife, she's tall and brunette. She's toned from years of cheerleading and her daily five-mile run. She's not a power hungry executive in the music industry who spoke of hiring nannies before a doctor could confirm her pregnancy.

She suggested marriage; I freaked and flew to Australia to learn to surf.

She miscarried two months in. I made a vow that we'd keep things professional from that point on and that is when I started my one night stand routine. Despite everything, she still loves me, and is waiting for me to change my mind.

"You know," the barfly from last night starts to say in between shuffling and her huffed breathing as she puts on her clothes. "I heard you were a dick, but I didn't believe it. I thought we had something special."

I laugh and shake my head. I've heard it all, each one thinks we have something special because of the most amazing night they've ever had.

"I didn't pick you for your brains." I walk into the bathroom and shut the door, locking it for good measure.

Leaning against the door I bang my head against the solid wood. Each time I tell myself I'm going to stop, and I think I have until something makes me want to forget. My hands rake over my face in pure frustration.

I'm not looking forward to going home.

The reason for returning is staring at me from my bathroom counter. The page-long article of the guy I used to call my best friend. Picking up the paper, I read over the words that I have memorized.

Mason Powell, father of two, was killed tragically when the car he was driving was rear-ended by an eighteen wheeler.

Dead.

Gone.

And I wasn't there.

I left like a coward when I didn't say goodbye.

I changed my cell phone number because *she* wouldn't stop calling. I had to make a clean break and Mason was part of that. *She* and Katelyn were best friends and he'd tell her where I was and what I was doing. It was better this way.

I was only meant to be gone a year. I told myself I'd return home after twelve months, make everything right and show her that I wasn't the same person she fell in love with. She'd see that and thank me, move on and marry a yuppie business man, one who wakes up every day and puts on a crisp dress shirt and pleated slacks that she'd iron in their *Leave it to Beaver* household.

I squeeze the paper in my hands and think about everything I've missed. I don't regret it, I can't. I did this for me and did it the only way I knew how. I just didn't think I'd care so much about missing everything.

I missed the day he asked Katelyn to marry him. Something I knew he wanted to do since we were sixteen.

I missed his wedding and the birth of his twins. He was a father and a husband. He had three people who depended on him and now he's gone. He'll never see his children grow up and do the things that we did when we were younger. All the things we said our kids would do together. I missed this because I had something to prove to myself. I gave up on their dream and the life we had all planned out.

And now I'm heading home to face the music.

ABOUT THE AUTHOR

Her grandma once told her that she can do anything she wants, so she is.

Originally from the Pacific Northwest, she now lives in picturesque Vermont, with her husband and two daughters. Also renting space in their home is an overhyper Beagle/Jack Russell and two Parakeets.

During the day you'll find her behind a desk talking about Land Use. At night, she's writing one of the many stories she plans to release or sitting courtside during either daughter's basketball games.

She's also an active book reviewer on The Readiacs.

www.twitter.com/HeidiJoVT
www.facebook.com/HeidiMcLaughlinAuthor
heidimclaughlinauthor.blogspot.com

This paperback interior was designed and formatted by

www.emtippettsbookdesigns.com

Artisan interiors for discerning authors and publishers.

Made in the USA
Middletown, DE
12 June 2019